Copperhead Summer

A Novel

by

GARRY BARKER

KENTUCKE IMPRINTS • BEREA, KENTUCKY • 40403

KENTUCKE IMPRINTS
Berea, Kentucky 40403

LIBRARY OF CONGRESS CATALOG CARD NUMBER 85-050639

ISBN 0-935680-15-2

To Greg and Beth

FOREWORD

Cox County, and the characters in this book, are ficticious.

To my knowledge, no copperhead ever behaved as do those in *Copperhead Summer*, but it *is* true that they are commonly referred to as "them mean old snakes"—as compared to the rattler, who kindly sings out a warning before he strikes.

Who knows? Any Eastern Kentuckian who spends time in the woods will attest to the eerie, chilling quiet which warns of danger; most often, that danger is a fat copperhead sunning or hunting.

As I wrote parts of *Copperhead Summer*, I found myself anxiously eying dark corners and dim hallways, half expecting a thick copperhead to come slithering out, nervously reassuring myself that no self-respecting snakes would ever crawl inside an air conditioned house.

They wouldn't, would they?

Garry Barker
September, 1985

Mark 16: 15-18

"And he said unto them, Go ye into all the world, and preach the gospel to every creature."

"He that believeth and is baptized shall be saved; but he that believeth not shall be damned. And these signs shall follow them that believe; In thy name shall they cast out devils; they shall speak with new tongues."

"They shall take up serpents. . ."

CHAPTER 1

"GLORY BE TO GOD!"

In a gray dawn the dusty pickup crossed Cumberland Gap, slowed for the descent into Virginia, then swung south into Tennessee, through Harrogate and upward toward Clinch Mountain. The driver–stocky and solid–downshifted and clenched the wheel during the final steep climb, then parked at the overlook to peer down through the fog at the spreading fingers of Cherokee Lake.

Then he was back in the truck, knobby tires singing as he steered quickly off the mountain and into the crossroads of Bean Station. At the small restaurant there was ham and biscuits with steaming coffee; as he left, he stopped to buy a Sunday Knoxville newspaper. Parked in a vacant picnic area two miles east, the placid man smoked and leafed casually through the bulky paper, basking in the warm sunshine, at peace with himself.

He froze, growling, staring at the cover story of the sports section. He read quickly, angrily, crumpled the paper and slung it to the cluttered floorboard. "The bastard," he hissed. "The son of a bitch is comin back."

The paper slowly crackled open on the floor, and a ray of sun lit the photo. It was of a lean, sweaty basketball player draped in a torn net and waving a champagne bottle. He was laughing and hugging an adoring blonde. The caption to the story read: "WILD BILL CALLS IT QUITS." Billy Cox, "Wild Bill" to a decade of sportswriters, had announced his retirement after 15 years of professional basketball.

He reached for the paper and read again. "Billy Cox is going home to Kentucky, back to the hills where he learned to shoot a basketball as good as anybody who ever played the game, where he learned to drink raw moonshine and charm the ladies. Billy Cox will soon be back on the hillsides, working the south end of a northbound mule team, growing the corn for his favorite drink. Billy is Cox County's most famous son, still a hero to the homefolks, a folk legend who is bigger than life."

"Imagine Wild Bill in overalls, laid back in a rocker, chewing and spitting and chasing the hounds. There's one thing for certain; close by there'll be a jug, a blonde and a basketball, the tools of Billy's trade."

"Damn!" The paper slid back to the floor. "Damn him to hell." He lit a cigarette with trembling hands, sat impassively for a half hour, then reached for the ignition. The truck jerked away from the roadside in a rattle of gravel. At the forks he braked and veered left, climbing, slowing as the pavement gave way to gravel and then became a worn dirt track. He relaxed as he guided the groaning pickup higher up the mountainside. In the churchyard he parked and waited.

They came in dusty battered cars and pickup trucks, families dressed in coarse clothing and heavy shoes, redfaced from working outdoors, somber and serious. No one met the gaze of the man in the pickup except one bosomy teenaged girl; she stared, frank and boldly interested, then lowered her eyes as she climbed the rickety steps.

He followed, slipped inside during the opening hymn, and took a seat at the rear of the room.

The singing staggered to a stop, and the preacher, a scrawny beanpole of a man with a bobbing adam's apple, stood before the congregation. Already, sweat beaded his upper lip, and he swallowed heavily as he prepared to speak. He nodded toward the stranger.

"Ya'll know Brother Wilde, yonder," he said softly. "He's come down from Kentucky to worship with us again."

There was a quiet shuffling and creaking as heads turned and bodies shifted. Wilde nodded a greeting.

"I'm a talkin today," gasped the preacher, "from the Book o' Mark. Jesus, he said to go out and preach the gospel to ever critter. Ever one." He punched the air with a bony finger and swayed gently, building his rhythm. "Brothers and sisters, I'm a tellin ye, he was a talkin the gospel. The word o' the Lord. He said to preach to ever critter, big uns and little uns alike, them what's tamed and them that's a runnin wild up on the mountain."

He loosened his starched collar and wiped sweat from a shiny forehead. "They ain't none of us, nary a one, what believes *enough.* They ain't one person in this here room—not one in all these here hills and hollers—so good but what ye don't got to prove yerself, over and over, prove that ye believe in the Lord Jesus Christ and his Holy Word."

He paused.

"Amen," whispered the teenage girl.

"Yes! Amen!" The preacher glared. "Ellie Sue Jackson, do you believe? Are you warshed in the blood of the lamb?"

"I believe!" she gasped. "Lordy, I believe." She half stood, trembling before the stern pointed finger, heavy breasts heaving.

Softly, a strong voice started the singing. The others picked it up, voices and tambourines joining in a quickening chant. The preacher swayed, eyes closed, his grave voice leading. The girl slowly rose fully to her feet, arms open to the pulpit, face flushed. "Lord, I'm a comin," she groaned.

The clapping, singing, shouting rhythm swelled and filled the little churchhouse. The congregation was standing, sweating, convulsing in the Holy Spirit and the heat of the moment.

The girl shrieked in pain and emotion, ripped open her dress and danced down the aisle, breasts flopping, arms and legs flapping wildly.

The church was now a stormy sea of emotion, of dancing and singing and screaming, alive with raw spirit. Men, women, and children joined in the outpouring, the orgasm of the mountain.

The preacher smiled and turned to reach for the heavy cardboard box. He spun, lifting his arms to the heavens, a thick four foot long copperhead squirming in his prayerful hands.

"I'm a comin through, Lord," screamed the barebreasted girl. "Yes, Lord, I'm a comin."

The preacher draped the snake over her slender neck and the coils wrapped around tender young breasts, heaving and shaking and sweating.

Other hands reached for the copperhead and the girl slumped to the floor, whimpering softly. The believers passed the snake from hand to hand as the congregation shouted and danced its approval.

The scared copperhead struck, and a lean barearmed farmer sunk to his knees. The snake slithered across the wood floor and coiled around the body of the quivering girl. It poised, ready, head swaying and tongue flickering.

Then, from the back of the church, the crowd parted.

Brother Wilde, slow and calm, made his way up the crowded aisle to face the lethal copperhead.

He knelt, heavy and awkward before the serpent, and reached out strong hands. The copperhead, swaying gently with tongue darting, moved closer.

There was silence except for Wilde's hoarse breathing.

"Come," he whispered. He stretched closer, and his big hands caressed the copperhead's dry coils. "Come."

Slowly, cautiously, the copperhead uncoiled into the big arms and hands; Wilde gently lifted his precious burden. He raised his arms aloft and turned, beaming, to face the hushed congregation.

"Glory be to God!" squeaked the preacher. He bent to his knees, worshipful before man and serpent.

Quietly, the others joined the preacher. They knelt before Brother Wilde and the copperhead. The half nude girl crawled to his feet, clung to his thick legs, and moaned her adoration.

††††††

Wilde backtracked whistling happily, crossed back into Kentucky and drove steadily north through Pineville and Corbin, up I-75 past Berea and across I-64 to Morehead; then left the main road to follow the winding creekbed. He was home, in Cox County, shortly after midnight.

CHAPTER 2

COPPERHEAD MOUNTAIN

On Monday morning Jake Wilde, Editor and Publisher of the Cox County News, wrote studiously about the season's uncommon rise in reports of copperhead bites in the county:

The common copperbelly (copperhead to town folk, Agkostroden Mokasen to you college graduates) is a peaceable critter when left to his own ways. But. . .if you insist on crossing his path, be prepared for the consequences. So far, just this summer, a dozen or so of you have found out the hard way that old brother copperbelly is a nasty bundle of poison. Over the past month we've had two dozen reports of bites and near misses, and some imaginative Cox Countians even insist that the copperheads attacked—in broad daylight.

Hogwash!

Copperheads don't work that way. Now, they'll sneak up on you in the dark and bite your britches, but they won't crawl up to you in the middle of the day and come out chewing.

According to Sam Cox, my most reliable local folklore expert, the dry weather is bringing the copperheads down lower. They need water, same as you and me. So you'd do well to watch your step around ponds and springs, anywhere there's water. But don't go running around yelling that the copperbellies are attacking.

It just ain't so. Be careful, especially around water, but don't feed into the panic. We've shared these hills with the copperheads for 200 years, and nothing has changed that fact.

Wilde rolled the yellow paper through his typewriter, studied what he'd written, and frowned. "I don't know," he mumbled. "It may make it worse." He lit a cigarette, stubbed it after a single puff and stared balefully out his window at the dark slopes of Copperhead Mountain. After a minute he sighed and turned back to his typewriter.

††††††

Brooding, scrubby Copperhead Mountain is the uppermost point of Cox Ridge in Northeast Kentucky, a dark thicket shunned by man since the early settlers discovered the dangers lurking behind the rocks and dense underbrush.

The mountain is harsh. Great jagged rocks, deep crevices, gnarled scrub timbers and a tangle of briars make the terrain nearly impassible to man, and there is no coal buried in the mountain's hard belly to spur the exploration. A series of fresh-water springs erupt across the mountainside, and man's absense has let nature create a safe preserve for small game.

Rabbits, squirrels, possums, foxes and even the elusive wild-cat call the mountain home. The smaller animals feed on lush crops of berries and nuts and green plants; the larger predators are sleek and healthy, arrogantly efficient in their hunting.

Hunters shun Copperhead Mountain, thwarted by two centuries of dark legend, frightened by visions of dens of writhing lethal copperhead families, hordes of Appalachia's most deadly, legendary serpent.

The snakes *are* thick on the mountain. Fed by the ample flocks of birds and frogs, the copperheads live free from natural enemies, undisturbed by any other animal. Hundreds of dens, tucked under the rocks and buried in the dark crevices, conceal thousands of the feared and awesome serpents. On the mountain the copperhead is truly king, ruler of a lofty domain, a legendary serpent who lives in peace and seldom strays close to the homes of men.

††††††

Copperhead Mountain is the eastern boundary of the Cox farm, nine hundred acres claimed in the 1700's by gritty Irish immigrant Mark L. Cox. He was the man whose name was taken for the ridge, the county and the hundreds of direct descendants who now cover a six county area of Kentucky. The whole of Cox Ridge covers a winding forty mile crest from Skaggs Gap to Dogfoot Creek; it is home to two hundred families and the crossroads village of Hogtown, named for its once plentiful herds of wild pigs. Hogtown–the community–is a general store, service station, church, half a dozen houses, and an empty schoolhouse.

Coxes still farm the family land, though many of the younger men moved north to the Detroit auto factories or the paper mills near Cincinnati. Others have opened small businesses, joined the work force of nearby factories, or are even teachers in the county school system.

Cox Ridge, and most of a thirteen state region labeled Appalachia, exists in a peculiar time warp, caught halfway, hung between the space age and a deep rooted mysticism. The southern mountains were ignored by the world for two hundred years, important only to its inhabitants and to the coal corporations, absentee landlords who built company towns and railways to mine and remove the rich black seams. There was little change, through the 1930's, in a way of life dating back to medieval England.

WW II brought the new world home to Cox County and the rest of Appalachia. Ex-GI's, home from the cities of Europe and the streets of New York, had new expectations. Many simply packed up and left, joining an outward migration which lasted for thirty years. Those who chose to stay built usable roadways, schools, electrical systems and more modern homes, cleared more land and bought more trucks, slashed the timber and strip mined the coal, working relentlessly, forever ending the physical isolation of a region.

Lyndon Johnson's War On Poverty focused on Appalachia,

spewing forth vast programs of social and economic development, swinging international attention and billions of dollars to bear on the people and problems of America's southern mountains. The Appalachian Regional Commission was legislated to build highways, hospitals, vocational schools, water systems and child care centers. New houses sprung up as federal funds made building possible, and community colleges brought advanced education close to home. Television suddenly brought the world to every fingertip. A flood of eager young volunteers spread the gospel of human rights and individual freedom. Appalachians were studied, trained and retrained, surveyed and dissected, and widely publicized; ironically they were given little voice in deciding just *how* their poverty would be erased.

Despite the cash and the concentrated effort, much of Appalachia remains unchanged. Family loyalty, religion, personal freedom and the right to bear arms are values stubbornly maintained, and a culture which fought the elements and survived has outlasted the government dollars.

By the spring of 1980, Cox County, Kentucky was a world within a world, a paradoxial marriage of tradition and technology, a world where intellect and superstition mingled freely.

††††††

The drought began in February, and by late April the uppermost springs on Copperhead Mountain were dry. The copperheads moved slowly down, following the sinking water level, moving steadily closer to the people of Cox Ridge.

Jessie Cox, clearing the family graveyard at the foot of the mountain, discovered a pair of fat copperheads near his uncle's headstone. He warned the rest of the family to watch closely, then went on about his business. Snakes, poisonous or otherwise, were plentiful on Cox Ridge, and Jessie saw no reason for alarm.

An elderly widow, whose cabin was close to the base of the

mountain, was the first victim. Her body, stiff and twisted near her well, was found after she had been dead for over a week. No special significance was given to her death; the old and the very young seldom survive the copperhead venom.

Still the rains did not come, and, in early June, the migration quickened. The copperheads moved relentlessly down the ridge seeking water. A two year old boy died quickly after being bitten twice while playing near a creek. Tales of daylight attacks circulated, stories of aggressive and angry behavior. Officials scoffed. The copperhead is clearly a night hunter, a non-aggressive snake dangerous to man only when disturbed.

Jake Wilde's column stirred the discussion.

Most agreed with Wilde and laughed at the reports. Sam Cox, seventy-nine year old patriarch of the Cox clan, reluctantly offered a differing view.

"Them copperbellies from the mountain is different," he warned. "They been up there so long they ain't afraid no more. They don't know they ain't supposed to chase atter us, damnit. Them copperheads is comin to kill."

"Yeah, Pap, we know," groaned Jessie. "You're the same one that's seen hoop snakes a rollin down the road and milk snakes milkin the cows. Pap, copperheads don't go huntin fer people to kill, and that's that."

"See fer yerself," growled Sam. "Jist wait, damnit. I'm right, Jessie, and afore the summer's over you'll be wishin ye'd listened to me."

Jessie's oldest son, Obie, sat and listened quietly. He offered no comment, made no effort to voice an opinion. He was thoughtful, remembering the stories he'd heard as a youngster, remembering how his namesake had died at the hands of the mountain copperheads.

††††††

Samuel Mark Cox had been born in 1901, the second son of

a ninth generation descendant of the ridge's original settler. At the turn of the century, Cox County was little changed from a hundred years earlier; the family was self sufficient, growing their own foodstuff and selling tobacco and timber for a meager cash income. Sam's father, Will, taught his sons farming, carpentry and the other skills necessary to survival in the hills. All five boys were superb marksmen and master distillers.

From his grandmother, young Sam learned the secrets of the herbs and roots used as Appalachian medicine, and at the old Hogtown School he learned to read, write and cipher. As the second son, he was not expected to follow in his father's footsteps as the clan's leader, and so had time to study the music, legend and wildlife of Cox Ridge. His energy and inquisitive nature soon led him to Copperhead Mountain, and during the summer of his fourteenth year, Sam decided to make the climb and see for himself what was on top.

With Obie, his twelve year old brother, he slipped away late on a Saturday afternoon armed with a .22 rifle, an axe, a .32 revolver and a supply of herbs for treatment of the copperhead venom. By sundown the boys had neared the crest, climbing carefully, tongues dry with fear and excitement. The mountaintop was a wide flat rock, and, in the center, Sam and Obie quickly stacked enough wood for an all night fire. In a cowboy novel Sam had read that new hemp rope would fend off snakes by scratching their tender bellies; he spread the coil in a rough circle around their campsite. They ate as the sun dropped, and the cool darkness came swiftly. Sam and Obie huddled close to the fire, back to back, weapons ready.

Bright moonlight flooded the area and a swell of creature noises filled the damp air.

"I'm skeered, Sam," whimpered Obie. "Let's go home."

"We can't, Obe, said Sam. "The copperheads will be out huntin by now. We're safe right here, iffen we stay put."

Flickering movement, real or imagined, busied the outer reaches of the flat rock. Obie, whimpering softly, clutched his rifle close. Sam casually tossed a fresh limb on the fire. Obie squalled, jerked the rifle and fired. "Damn you, Obe," bellowed Sam. "You like to have shot me!"

Obie was shaking. "I'm a leavin, Sam. I'm tellin Pap. You made me come up here, and I'm tellin."

The shriek of a screech owl was the last straw. Obie scrambled and ran, Sam close behind, and they slid to a stop near the ring of new rope. "Look," hissed Obie. He pointed.

Two feet away a thick copperhead moved slowly past, a dark, slithering shape in the blackness.

"Git back here, Obe," Sam whispered hoarsely. He dragged Obie back to the fire. The boy lay trembling, gasping, whimpering and struggling to breathe. Sam held him throughout the night, huddled close to the flames, wide awake and fearful. At dawn a welcome foxhorn blared from the lower slopes of the mountain.

"Pap!" screamed Sam. "Pap, we're up here!"

Before the rescuers arrived, Sam used his Barlow to scratch on the soft rock. He carved his name and the date: July 15, 1915.

An angry Will Cox carried Obie off the mountain, home to his bed and his mother's tender care. Then he led Sam to the barn, thrashed him with a length of brittle harness leather that brought blood through the thin shirt.

A few days later when he finally spoke, Obie had acquired the stutter he carried to his grave.

††††††

Sam and Willie, Sam's older brother, were part of the first wave of American troops to reach France during WW I. Sam was a medical corpsman; Will fought with the cavalry.

Willie died at Argonne.

Sam came home to Cox County in early 1920, a strapping nineteen year old with lusty stories of French bordellos and

German maidens, a robust youngster with plans for a trip back to New York and a career in medicine. Instead, he found he'd acquired new responsibilities–the role of eldest son, future leader of the Cox families. After a year he married a neighbor girl, Lily Skaggs, and built a small house near the homeplace. He settled into farming, doctoring the neighbors and rearing a family of his own. Jessie, the oldest son, was born in 1921.

Obie, an awkward and stuttering youth, also became Sam's charge, a willing helper who doted on the children.

Will Cox died in 1927, shot from ambush. After the funeral Sam loaded his Army revolver, rode to the neighboring farm and shot Buck Waggoner six times. Jessie, only six, rode with Sam to Hogtown to await the sheriff. The boy carried a .22 rifle, tucked under his saddle, and was grimly determined to protect his father.

The sheriff, reluctant to interfere, sent a message. There would be no arrests. Sam and Jessie started for home at midnight, letting the mules pick their way along the narrow trail. Half a mile from home they heard the gunfire and kicked the mules into a loping gallop. Jessie fell behind and reined his mule into a thicket above the hillside. He pulled out the rifle and ran to an overlook, saw old Kate falter and collapse, and watched as Sam rolled clear of the dying mule.

Hoarse yells shattered the night, and shadows crossed the hillside. Jessie aimed cooly, fired, and grinned as a scream of surprised pain answered him. His second shot clipped Jim Waggoner's hat. "Let's git!" yelled Waggoner.

Sam's pistol came to life, firing into the dark hillside, and chains rattled as the Cox hounds broke across the field in full voice. From the house a shotgun roared, and buckshot splattered the leaves. The Waggoners retreated quickly.

Jessie and Sam reached the house, found a sputtering Lily Cox on the porch with a smoking shotgun, and watched as flames flickered on the ridge above them. "It's the barn," said Sam. He caught Jessie. "Leave 'em be, boy. Is anybody hurt, Lily?"

"They busted my winders," she sobbed. "And shot up the Motorola radio, Sam. Go kill them sons-a-bitches." The smaller children were peering over from the sleeping loft, fascinated.

"Fergit it," Sam said softly. "They ain't nobody hurt. They's been enough killin fer one day."

"But Pap," protested Jessie. "Them bastards shot old Kate."

††††††

The next day Sam rode alone to the Waggoner farm and convinced Jim that no further good could come of fighting. Waggoner hesitated, grinned sheepishly, and offered his hand. "They's jist one thing," he said. "Who in hell was that hidin up in the rocks shootin? He winged Rich and near took my head off."

"That was Jess," Sam said softly.

"That little squirt? Hell, he ain't nothin but a baby." Waggoner shook his head admiringly. "He's gonna be a mean one, Sam, iffen he lives to be a man."

"Iffen he don't live," Sam said gravely, "me and ever damn Cox in a hunnert miles of here will be comin back, Jim."

Waggoner stared. "I hear ye, Sam," he said quietly. "They won't be no more trouble."

A precarious peace was restored. Sam worked the fields and cared for his mother and Obie, still much a child. Obie was a strong and willing worker, a gentle giant who loved Jessie as if the boy were his own.

"M-me and y-you," he told Jessie. "We're Sam's m-mules." He laughed happily. "Sam, he's the d-damn mule driver, and w-we're the t-team."

Jessie finished the eighth grade when he was fifteen and took on more of the farm work. To earn cash money he cut timber, snaking the logs off the hillsides with a skilled team of mules and his and Obie's strong shoulders. From the Sears and Roebuck catalogue Jessie ordered a shiny Winchester .30-.30 carbine; at Skaggs Gap he bought, for $35, a black Model A Ford.

In the back seat of the Ford he bedded Georgie Waggoner, and at the age of eighteen he became—in less than a month's time—both reluctant husband and proud father.

Obie shared the pride. "J-Jess," he beamed. "We g-got us a girl. She's the p-purtiest baby I ever s-seen."

Georgie was expecting again, less than a year later, when Obie found the copperhead den.

Jessie and Obie had worked since dawn clearing new land near the barn, making way for ten more acres of corn. At midmorning Jessie walked to the spring for a drink, but Obie's bellows brought him running back to the field.

Obie, frozen, was screaming senselessly, his arms wrapped around his chest and his eyes bulging. Jessie ran harder, swinging the axe, wishing he'd brought the rifle. Sam, from the next field, dropped the reins and came at a frantic run.

Obie, slashing at the roots of a thicket, had uncovered a nest of baby copperheads, a squirming ball of baby vipers. "I wanna go home, Sam," droned Obie. His voice was soft, younger. "You made me come, Sam, and I'm a tellin Pap."

"Take it easy, Obe," whispered Sam. "Jist back away, Obie. Come on home with me."

Obie's vacant eyes found Jess, standing close, puzzled and tense. "Pap?" he asked plaintively.

"It's Pap," Sam said quietly. "He come fer us, Obie. Let's go now." Gently he pulled Obie away.

"No, muttered Obie. "No, it ain't Pap." He twisted and broke away from Sam's grip. "That ain't Pap," he screamed. He ran, arms flapping, his long strides carrying him quickly across the stubbled field.

"Ketch him, Jessie," yelled Sam. "Don't let him git away."

Obie's screams of terror came from a nearby gully.

"God a mighty," moaned Sam.

In his flight Obie had not seen the deep ditch. He had run

into mid-air, legs pumping, then tumbled headfirst into the brush. The copperhead struck quickly, then bit again, and Obie's wail filled the muggy air.

Jessie's axe flashed as he killed the snake, but Obie was running again. "No, Obie," yelled Jessie. "Come back here."

He ran wildly, moaning, his arms flailing as he went.

"Come on," growled Sam.

They found Obie's body a half mile across the ridge.

"Git the sled, Jess," Sam said softly. "He wants to go home."

Jessie stared at the limp body. "Pap," he mumbled, "Obie quit stutterin. He was talkin good. What was he sayin?"

"He was rememberin," said Sam. "Rememberin somethin that happened a long time ago."

Two weeks after Obie's funeral Jessie's first son was born. "He'll be Obie," said Sam. Jessie nodded agreement.

The second son, William Samuel Cox, was delivered six months after Jessie's regiment left New York bound for London and the battlefields of France. Sam cared for Jessie's family during WW II, and in 1944 he hitched up the team, drove the wagon to Skaggs Gap, and proudly presided over young Billy's first haircut and the buying of new hardsoled shoes.

"You're too big fer the sugartit now," he told Billy. "It's time you was bein a little man." He chuckled. "He's a goodun, Georgie."

"I reckon you think so, Sam," she said. "You done carried him over ever hill on the ridge, talkin and singin to him. He ain't gonna know his real daddy."

Georgie was right. Jessie came home the following year and three year old Billy hid under the bed and squalled for Sam. "*That's* my daddy," he yelled angrily, pointing to the tinted photograph on the mantle. "Make the man go away, Mamma."

"Damn, Pap," Jessie laughed. "You done got yerself a new youngen to raise."

Billy did stay close to Sam as he grew and shared his grandfather's love for the land and the legends. Jessie protested.

"Damnit all, Pap," he complained. "You're fillin the boy's head fulla old tales and junk. Hell, you're gonna make him into another Obie. Times is changin, Pap. It's 1948. The boy, he's got to change, too."

Sam leaned on his hoe.

"Jess," he said. "I know that they's different times now. I been watchin. All them Fords and Chevies and electric radios and sich. I reckon Billy, he'd do anything you wanted him to. What me and him does, it don't hurt nothin. He ain't gonna have to fight no wars. Billy's gonna be a lawyer or doctor or sich. Leave us be, Jessie. Billy gits his work done, same as Obie. He's jist a little different."

"He sure is, Pap," agreed Jessie. "Always a readin and askin. Other night he wanted to know about the fight we had with the Waggoners." He chuckled. "Georgie like to died when she heered it was me that shot old Rich." He frowned. "Then he was askin about Uncle Obe and the mountain. You ain't been tellin him about climbin there, have ye?"

"No," Sam said quickly. His eyes lifted. "No, Jess, I ain't ever gonna send another'n up that hill."

††††††

Jessie Cox evaluated his two growing sons with cool detachment.

Neither, in his mind, was a worthy heir to the Cox leadership. Neither, thought Jessie, could have taken the rifle and fought against the Waggoners, and neither could have performed cooly under fire as he had done in the war.

Jess loved Obie in much the same way he prized his work mules. Young Obie was steady, uncomplaining, quiet, strong, and durable. But there was no fire in Obie, and Jessie grieved. For a man to live without knowing the chill of near madness, the gut-wrenching excitement of a dangerous act, was for only half a man to exist.

Billy was too free to act on impulse. Brash, full of fire and devilment, the boy acted totally on emotion, running roughshod over anyone who was less determined. Under the brash exterior Jessie saw weakness. Billy, he thought, would be unable to dig in, to face reality and perform under pressure. "But he's plenty stubborn," mused Jessie. "So they's hope he'll grow up and be a man someday."

Jessie blamed Sam for Billy's flighty attitude. The years Sam had cared for Billy and the subsequent closeness of the two had spoiled the boy, and conditioned him to expect everything to come too easily.

As the boys grew, Jessie shared Obie's sufferings. The awkward outcast, happy only when home on the ridge, was a good-hearted and humble youngster, totally the opposite of the noisy and explosive little brother.

There were times when Jessie detested Billy. The arrogance, easy athletic prowess and angry defiance offended Jessie, and their loud confrontations became more frequent.

Though at times Jessie worried about Obie's long rambling disappearances, his grief with Billy was much more difficult. He was always awake, far into the night, anxious to see if the rowdy son would make it home alive again.

The daughters, to Jessie, were a pleasant footnote. They were cuddly and loving, decorative and entertaining. He enjoyed them; he hoped neither would get pregnant before she was married.

††††††

Georgie Cox, from the night she had opened her legs to Jessie, had accepted her role in his life.

She was his helper. Georgie was Jessie's cook, housekeeper, farm laborer when needed, and breeder. There was no intimate sharing of problems, no casual and easy affection. Sex was a periodic release for Jessie; Georgie was the convenient receptacle.

She was given full responsibility for the house and garden, and for the rearing of the daughters.

The sons, by Jessie's code, were another matter.

The boys were not to be babied, fussed over, or otherwise weakened by female coddling. When they were old enough to work, sons were the man's domain. The father was firmly responsible for training, discipline and the intense preparation for manhood. But Georgie managed to form close, almost secret bonds with both sons, and was the buffer which protected them from Jessie's bruising expectations. Her evaluation of the boys, in no way objective, differed greatly from Jessie's harsh assessment.

For Obie she had a special love, shielding him from the cruelties of the world. There were special small favors—extra helpings of his favorite foods, the selection of his clothing, secret aid with school homework, and daily assurances of love and security.

She was Billy's sounding board, the soft mat to cushion his frequent falls. More than Billy was ever to know, she defended him from Jessie's quick wrath. Quietly, Georgie discarded the many rumors and accusations which followed the growth of her mercurical son and was sure to let him know how proud she was.

She blushed with pleasure at Billy's athletic accomplishments and suffered in silence whenever he caused trouble. Never did she doubt that Billy would make his own way in life; she wished, often, that his stubborn independence would bend enough to make room for a mother's love.

CHAPTER 3

"THE ONE AND ONLY"

"We can't, Billy!" She squirmed free and jerked his hand away from her thigh. "We're cousins."

"So what?" Fourteen year old Billy Cox, grinning and determined, slipped his hand back to Linda's plump thigh. Her cotton dress was pulled up to her waist, and white panties covered a soft rounded mound. They lay in the hayloft, streaked by sunlight, straw clinging to them.

"You want to, don't you?" persisted Billy.

"Well. . .yes, but it ain't right for us to. . .to do it, Billy, us bein cousins and all." Linda blushed brightly.

"Damn." Billy crawled to the window and stared out at Copperhead Mountain, looming tall at the end of the ridge. "You done it with Timmy Harper, didn't you?"

"No." Linda frowned. "Well, yes. But just once."

"Ain't I as good as him?"

Billy rolled over to lean against the wall. Already he was six foot three, a lean muscled and wiry athlete, darkly bearded and impatiently virile. "Ain't I?" he asked again.

"You know I like you better than any old Timmy Harper," said Linda. "It's just–us bein cousins–I want to, Billy, but it ain't right."

"It ain't like we was gonna git married and have idiot youngens," argued Billy. "I got rubbers."

"It still ain't right," she insisted.

"Then just take off your dress," whispered Billy. "Just let me look. You sure are pretty, Linda."

She blushed. "Just to look? You promise?"

"I promise," swore Billy. "Cross my heart."

Linda unbuttoned the dress and tugged it up over her blonde hair. She sat, redfaced, in her underwear.

"That thing too," said Billy. "The br–brassiere."

"I–Billy–no, I can't."

"I'll help you," he said. His arms were around her, his fingers fumbling with the clasps. Exposed, her breasts were milky white, firm but soft, with hardening pink nipples.

"God." Billy's whisper was hoarse.

"Do you think I'm pretty?" asked Linda.

"More'n that." His breath came in ragged gulps.

"Prettier than your girlfriends here?"

"Lots."

Linda giggled. Billy bent and tentatively licked a nipple.

"Ooh," gasped Linda. "Don't do that."

He circled the nipple with his thick tongue, his heart pounding, then moved to the other.

"Oh, Billy, that feels so good."

He pulled her close, feeling the warm softness of her breasts against his bare chest, and parted her legs. "No," she gasped, arching to him. "No, Billy."

He slid the panties down over soft hips and she was wet when he reached for her. He fumbled with his jeans.

Linda shuddered and slowly lay back, her eyes closed, and moaned as he eased himself down. Their mating was frantic and awkward, and then they lay quietly.

Linda twisted to stare frankly at his body, then squealed. "You never used no rubber!" she wailed. She was up on her elbows, her breasts shaking as she angrily snapped at him.

"I forgot," grinned Billy.

"What if I get pregnant?"

"You won't," assured Billy. "I ain't old enough fer all that stuff."

As she sat, trembling with anger, he reached for her again and roughly bent her down into the straw. They moved easily together, and her squalls of pleasure echoed across the empty barn.

Later they dressed and walked to the house, hand in hand. Linda's father met them halfway. "I was lookin fer you, Linda," he said. "We gotta git goin if we're gonna make it to Cincinnati before dark."

"I was showin Linda the new tractor, Uncle Jack," smiled Billy. "We didn't know what time it was."

"Hell, that's okay, Billy," said Jessie's youngest brother. "Are you gonna be playin ball this year?"

"Yessir," said Billy. "I'll be starting at forward. We got us a good team this time."

"Maybe we can come and watch you play sometime," said Jack.

They did come.

The night Billy made his first appearance for the Cox County varsity team he scored twenty-seven points. Two hours later, his Uncle Jack led him to the barn and beat him senseless.

Linda, four months pregnant, had confessed.

††††††

"Grandpap," Billy asked quietly. "What happened to Linda's baby?"

"Her's and yourn?" Sam's eyebrows lifted.

"How'd you know?"

Sam sucked at his new false teeth. "Jessie told me, last winter when she was havin it. It was give away, Billy. She never even seen it."

Billy was silent.

"What do they think, Grandpap?" he finally asked. "Mamma and Daddy, and the others?"

"What do ye expect?" asked Sam. "They think you're damn half crazy, Billy. Worthless."

"What should I do?" asked Billy.

Sam grunted. "Git castrated, most likely." He chuckled. "I heerd about that cheerleader, too, and the principal's girl. Damnit, Billy, it's all too easy fer you. School, and ball, and girls—damn near everthing." He stared somberly at his grandson. "How old are you now, Billy?"

"Fifteen," said Billy. "I'll be a junior."

Sam shook his head. "Maybe your daddy's right, that some of your trouble is my doin. I was always partial to ye, raisin you when Jessie was gone to the war and all. Your daddy, he's still mad over that."

They sat without speaking for five minutes.

"Billy," Sam finally said, "you got to finish yer schoolin and then git away from here for a while."

"I'm goin to," said Billy. "I'm going to get a basketball scholarship to Kentucky."

"Good," nodded Sam. "What if ye don't?"

"I will," promised Billy. "Grandpap, did you know Uncle Jack beat hell outa me?"

"Yep, I knowed." Sam grinned and spat. "I was the one that told him to do it."

††††††

"He's out there," the coach said nervously. "Up in the bleachers."

"Rupp?" asked Billy. "He's here to watch me?"

"Adolph Rupp himself," said the coach. "Billy, tonight's your chance. Play a good levelheaded game, and you'll be at UK next fall."

Billy grinned. "I'll show him. What's the state scorin record?"

"He ain't lookin for a gunner," warned the coach. "Just show him you can pass, handle the ball and rebound. Play a smart game, Billy."

"Hell," scoffed Billy. "I'm gonna show him how to put that ball in the basket."

At the end of the first quarter Billy had sixteen points.

"Back off," warned the coach. "Rupp don't like a gunner, Billy."

"Hell," said Billy. "Tonight I'm gonna git sixty."

He did, and the legendary Rupp left midway through the final period. "We don't need him," he told a local reporter. "Cox is good, but he's a hot dog. Small college material at the best."

Billy fumed, denounced Rupp as an old fashioned bigot, and signed to play for a university in the Midwest.

††††††

The 1964 UPI All American team was announced in March. Listed in the second five was Bill Cox, with the following notation:

Flambouyant, unpredictable, incredibly talented, Bill Cox led the nation in scoring as a sophomore, spent most of his junior year on probation, then came back this season to average 32 points per game. The 6' 5" Cox is an offensive machine, capable of scoring at will, held back only by his explosive personality.

Against Marquette he poured in 39 points, grabbed nine rebounds, dished out 11 assists, and held his man to seven points. But in the NCAA Regional Finals against Kentucky, Cox scored only 13 points on 23% shooting and was charged with eight turnovers. When he picked up his fifth foul, midway through the second half, he charged the UK bench, screaming at Coach Adolph Rupp. He was evicted from the fieldhouse.

Pro scouts rate Cox as a gamble. His talent is unquestioned, but his lack of discipline may exclude him from an NBA career.

Jessie threw the paper to the floor. "He ain't changed none," he growled. "Pap, you raised you a heller. Billy ain't never gonna amount to nothin."

"He's gonna grow up someday," Sam said. "I shore would

like to see the youngen. Been five year now."

"If he walked in that door I'd have to whup his ass," said Jessie. He smiled. "Then, I reckon he'd be welcome to stay." He kicked at the folded newspaper. "You remember when the little bastard tried to run me off? After the war? Hid under the damn bed, kickin and a cussin and tellin me to git, not lettin me git close to Georgie without a throwin somethin at me?"

"I remember," said Sam. "And I wisht he'd a come to Lilly's buryin."

††††††

Billy Cox, "Wild Bill" to appreciative sportswriters, played for nine NBA teams in sixteen years. The mercurical athlete was too good to cut, too unpredictable to become a lasting star. During the 1970-80 season he was a backup guard for the Denver Nuggets scoring sixteen points per game despite limited playing time, barely half his career average of thirty.

"Why don't you quit?" asked Lucille. She wiped his sweat from her heavy breasts.

"Lucy!" he protested. "What the hell else can I do?"

"Go home. To Dogpatch, or wherever it is you came from, and do what you always threaten. Be a farmer." She nuzzled close to his chest. You don't need good knees to follow a mule, do you?"

††††††

UPI . . . Denver, Colorado . . . "Wild Bill" Cox, a sixteen year NBA veteran, today announced his retirement.

Though acknowledged to be one of the greatest scorers in basketball, Cox has been a transient player, moving from team to team, always scoring points but never living up to his enormous potential.

A series of knee injuries and a tumultuous personal life—

three divorces and a bankruptcy—hindered Cox even more. The past three seasons he has been a reserve and a shooting coach.

Cox has sold his Las Vegas home and is returning to Kentucky. "I'm gonna help my grandpappy raise corn," he told reporters, "and then I'm gonna drink it."

The personality of the NBA will suffer from the loss of "Wild Bill"; certainly Cox County, Kentucky, will be a livelier place from now on.

††††††

The impending return of Billy Cox, after twenty years, took the minds of Cox Countians off their problems with the drought and the copperheads. The NEWS dug out photos of the county's first and only All State and All American athlete, and ran a season by season summary of his high school, college, and pro careers.

Sam Cox was interviewed, but could offer little current information. "We ain't seen Billy since he left," he said. "He was a good youngen, though. A little wild, sometimes, but he was a good boy. Was he a good ballplayer?"

"A little wild, indeed," sniffed Ellie Clark. "Fathered a baby by his own cousin when he was jist fourteen, and there was Principal Brown's girl, and the Rose girl what was a cheerleader. And drunk at his graduation! A little wild!"

"Don't fergit," reminded Elmira Jakes, "they's Annie Clark, still a pinin after twenty year."

"Shut up, Elmira," snapped Ellie.

In Cincinnati, twenty-three year old James Farley read the sports page announcement of Billy Cox's retirement and phoned his mother. "Mamma," he said, "I'm going to Cox County."

There was a long silence on the line.

"Don't go, Jimmy," Linda Hamilton finally said. "You'll get nothing but grief." She paused. "It was bad enough, Jimmy, when you found out about me. You've got a good home. The Farleys have been better to you than I could ever have been. Please, don't go looking for Billy. You'll only get hurt."

"It's high time," Jim said cooly, "that the Coxes found out about me. And it's time I met my real father. I'm going, Mamma."

"I'd rather you wouldn't," she whispered. "But . . . Jimmy, I wish that you'd . . . if you do . . . I'd like . . ."

Jim laughed. "I'll call and tell you all about him, Mamma. I know about your scrapbook. You're not a basketball fan. He must be pretty special for you to still care so much after all these years."

"He is, Jimmy." Linda giggled. "Daddy nearly killed him, once."

"You told me," said Jim. "I'll call, Mamma."

"He's probably still a little boy," said Linda. "Not a man, like you."

"I'm going to find out," said Jim.

††††††

UPS delivered four trunks to Hogtown.

"I reckon he really is comin," said Jessie. He helped Sam carry the load inside.

"He'll be here," said Sam. "My boy, he's a comin home."

††††††

Obie Cox, chunkier than his namesake and ploddingly efficient in his farmwork, was up at daybreak to get a head start on the plowing. He eased his gray tractor slowly past the old Cox homeplace, empty for the past ten years since Sam had moved to the small new house in Hogtown. Near the abandoned house the morning sun flashed off the windshield of the dirty bronze Corvette, and Obie idled the Ford to a crawl for a closer look at the strange car.

The dust covered Corvette, sporting Nevada tags, was pulled across the yard, its front wheels resting on the fieldstone walkway, and its long nose jammed into the rosebush. Obie slammed the brake and slid the tractor to a sudden stop. A limp body was sprawled with feet out the passenger side window and head pinned loosely against the leather steering wheel. "Lord God," muttered Obie. "Somebody's done got drunk and drove back in here to die."

He scrambled off the tractor and ran closer, but slowed when he realized the man was breathing. "Stinkin drunk," he growled. Obie reached for the door handle and jerked angrily. The wide shoulders shuddered and the limp body slid to the dirt, head first, feet tangling with the stubby gearshift. One bloodshot eye cracked.

"Goddamn, Obie," croaked Billy. "You still don't know nothin about handlin a sufferin drunk."

Obie recoiled. "Billy?"

"The one and only." Billy rubbed his smeared eyes. "Well, help me up from here. Don't just stand there a gawkin."

"Billy." Obie offered a gnarled hand. "Where did you come from? And when?" He stared.

"From the other side of hell," chuckled Billy. "About four this mornin." He stood, shaky, and leaned on the dirty car. "Hell, Obie, want a drink?" He pulled a pint bottle from the door pocket. Obie shook his head.

"You're lookin good, Obe," said Billy. He took a long pull from the bottle. "Course, you always was mighty healthy." He offered his hand.

Obie responded. He clasped Billy's hand and shook heartily, still staring in disbelief.

"Hell, it's jist me," laughed Billy. "Twenty years worse for the wear, but lovable as always."

"I'll jist be damned," Obie finally grunted.

Billy chuckled. "Where is Grandpap? I come here lookin

for him."

"H-he moved," stammered Obie. "Ten year ago, to Hogtown." He recovered. "Pap, he's jist up the road there. He'll be wantin to see you, Billy."

"I doubt that," grinned Billy. "Besides, right now I ain't in no shape for a fight. Is Mamma at the house?"

"Yeah," said Obie. "Same place." He wiped the sweat from his brow. "Look here, Billy. My place is jist over the hill there. You'd be welcome to go there first, to git cleaned up and to rest some."

"Look like hell, don't I?" asked Billy.

"Yes," Obie said truthfully. "You shore do."

Billy Cox, the NBA's "Wild Bill," looked two decades older than his thirty-seven years. His eyes, sunk deep in their sockets, were red and swollen. A heavy stubble covered his jaw, and his coal black hair—graying now—hung in coarse, greasy strands. His silk shirt was rumpled and stained; the tailored pants were bagged at the knees and roughly wrinkled. The ornate boots were scuffed and dusty, and a slim gold chain hung crookedly around his slim neck. He looked much shorter than his six five, and his shoulders sagged wearily.

"I drove straight through," he mumbled. "From Vegas."

"You look it," chuckled Obie. "Are you able to drive jist a little bit more?"

"Sorta," grinned Billy. "Long as they ain't no traffic."

"Then go back up yonder," said Obie. "Take a right jist past the old graveyard. My place is half a mile. Tell Annie I sent ye."

"Annie?"

"Annie Clark, she was. You know her."

"Annie Clark?"

"That's what I said, Billy. Git goin. I don't want Daddy to see you whilst yer like this." Obie pondered. "Are ye sure you can drive?"

"I can do her, Obe," laughed Billy. "Watch."

He eased into the Corvette, found the ignition, and spun the big V-8 to life. Twin exhausts rumbled, and the engine clattered smoothly.

"Runs purty good," observed Obie.

"Does alright," said Billy. He eased out the clutch and the Corvette lurched forward. "Wrong way, damnit," he growled. He found reverse and rolled backwards. "Obie," he said, "if ye see Daddy you tell 'im—if you don't mind—that if he don't care I'll be comin for supper."

"I'll tell 'im." Obie crawled back on the waiting tractor. He stopped and yelled, and Billy shut down the Corvette to listen. "I said," roared Obie, "welcome home, Billy."

Billy grinned, saluted, restarted the Corvette and rolled away, Willie Nelson wailing through the four-speaker stereo system. Obie drove the tractor on to the field and met Jessie there.

"Mornin, Daddy," he called. "Wait up a minute."

Jessie held the mules and waited impatiently.

"He's here," said Obie.

Jessie paled. "Billy?"

"Yeah. I found 'im asleep in his car over by the homeplace. I sent him up to my house to git rested."

"What's he like?" asked Jessie.

"Drunk," grinned Obie. "And seventy years old."

"Damn," said Jessie. He turned to the plow and clucked to the mules. "He never changed none, did he?"

††††††

Billy eased the Corvette up the narrow graveled drive to Obie's house, swerving to miss the potholes and to soothe his throbbing head. He pulled to the side to let the yellow school bus pass, then drove on slowly. He parked in the yard beside a blue Mercury and wearily swung out. The woman working in the flower beds stared, quickly stood, and ran to meet him.

She stopped short, cupped her hands over her mouth, and stood trembling.

"Hello, Annie," Billy said quietly. "Been a long time."

"It is you," she gasped. "Billy Cox."

"Wild Bill Cox, ma'am. At your service." His eyes sparkled. "Mrs. Obie Cox, I presume?"

"God!" Annie was still staring, her eyes wide. "They said you was comin home." Her hands smoothed her hair and she fussed with the buttons of her dress. "Billy, I . . . I'm . . ."

"Obie told me," grinned Billy. He walked closer and hesitated. "Any more youngens here?"

"N-no."

He swept her off the ground in a bear hug, reached down and squeezed her ample rear.

"Billy!" she squealed happily. "You stop that!"

"Ain't you gonna say hello?" he asked, "to an old friend?"

An hour later, freshly scrubbed and shaved, he slept.

In the kitchen Annie sobbed into her apron. The phone interrupted her private thoughts, and Sam Cox was screeching into the receiver. "Is Billy over yonder?"

"He's here," Annie said quietly. "He's sleepin now, Sam, and it might be night before he's up."

"I'm a comin over there," cackled Sam. "Soon as I can find me a ride."

"He's sleepin," protested Annie. "Sam, wait 'till after two or three o'clock and let him rest up."

"Aw, hell," grumbled Sam. "Okay, Annie, I'll wait a while. But if he wakes up you call me."

"I will," she promised.

††††††

Jessie paused over his lunch. "Billy's home," he said softly. "He's over to Obie's, sleepin. Sent word he was comin here fer supper."

"Law, Jessie, why didn't you tell me first thing?" Georgie spilled her water as she lept excitedly to her feet. "I'm fixin chicken, and beans, and—Jessie, why didn't you tell me?"

Jessie chuckled. "I like to surprise you, Georgie. Hell, Billy didn't tell ye neither."

Georgie was already busy, bustling around the kitchen.

"Better fry 'im up a pan full of crow," laughed Jessie, "cause that's what he's gonna have to eat first."

††††††

At three Annie slipped the door open. "Better wake up, Billy," she whispered. "Sam's comin."

"Aw, Annie, I just got to sleep." Billy rolled over, grinning, and reached for her. "It'll be two more hours before old Obe gets home."

Her freshly washed, powdered, and excited body still fit snugly in the curve of his elbow, and she wiggled with intense pleasure as he pulled her down in the sheets and renewed their old friendship.

††††††

By four-thirty Billy was dressed, relaxing in the parlor to meet Annie's children as they ran in from the bus. "Youngens," Annie said proudly, "this here is your Uncle Billy. Your daddy's baby brother."

Billy winked at the four speechless youngsters. "Out in my car is a ball I brought you. The whole team signed it."

Twelve year old William Samuel Cox whooped and ran for the Corvette.

Ten minutes later Sam arrived, sweating and cursing. "Damn fool Jake Wilde," he fumed, "made me walk. I told him he couldn't see Billy yet and he put me out at the highway."

"Grandpap," yelled little Billy. "Lookit this! He brung us a ball, and it's got Dan Issel's name right here."

"Where's he at?" bellowed Sam.

"In the house with Mommy."

Sam hobbled to the door. "You crazy bastard!" he yelled. "Don't you know your old grandpappy's out here a wantin to see you?"

††††††

Obie, tired and dusty, came home at five-thirty. "Found two more copperheads," he told Sam. "Right out in the cornfield." He smiled slowly. "You're lookin better, Billy, than you was this mornin."

"Feelin better, too," smiled Billy. "I slept all day, 'till Grandpap here come in a cussin and yellin."

"Take him with ye," said Obie, "and git on over to the house. Mamma's done fried enough chicken to feed a army fer a month."

"Let's go, Billy," croaked Sam. "I can't drink no more of your fancy moonshine nohow."

Obie waited until the Corvette was gone, then spun to glare at Annie. "You couldn't wait, could ye?"

"Now, Obie," she said, "don't go thinkin—."

"I can tell, damn you!" hissed Obie. "You couldn't even wait for dark." He slapped her, hard. "You're worser than Billy. Least he don't pretend to be nothin he ain't."

"Obie?" Annie's voice quivered. "What are you gonna do?"

"Nothin." He grinned. "Not to Billy." His smile flickered.

"No, Obie," pleaded Annie. "Please."

"S-shut up!" he snapped. "B-bitch!"

CHAPTER 4

COPPERHEADS AND OLD BASKETBALL PLAYERS

In her dim office in the basement of the Cox County Courthouse Brenda Higgens drained the last of the coffee from the yellowed pot. "Jesus, Becky," she grumbled, "you could use this stuff in your car motor."

"Sorry, boss." Becky grinned broadly. "You lady lawyers are all alike—bitch, bitch, bitch."

Brenda chuckled. "It's a good thing it's quitting time," she said. "You've got sassy again."

"Horny." Becky crossed her legs, stretched, and smiled.

"Then I wish you good hunting tonight," said Brenda. "If you get in trouble and need a lawyer, don't call me. You know that all I'm good for is drawing up deeds." She laughed and slung the coffee into the garbage. "Lord, what I wouldn't give for a nice juicy, scandalous lawsuit."

"Don't worry, honey," consoled Becky. She tugged at her bra straps. "Someday some poor sucker who can't afford a real lawyer will come walkin in here and you'll be in business."

Brenda scowled and stuck out her tongue.

"Speakin of men," grinned Becky, "did you hear that Billy Cox is comin home?"

"Who's Billy Cox?" Brenda was busily loading her briefcase.

"Law, honey," sighed Becky. "He's just the sexiest hunk of man I ever laid eyes on. He'd be as welcome in my bed tonight as he would have been twenty years ago."

"He's one of ours?" asked Brenda.

"Jessie's boy," said Becky. "Younger than Obie. His pictures are all over the school gym. He's been a professional basketball player for fifteen years." She smiled, remembering. "God, he cut him a wide path when he was here! Knocked up his cousin when he was just fourteen, and then he got busy. Lordy, what a body."

"Well, he's probably fat and bald now," said Brenda. "But I wish you luck all the same. Maybe he'll want to renew old friendships."

Becky shrugged. "He never got around to me. But I'm still willin." She flipped the light switch and opened the door. "I guess you got a hot date tonight, huh?"

"Go to hell, Becky."

"I will," said Becky. "If that's where Billy's waitin." She yelled back as she left. "You orta come with me. He'd shake them curls outa your hair and put 'em in your toes."

Brenda, smiling, finished packing her briefcase and locked the door. Outside, as always, she stopped to look at her window.

The sign read "BRENDA M. HIGGENS, ATTORNEY AT LAW."

"Took long enough to get," she mumbled as she walked away. "Maybe someday I'll get to do something besides shuffle papers."

In the parking lot she located her gray BMW and drove to the Cox Ridge Road. Three miles out she braked hard, turned sharply left, and sent the lively sedan scrambling up the steep gravel drive. At the top she shifted, straightened the skidding rear wheels and drove the final half mile at full throttle, dust billowing. The two large hounds ran barking to greet her and leaped happily as she climbed out of the car. "Down Buck," she yelled, "and git, Sam!" She walked briskly to the cabin, a two story restoration that overlooked the ridge and valley, and ducked inside to escape the eager hounds.

She changed quickly. The severe suit gave way to soft jeans and a baggy sweatshirt, and her hair was freed to flow to her shoulders. Her breasts swung as she ran back outside to romp with the hounds.

Brenda M. Higgens, attorney, was home, and she relaxed into a very different role.

She was thirty-four, a leggy and slender brunette, a native West Virginian who slipped back into her mountain drawl as easily as she pulled on the loose shirt.

Brenda had been born in Number 9, a coal camp near Morgantown, two miles from Camp Number 7 and light years removed from the modern world. Her father was an underground miner, illiterate and unquestioning, who was killed in a cave-in to leave five growing daughters and a penniless, tubercular widow. Brenda was eleven when her mother died. For the next seven years she lived with an aunt in Beckley, more of a live-in babysitter and maid than family member, a handy whipping post for her mother's frustrated sister. A week after Brenda's thirteenth birthday her uncle raped her; she lived the next years in terror of his rough, groping hands and foul breath. She finished first in her high school class and earned a full scholarship to begin her escape.

She earned her degree in history and political science and enrolled in the West Virginia University School of Law; in 1972 she passed the bar exams.

For four years Brenda worked in the offices of the West Virginia Attorney General, and during a mineral rights case met courtly, seventy-three year old Zachariah Cox, Sam's brother, who persuaded her to move to Skaggs Gap and take over his law practice. She came to Cox County in 1976.

Brenda carefully cultivated her image as a no nonsense professional; she dressed in conservative, expensive suits and dresses, and maintained an air of rigid competence. The younger Cox County men were intimidated by her cool presence, and the courthouse philanderers soon learned that Brenda was not interested.

She used her savings to buy the twenty acres from Sam Cox,

and in six months completed the restoration of the old cabin. The hounds were Sam's gift. "It ain't fittin," he said, "fer a woman to live up yonder all by herself. You be a good lawyer, Miss Higgens, but you don't look to be much of a hand at shootin critters or fightin off roughnecks."

Sam was wrong. Brenda Higgens was a crack shot, with rifle or revolver, and her only inheritance from her father was the well oiled old .30-.30 carbine hung over the fireplace.

Secretary Becky Skaggs had come with Zack's law office. Zack had hired her out of high school, trained her as a legal aide, and somewhat toned down her openly aggressive sexual drive. Becky, a divorcee with a pretty daughter, drew business to Brenda as she struggled to establish her practice. Brenda handled all legal affairs for the sprawling Cox family, and word of her reliability and discretion helped draw new clients, but to her frustration, the work was mostly routine—deeds, contracts, uncontested divorces, and work with state and private agencies in Cox County. No man would hire a female lawyer for courtroom work; even the brawlers who used public defenders asked for a man—"a real lawyer," they said.

Except for Zack and Sam Cox and an occasional evening with Jake Wilde, there were no men in Brenda's life. She used her money to travel, and over the years had located and helped educate her four sisters. She was content, happy with her simple life, only vaguely aware of the emptiness.

††††††

After feeding the dogs she stretched out on the sofa and dozed until the phone buzzed her awake.

"Godamighty," giggled Becky. "I jist had to call, Brenda. He's already here."

"Who's here? From where?" Brenda tried to shake away the sleep.

"Billy," said Becky. "Billy Cox. He come in last night."

"So?" Brenda yawned.

"He's by hisself. No wife, drivin a big yeller sport car. He's out to Jessie's right now."

"Becky, did you wake me up just for this?"

"Wait'll you see 'im, Brenda. Just you wait. You'll see."

"I can wait," groaned Brenda. "I'll see you tomorrow, Becky, if you live through the excitement."

Brenda fixed her evening meal, and as she sat down to eat opened the Cox County News. Billy Cox was the front page feature. The half dozen photos–none recent–showed a lean young man, graceful and powerful, always with a basketball.

Another small town jock, thought Brenda. She read on. He was a college All American. "Probably never did graduate," she snorted. Sixteen years as a professional. Thirty-seven years old and still "Billy." Obviously, Sam's errant grandson was not one of the solid, stable Coxes she'd come to deeply respect after four years in Skaggs Gap.

She tossed the paper aside and finished supper. At least, she conceeded, Billy Cox's arrival would divert attention from the copperheads. The paper contained reports of three more incidents. The victims survived, after quick treatment, and all three swore the snakes had aggressively attacked them in daylight. Specialists from the university had been requested to study the situation, and local residents were again advised to exercise extreme caution.

Brenda sighed. Copperheads and old basketball players.

She read for an hour, and was fast asleep by nine.

††††††

Jessie met Sam and Billy on the porch. "Pap, you been drinkin," he said accusingly.

"Yep," grinned Sam. "Ever since I was a pup. My pappy wouldn't let me have none 'till I was up walkin on my own."

"Hello, Daddy." Billy, suddenly awkward and bashful,

offered his hand. Jessie gulped, frowned, and finally reached out.

"You're lookin good, son," he said quietly. He frowned again as he smelled Billy's breath. "You know your mommy don't like likker in the house."

"God damn," blurted Sam. "We ain't gonna spill none, Jess, cause it's all in our bellies." He shoved past Jessie. "Georgie! Your baby's here! Where in hell are you?"

Frail, white skinned Georgie Cox came from the kitchen, swiping at her hair and wiping her hands on a gingham apron. "Billy!" She smiled and reached for him, and as they embraced her hands ran lightly over his broad shoulders. She sniffed and pulled away, dabbing at her eyes. "You're so thin, Billy! You ain't been takin good care of yourself."

"It's a hard life," chuckled Billy, "and I been drivin for three days. I'll be fine, Mamma, soon as I eat a plate of your chicken and biscuits."

"Then let's eat," growled Sam. "I'm so damned hungry I could eat a whole hog."

Supper was a platter of fried chicken, white gravy and hot biscuits, fresh beans, corn, and tomatoes, homemade jelly, and a crusty blackberry cobbler. Sam's teeth clacked and gravy dribbled down his chin. "I ain't et so good," he said, "since Lily passed away."

He turned to Billy. "How's come you never come home fer the buryin?"

"I meant to, Grandpap," said Billy, his eyes averted. "I just couldn't get away. There was school, and practices, and. . ." His voice trailed away.

"I reckon you've stayed plenty busy, boy," said Jessie. "For damn near twenty year now."

"Yeah, I guess so." Billy found his mother's eyes. "You know how I ain't much for writin or callin, and I was always on the road somewhere."

"And laid out drunk mosta the time," added Jessie.

"Jessie Cox!" Georgie was half standing, her eyes snapping. "You stop that right now! Billy, he's come home. You stop pickin at him."

"It's okay, Mamma," laughed Billy. "I'm used to it. It makes me feel right at home to hear Daddy yellin at me again. We never did get along real peaceful." He smiled, and Jessie squirmed. "How's the rest of 'em doin, Mamma?"

Georgie lit up. "Obie, you done seen, he's helpin here. Georgie Sue is up in Cincinnati, she's got three boys. Louvonna's over to Skaggs Gap—her man's got a garage—and Margie, she went to Youngstown and made a teacher."

"All doin real good," grinned Billy. "Uh, what about Uncle Jack?"

"Iffen ye mean Linda," scowled Jessie, "she lives in Hamilton. Her husband is a bookkeeper and she's got three younguns."

Billy stared cooly at his father. "Thank you," he said.

The cold silence gave way to a discussion of the doings of other aunts, uncles, cousins, nieces, and nephews, and for an hour the lively and laughing conversation bubbled. Then Jessie, from his armchair, asked the question he'd held back. "What are you plannin to do now, Billy? To make a livin?"

Billy squirmed, and grinned sheepishly. "Well, Daddy," he said, "I'm not real sure just yet."

"I reckon you ain't hurtin, are ye?" asked Sam. He spat into a grimey coffee can. "You made damn good money, bein a ballplayer. That yeller car, she's worth a bunch, ain't she?"

"It cost $16,000 new," admitted Billy.

"You'll stay with us, won't you?" asked Georgie. "Until you decide?"

"I. . .I don't know, Mamma," said Billy. "It all depends."

"Hell, you can stay," grunted Jessie. "Leastways until ye find work."

"Damn!" Sam snorted and slapped his chair. "Come over and stay with me, Billy. Let's batch it. I got the house over in

Hogtown and they ain't nobody there but me. Hell, I need some company worser'n anybody."

"No, Sam," pleaded Georgie. "Billy's stayin here."

"Let him go." Jessie's voice was strained. "That's what he wants to do. Then him and Pappy can lay drunk together and neither one of 'em'll have to work any."

"Jessie!" Georgie was angry.

"He ain't changed none," Jessie said softly. "Billy, he's still playin." He stared at his tall son. "You ain't got no money, have ye?"

"Not a whole lot," admitted Billy. "Enough to support myself and get started. The car's paid for. I was plannin. . .well, I'd like to. . .to fix up the old homeplace and live in it, and help with the farmin."

Jessie's cackle hurt Billy's ears. "You're crazy as ever, Billy," he laughed. "Still a dreamin." He shook his head. "Me and Obie don't need no help on the farm. And that old house, it's been settin empty for ten year. Forgit it, Billy. Go on back and do your playin somewheres else."

"This time I'm not playin," muttered Billy. "I mean what I said."

"You ain't worked a lick since you was sixteen," chuckled Jessie. "How am I supposed to believe that now you're wantin to bust your ass on that grubby hillside?"

"Don't talk like that," said Georgie. "Billy's your son."

"That he is," grinned Jessie. "And the land, it's mine, too."

"And mine, Jessie." Sam was stiff in his seat. "Don't you fergit that. You gonna give Billy a chanct or I'll give him the damn land myself."

Jessie glared. "No, you won't," he growled.

"Billy," said Sam. "Tomorry mornin I'm givin ye a hunnert acres."

"What hundred acres?" demanded Jessie.

"The homeplace, the fields around it, and the mountain," said Sam. "That part you don't own none of."

"Forget it, Grandpap," Billy said softly. "I'll just be movin on."

"Damn if you will!" spat Sam. "You got a right, boy. You're a Cox, by damn, same as the rest. It's my land, and I'll damn well do as I please with it."

Jessie chuckled. "Take 'er, Billy. Give it a try. I wanta see you scratchin a livin outa that hillside and fightin off the snakes. You and them damn copperheads. Hell, you make a good match."

Billy stared quietly. "Okay, I'll take it. Daddy, you're in for one hell of a surprise."

"I hope so, son," Jessie said softly. "But I doubt it."

Their eyes met stubbornly, and it was Billy who looked away. "Where's the stuff I shipped?" he asked.

"Over at Sam's," Georgie said. "Billy, you stay right here. I want you to."

"No," said Billy. "But don't worry, Mamma. I ain't goin anywhere. Before winter I'll be livin in the homeplace."

He shoved himself up from the chair. "Let's go, Grandpap."

On the porch Georgie clung to him. "He don't mean all that," she whispered. "Your daddy jist has to. . .to show ye he's still your daddy."

"I know," said Billy. "He's a tough man, Mamma. But a good one." He smiled. "We'll work it out."

"Let's git, Billy," roared Sam from the darkness. "Take me fer a ride in this here yeller car."

"All right, Grandpap." He opened the door and slid down into the seat. "I'm glad to be home, Mamma," he whispered. He grinned, started the engine, and spun the Corvette in a circle. Sam whooped in fear and fun as Billy hit the roadway and accelerated.

"Hot damn, Billy," yelled Sam. "This thing's better'n the one the lawyer woman's got."

Billy shifted and the Corvette leaped forward. "What lawyer woman?" he asked.

"One that took Zack's office," yelled Sam. He covered his ears. "This thing always make so much racket?"

"Sure does," said Billy. "Is she pretty?"

"Fergit it," said Sam. "She's too damn good fer you."

Billy laughed and drove swiftly; he parked at Sam's small house and pulled a duffel bag from behind the seat. "You got more of that fancy drinkin whiskey?" asked Sam.

"Just half a case of it," laughed Billy. "Closest thing I ever found to your drippins."

Inside they opened a bottle and drank, and remembered and laughed for two more hours. "What's all this I hear about the copperheads?" asked Billy. "Last night I stopped for gas and the feller told me I was headin right for a snakepit. What's goin on?"

"They're bad," said Sam. "They ain't no water up on the mountain, and they come down to drink. They done kilt three, and it's gonna git worser."

Billy shuddered. "The bastards scare me. Ever since that time you told me about your brother Obie gettin killed."

Sam was suddenly gloomy and brushed aside further discussion. "Gimme some more of that stuff," he said.

"You're gettin high," laughed Billy.

"I'm seventy-nine year old," grunted Sam. "Old enough to do as I damn well please." He giggled. "Course, *you* been doin as ye pleased ever since ye was borned."

"Pretty much," chuckled Billy. "And look at what it's got me." He took a long pull from the bottle. "Now," he said, "tell me the truth. Are the copperheads really attacking people?"

Sam shrugged. "They say so, but I ain't seen none myself. Folks that has, they say the bastards is comin right after ye, not skeered o' nothin."

"I'll be damned," Billy said quietly. "What's gonna happen, Grandpap?"

"I dunno," Sam said wearily. "I jist know a damn copperbelly can be awful mean. The one that got Obe, it musta bit him six times fore he got loose."

"Daddy told me," said Billy. He stared off into space. "He also said Obie stopped stuttering before he died, and kept yellin that he wanted to go home."

"He was jist rememberin," said Sam. "Recallin the night me and him spent up on the mountain. That's what got him to stutterin to start with."

"You stayed up there? All night?"

"Me and Obe," sighed Sam. "Night of July 12, 1915. I scratched it in a rock up there. I tooken Obie, him jist twelve, up in them snakes. He never was the same after. . .it were my doings, Billy. I kilt Obe, sure as if I'd a shot him."

Billy leaned to gently pat Sam's shoulder. "No you didn't," he said firmly. "Obie didn't have to go with you."

Sam sat forlornly. "He was gonna tell Pap unless I took him along."

"See? He made up his own mind." Billy stood. "Let's get some sleep now."

Sam waited. "I mean it, Billy, about the land."

"I do too," smiled Billy. "Thanks."

"I got some cash, too," said Sam. "Near $10,000. This place is all paid for. We can do 'er, Billy, if you really want to."

"I want to," said Billy.

"How much money have you got?" asked Sam.

"Oh, maybe $25,000. I'll sell the car. I get money from endorsements–about $5,000 a year. Is that enough?" He grinned. "Hell, I can always go play another year."

"Why'd ye quit ball, Billy?"

Billy sighed and slumped in the chair. "Old age," he grinned. "For a ballplayer, I'm old. My knees are patched together, and I just can't play anymore."

"That all?" asked Sam.

"Hell, no," laughed Billy. "I got tired of all the travelin and the runnin and drinkin. I want to stay here, Grandpap.

Maybe I finally grew up."

"I'm gonna help you," said Sam. "I'm awful tired of settin around. We'll be partners."

"It's a deal," said Billy. "Now damnit, let me get some more sleep."

††††††

The dark man walked the mountain, guided by soft moonlight, passing silently through the brush and fallen logs, gliding over the jagged rocks. He moved with the copperheads, skirting the thickets and climbing steadily. Atop the mountain, in the barren clearing, he sat motionless. He raised his eyes to the heavens, and the restless copperheads were soothed.

At dawn the man left, vanishing quickly down the slopes, making no sound as he moved.

Copperhead Mountain greeted the new day.

CHAPTER 5

"HE'S ONE OF OURS, SURE AS HELL"

Jim Farley eased the Volkswagon into a parking space and checked his watch. He'd left Cincinnati at six; it was now eight-thirty. He swung out the door, looking for someone to ask directions to Sam Cox's house, as Becky Skaggs rounded the corner. She froze, blinked, then shrieked with delight.

"Billy!" She screamed, and ran toward Jim with her arms waving and her hair bouncing. "Billy Cox! You ain't changed one bit."

Jim backed away, pushing Becky back. "What did you call me?" he sputtered.

"Billy," she said. "You *are* Billy, ain't you? Billy Cox?"

"N-no," stammered Jim. "I-I'm Jim Farley."

Becky stepped back and studied him carefully. "Well," she decided, "you are a mite young to be Billy. But I swear you're the spittin image of him. Are you kin?"

Jim blushed. "Maybe. Sam Cox is my great-grandfather. Could you tell me where he lives?"

"Sure can," grinned Becky. She stared intently. "Go down two stoplights and turn left. That road'll git you to Hogtown. It's about five miles and Sam's house is the little white one on the right, just as you git there."

"Thanks," said Jim. "Sounds easy enough."

"Your daddy's already here," blurted Becky. "He come in yesterday."

Jim's smile was cold and tight. "My father's still sleeping in Cincinnati," he growled. "I told him goodbye two hours ago. But I still thank you for the directions."

He jerked his car door open and sat down quickly, fumbled with the controls and lurched away. Becky ran inside and grabbed the phone. "Susie?" Becky giggled happily. "You remember Billy Cox gittin his cousin pregnant? Linda? Jack's girl? Well, their baby just drove off lookin for Sam. The boy is the spittin image of Billy, tall and good lookin and shy. He was gittin out of his car as I come to work."

††††††

As he drove, Jim Farley cursed his family resemblance. He must look even more like his father than Linda had said, judging from the reaction of the trampish woman he'd just met.

"Damn," he muttered. "Maybe I should have left well enough alone."

He gritted his teeth and drove on, remembering.

Jimmy Farley had been thirteen, a budding young basketball star, and summer camp at the university cost two hundred dollars. James Farley, senior, had refused; Jimmy listened from outside as his mother took up the battle. What he heard sent him fleeing, terrified, his illusions of his own life shattered.

"Damn him to hell!" James Farley had screamed. "He can pay his own way! I will *not* be a part of encouraging him to be like his good for nothing father."

"Be quiet," hissed Jimmy's mother. "He'll hear you."

"Let him," snapped Farley. "Hell, maybe you ought to bring him in here and tell him the truth—that his mother is a whore from Hamilton and his father is a basketball playing sot!"

"Please," she begged. "Jimmy might hear you."

Jimmy, running, blinded by angry tears, heard no more.

When he returned, late in the night, his mother reluctantly confessed. The Farleys had taken Jimmy at his birth; they knew his mother and her family. She would not give Jimmy names, refused to identify the father. He sulked, suffered, and finally accepted his own version of the truth—he was a bastard, an inbred offspring of cousins, a direct descendant of the dreaded hillbillies he and his friends so openly ridiculed.

Jimmy quietly continued his search and, two years later, located Linda Hamilton—married now with other children—and was able to meet with her. Finally she identified his father; Jimmy watched Billy play a month later. He stared as the lithe athlete dazzled the crowd with a display of long range shooting, frowned as Billy played lazily. He left frustrated but determined to become an even better player than Billy Cox.

At seventeen he was an All Cincinnati player, and for the next four years he starred at Xavier University. Pro scouts liked his cool floor presence and he was drafted in the early rounds. Jim declined the NBA contract, returned to school for an advanced degree in biology, and had completed a year of high school teaching when he read of Billy's retirement and return to Kentucky. He was at once angry and curious; he decided it was time to meet his father and the family he knew nothing about.

Now, enroute to his great-grandfather's house, he was having second thoughts.

††††††

"Damn fool!" Jimmy yelled and braked, swinging his car into the thick roadside grass to miss the thundering Corvette that swept around the curve sideways. He glimpsed a lean, younger man driving; the passenger was a strawhatted old timer.

He trembled over his steering wheel, looking after the Corvette. "That son of a bitch shouldn't be driving," he muttered.

He shook his head, accelerated, steered the VW back out onto the roadway and was in Hogtown in 10 minutes.

††††††

Billy parked the Corvette near the courthouse and chuckled as Sam struggled to lift himself out. "Damn newfangled cars," grumbled Sam. "Fer my money, the Model T was the last goodun."

Billy, watching Sam, stumbled headfirst into a blushing teenage boy. "Jesus," the teenager whispered. "You're Wild Bill Cox."

Billy grinned. "In the flesh, son."

The boy, dressed in a Cox County High School jersy, stood and stared blankly. "You play?" asked Billy.

"Uh, yeah, but mostly football."

"They didn't have that when I was your age," said Billy. The youngster still waited, blocking the way. "Mind if we go on?" asked Billy.

"Oh. I'm sorry." The boy moved aside. "I never seen a real pro before."

"Son," laughed Billy, "you still ain't. Just ask any sportswriter." He slapped the boy's shoulder. "Me and Grandpap got to be going. See you around." He guided Sam quickly forward.

Sam hobbled and cursed. "Damnit, Billy, slow down and let 'em look at ye. Might as well git it over with so's ye can be left alone. Folks around here ain't used to seein a real live hero." He chuckled. "You are a hero, damnit, even iffen ye don't deserve to be."

"Some hero," grunted Billy. "This lady lawyer of yours in Zack's old office?"

"Yep," said Sam. "Right down them steps."

Sam shoved away Billy's offer of help with the steep concrete stairway. "Let me be," he snarled. "I ain't so fer gone as to need carryin." He drew himself to his full height and threw the door open. Becky looked up from her typewriter, squealed, and came running.

"Billy! It *is* you!"

"You remember Becky," said Sam. "She's Oney's youngest girl."

Billy smiled, hugging Becky tight, his hands exploring her full body. "Hell, Grandpap," he asked, "why didn't we come to town last night?"

"*Do* you remember me, Billy?" asked Becky.

"Sure I do." He winked at Sam. "It's been a long time, Becky."

"I just *knew* you'd remember," gushed Becky. "I was just thirteen when you left, but I watched ever game you played." She stepped back and appraised him. "Are you married, Billy?"

"Not any more," he chuckled. "Three times was plenty."

The door behind them opened. "Is this a family reunion, Becky?" asked Brenda. She saw Sam. "Hello," she smiled. "How's my favorite moonshiner?"

Sam cackled. "Still gittin around," he said. "Still a waiting fer you to come and marry up with me."

"I will," she promised. "As soon as you settle down and act like a grown man." She eyed Billy cooly. "This must be Cox County's illustrious basketball playing son."

"I'm Bill Cox," he said. "I liked Becky's greeting better."

"I'm sure you did," said Brenda. "What can I do for you, Sam?"

"Draw me up some papers," said Sam. "I'm givin Billy some farm land."

Her smile was cold. "I'm sure he's an excellent farmer," said Brenda. "Totally dedicated to the land."

Billy scowled. "Look, lady," he began, "I—."

"My name is Brenda Higgens."

"Look, Brenda Higgens," snapped Billy. "I didn't come here for you to be cute. I doubt if you're capable of that. If you *do* know how, just draw up the deed."

Brenda glared, then reddened. "Come on in, Sam," she said. "I'll fix it up for you." She turned to Billy. "Maybe you'd prefer to wait out here. You wouldn't understand the language."

"Now looky here, Brenda," said Sam. "Don't go pickin on

Billy. He went to college too."

Brenda smiled. "And was an excellent student, I'm sure. Did you major in gym? Or skirt chasing?"

Billy grinned slowly. "*Your* skirt is safe, Miss Brenda Higgens." He sat on Becky's desk. "I prefer real live women."

Sam dragged Brenda into her office and pointed out the land to be transferred to Billy. "The old homeplace," he said, "and back to here, and down to the road. And the mountain."

Brenda frowned. "That's one hundred twenty-five acres, Sam. Plus the mountain. Why does he want that?"

"The mountain?" Sam grinned. "He never. I just decided it'd be good fer him to own it."

Brenda shrugged. "Not that it matters, Sam, but he doesn't seem to be a farmer."

"They's lots to Billy that don't show at first," said Sam. "He ain't nearly as damn crazy as he acts sometimes."

"I hope you're right," said Brenda. "How does Jessie feel about all this?"

"Ain't none of Jess's business," said Sam. "It's my land."

She smiled tightly. "You're absolutely right, Sam. I can have the papers ready this afternoon."

"Do that. Billy, he'll come fer 'em."

"About four-thirty," said Brenda.

Sam joined Billy and Becky in the outer office. Becky was red and squirming, totally absorbed in Billy, clinging to every word. "Ready to go?" grunted Sam.

"Yeah, Grandpap," said Billy. "Everything squared away?"

Sam nodded. "You got to come back at four to git the papers."

"Okay." Billy stood. "See you then, Becky."

"Sure thing," she said. Becky waited, then blurted: "Billy, your. . .your boy, he's in town."

"My what?" He laughed. "I said I'd been married, Becky. Not out of my mind. One thing I don't have is children."

"You got a boy," Becky insisted stubbornly. "He was right

out there, early this mornin. He looks just like you, only younger and not as tall. He was lookin for Sam, and asked directions to Hogtown. His name is Jim Farley, and he's drivin a white car. A little one."

Billy frowned. "We met a VW Rabbit on the way in."

"That was him," said Becky. "I swear, Billy, he's yourn. Maybe. . ." She blushed. "Maybe he's yourn and Linda's."

Billy glared. "Let's go, Grandpap," he muttered. "Things are gettin a mite too personal in here."

Becky followed. "Don't be mad at me, Billy," she wailed. "I was just tryin to help." She watched them leave, then wheeled quickly as she saw Brenda watching and smiling. "It's the damn truth," she spat. "That boy was here this mornin."

"Becky," Brenda said softly, "I think you just blew it." She smiled. "Help me get this deed ready. I feel sort of sorry for the copperheads."

††††††

Billy drove swiftly, eyes straight ahead. Sam watched, and finally spoke. "A body can't pay no attention to Becky Skaggs, son."

"I know," sighed Billy. "But, damnit. . .what if she's right?"

"Hell," said Sam. "If he's there we'll see what he wants."

"It's not that simple," said Billy. "I never knew. . .I forgot, sort of, on purpose. I haven't said a word, ever, about him. I guess it'll be one hell of a shock to meet my full grown son."

"He'd be about twenty-three," mused Sam. "But that don't mean thisun is him, Billy. Hell, Becky'd think any goodlookin young feller was him, just because of you bein back and her gittin so wild."

"Goddamn, Grandpap," said Billy. "I can't handle a grown up son. Maybe, if he was just a little kid. . ."

"That'd be easier," agreed Sam. He rubbed his chin. "You've always been worryin about him, ain't you?"

"Yeah," said Billy. "Lots." He stared glumly ahead. "Knowing I had a child somewhere. . .hell, I'm human."

"Damn," Sam said softly. "I don't know what to say, Billy."

They topped the hill and saw the white VW parked in Sam's yard. "By God," growled Billy, "we'll soon know." He laughed, a nervous chortle, and eased the Corvette in close. He was out quickly, walking toward the house, leaving Sam.

A tall young man, rocking gently on the porch swing, smiled as he watched. He swung easily to his feet and walked to meet Billy, who stopped and waited. Jim moved closer, recognizing the familiar features, and smiled again. He extended his hand.

"Hello, Daddy," he whispered.

The three men sat around the little kitchen table, tumblers filled with amber whiskey, awkwardly talking as they sipped. Jim slowly filled them in on his background, his adoptive family, his career.

"One thing's damn sure," said Sam. "You're a Cox, pure and simple. You're Billy plum over."

"I wasn't doubtin it," grinned Billy. "I'm just still a little shook."

"What about me?" asked Jim. "I had to work up enough nerve to come down here."

"Jim, I. . .I'm glad you did." Billy gulped the whiskey, and swallowed hard. "Welcome home, son."

"Thanks." Jim smiled. "I think I'm gonna like it."

Sam fixed lunch and they stayed at the table, talking more, remembering and filling each other in on the years of separation. Billy finally asked the question he'd held back.

"Jim, what did you—all those years—think about me?"

"For a long time I hated you," he said bluntly. "Maybe I still do." He grinned. "No, Mamma—Linda—told me that you were just kids, and that you wanted to marry her."

"He did," agreed Sam. "Jessie ner Jack wouldn't hear of it."

"I don't know," said Jim. "I just wanted to get to know you." He brightened. "I saw you play, once. At Cincinnati.

You were pretty good."

"Sounds like you did okay," said Billy. "I remember hearing about you, but I. . .I didn't know. . ."

"The Celtics offered me a contract," said Jim. "For a while I thought about trying it." He grinned. "I had this dream, where I played against you and really worked you over, then told you who I was."

Billy chuckled. "The last few years all the young kids worked me over. But I can still outshoot any of you."

Jim smiled lazily. "We'll see," he said. "Want to play some one on one?"

"Not today," growled Sam. "I don't want you and Billy to git to fightin over who's the best."

"Good thinking," said Billy. He turned to Jim. "Your mother. Linda. What did she think about you coming down here?"

"She told me to stay away," said Jim. "That all I'd get was hurt. She. . .I think she's still in love with you."

"Oh, lord," groaned Billy. "Does her husband know about all this?"

"He knows about me," said Jim. "Maybe you. I'm not sure. He was always gone when I visited her."

"Poor bastard," sighed Billy.

"Hell," laughed Jim. "Don't go wasting any sympathy. I'm the bastard around here."

"Damnit, Billy," laughed Sam. "We finally growed us another Cox what ain't skeered of laughin. You got spunk, boy. You're like Billy was, 'cept you got sense."

Billy blushed. "I guess you've heard about my wild life."

"Plenty," said Jim. "But I'm sure there's lots more."

"Are you planning to stay a while?" asked Billy.

"If you'll let me."

"What if I say no?"

Jim shrugged. "I'll stay anyway."

"Set another plate," Billy told Sam. "We just took in a

boarder."

"And find us another bottle," added Jim. "This one's dry."

Billy leaned back in his chair. "You still haven't asked me why I came back here."

"So I'm asking." Jim uncapped the fresh fifth.

"Me and Grandpap," said Billy, "are gonna farm the old homeplace. With mules, tobacco–the whole bit, the old way. You want to help out for a while?"

"Can ye handle a team?" asked Sam.

"Well, I coached a little," said Jim.

"I mean mules, damnit!" snorted Sam.

Jim laughed. "I never did. But I learn fast."

"We got us another set of hands," said Sam. "You got any cash?"

"What?" Jim stared at Sam.

"Money," said Sam. "We're needin to buy tools, and a good team, and all kinds of stuff. You want to buy in?"

"No thanks," chuckled Jim. "But I will help. Besides, I'm due twenty-three years of child support."

"Why not?" Billy shrugged. "I'll give you the names and addresses of your three stepmothers. Maybe they'll give you part of all they took from me."

At four Sam interrupted the gathering. "You got to go to Skaggs Gap," he told Billy. "Git them papers from Brenda, and bring some groceries for supper." He winked. "Bring her along, too."

"The lady lawyer?" Billy laughed. "You're kidding."

"No, I ain't neither," said Sam. "Me and her is friends. Tell her I'm cookin up a supper she don't want to miss."

"Hell, I'll try," said Billy. "Are you sure you wouldn't rather have Becky?"

"Git!" ordered Sam. "Don't come back here without Brenda Higgens."

††††††

Becky Skaggs had already gone by the time Billy arrived. He pushed the door to Brenda's office open quietly and stared. She sat wearily, her skirt tugged up over slim thighs, busy with a cigarette and a stack of papers. Her legs were curled over the desk and her hair was rumpled.

"Beautiful," he murmered.

Brenda jerked, spilling the papers to the floor, then recovered quickly, her face slightly red.

"Don't you ever knock?" she asked. "Everything is ready. Have Sam sign these, and bring them back for filing. There's no rush."

Billy did not move. "I'll bring them back first thing in the morning," he said, "if you'll promise to be sitting here again, just like you were."

Brenda blushed and tugged down the hem of her dress.

"Just for a second there," said Billy, "you were all soft and pretty."

"That," she snapped, "is no concern of yours."

"Yes it is," he grinned. "Remember? I went to college to study skirt chasing."

"Mr. Cox, I–."

"Billy. If we're going to do business, we might as well be civil."

"Very well. Billy." Brenda straightened her chair. "My personal life is no concern of yours. Obviously, you are very quick to jump to conclusions. Don't judge me by your standards, Mr. Cox."

"Billy."

"Billy." Brenda frowned. "I'm an attorney, a damned good one. Anything else there is about me is none of your business."

Billy found a chair. "Miss–Ms.–Higgens," he said, "I don't give one damn about your personal habits. I need an attorney, not a social partner. I *did* enjoy looking at you." He chuckled. "Hell, I still do, even with you trying to be all proper and official."

He stared solemnly and Brenda finally grinned. "I apologize," said Billy, "for anything I've said and done. Could we start over?"

"Okay," she said. "Start." She crossed her arms and smiled.

"All right," he said, "I'm Billy Cox. For the past sixteen years I've been a professional basketball player. I also have a degree in English from a damn good school. I came home, just yesterday, to get away from a world that was making me sick. Today I've almost thought I was back in the NBA. First you jumped on me, then I met my son for the first time and he's bigger than me. I'm giving up a two hundred thousand dollar contract to start farming a hillside, and I'm a little worried. I'm tired, sort of drunk, and in no damn mood to swap insults with an ERA Yankee girl with a hostile attitude toward men."

Brenda stared, giggled, then burst out laughing. "A degree in English?"

"Cross my heart," said Billy. "Hell, I can even write."

Brenda spun her chair around and stood. "I do apologize," she laughed, "for part of what I've said. Becky's report on you didn't include anything except basketball and sex. She didn't tell me you were arrogant, pushy, macho, and. . .sort of sweet and likeable."

"Apology accepted," said Billy. "But old Becky's right about some things."

"So I've heard," Brenda said dryly. "And, for your edification, I'm no damn Yankee. I'm from West Virginia, just across the line, and your family was wealthy, compared to mine."

Billy chuckled. "You sure as hell fooled me. I'm sorry I called you a Yankee. But I meant every word about you being pretty."

"Thank you," she said. "This is much better."

"I agree," said Billy. "I have an invitation from Sam. He wants you to join us—him, me, and my spanking new, twenty-three year old baby—for supper. Can you come?"

"Yes." Brenda smiled. "Sam is my favorite cook. Do I have

time to change?"

"Plenty," he said grimly. "I have to go grocery shopping. I could pick you up in about an hour."

"Fine. I live out. . .well, around here everybody calls it the old Boone place."

"Up on the hill?"

"That's the one."

"I'll be there," he said. "About six?"

He stood to leave, and she stopped him.

"This is just for supper," she said. "Nothing else."

His lip curled. "I don't recall," he said softly, "that I asked you for anything else."

††††††

He bought groceries from Sam's list and then stopped for gas. The attendant admired the Corvette as he scrubbed the bug spattered windshield. "Hell of a car," he offered. "It a 454?"

"That, and a little more," said Billy. "A shop in Denver built the engine for me."

"I bet she's fast," the young man said. He stepped back. "Need anything else?"

"Not for the Corvette," said Billy. "But tell me about that old truck with the 'For Sale' sign on it."

"It's a '57," he said. "Got good tires, runs real good."

"How much?" asked Billy.

The boy eyed the Corvette before answering. "Nine hundred."

Billy laughed. "I'll give you three."

"Hell, no," protested the attendant. "Daddy'd kill me." He studied. "Might let ye have it fer five."

"Sold," said Billy. "How do I make the check?"

"Don't you want to drive it first?"

"Should I?"

"Well. . .no, but most people."

"I trust you," grinned Billy. "How do you want me to make the check?"

"Jeff Bowles. I'll have the truck ready in the mornin." He looked at the check. "Damn," he said. "Are you Wild Bill Cox?"

"Yep."

"I mighta knowed." Jeff grinned. "The car, and all. I heard you was comin back. You gonna coach, or what?"

"I'm going to farm some," said Billy.

"Farm?" Jeff sneered. "Even we done give up on that."

"You quit farming?"

"Two years ago. We still got the place, but we don't work it. Me and Daddy, we're partners here."

"Do you still have your tools?" asked Billy. "The tractor? Plows? Wagons? I need everything."

"We got it all," said Jeff. "Even a team of mules. Why would you want it?"

"I told you," said Billy. "Make me a price. On the whole works."

"You serious?" Jeff peered intently.

"I sure am."

"Why?" Jeff shook his head. "Hell, you don't have to farm."

Billy laughed. "I've got over a hundred acres. The old Cox homeplace."

"Hell," said Jeff. "That's right in the middle of all them copperheads."

Billy sat down and pulled the door shut. "That's what I hear," he said. "Make me a price. I'll stop by tomorrow."

Billy drove quickly to the old Boone place, pulled the hill on the second try, and stopped in a cloud of dust. Two hounds bellowed at his door, and Brenda came running. "Down!" she ordered. The dogs fell in behind her. "Want a drink first?"

"Sure." Billy stared. Brenda's hair was loose and hung almost to her waist, and she wore tight, faded jeans and a soft velour shirt. "Damn," he said. "Are you sure you're the same woman?"

Inside the cabin she handed him a glass. "Mix your own," she ordered. He found bourbon and splashed it over ice.

"This is some place," he said. "When the Boones lived here you had to fight off the hounds and roaches for a seat."

"So I've heard," said Brenda. "All I kept was the hounds. Sam gave them to me. The Cox bloodline, he said."

"That's true," said Billy. "He's been breeding them for over sixty years, and the line goes back to his grandfather." He inspected the old rifle over the mantle. "Yours?"

"It was Daddy's," she said. "It's all I have of his. . ."

Billy finished the drink. "We'd better go," he said. "We're already late. Grandpap is gonna be madder'n hell."

He opened the heavy door for her. "Quite a car," she said.

"It's okay," grinned Billy. "Not a BMW, but it'll do."

"That car is my toy," laughed Brenda. "It's sort of cranky. Jeff, over at the garage, calls it the 'bastard mother whupper'."

"Jeff Bowles?"

"Yes. How did you know him?"

"I just bought his truck," grinned Billy. "And tomorrow I'm going to look at all the Bowles farm equipment."

"Are you really serious? About farming?"

"Yep." Billy hit the starter and the Corvette roared. "I've been on stage long enough. I'm tired of being Wild Bill. I'm going to farm, and Grandpap and Jim are gonna help."

"Jim?"

Billy blushed. "He's my son. Hell, he's a grown man. We just met. Jim's a biologist, or something like that."

"What a household," laughed Brenda. "The three of you need a cook, maid, and babysitter."

"And," added Billy, "a good lawyer."

At the house Sam sat immobile, bleary and solid. Jim grinned and tried to stagger to his feet. "Pleased to meetcha," he mumbled. "Miss Higgens, I'm sorry. I tried to drink with Grandpappy and I. . ."

"And you found out he's had eighty years of practice," said Brenda. "I think I better cook."

"Can ye?" Sam belched loudly.

"Just you watch, Sam," she said. "Of course, I will need an assistant cook and head dishwasher." She smiled at Billy. "Since you come closest to being sober. . ."

"I'll do it," grumbled Billy. He looked down at his large hands. "They fit a basketball better than they do a dish, but I reckon I can learn."

"Come on," ordered Brenda.

††††††

Supper was a feast. "By God," said Sam. "You cook as good as Lily did. Marry up with her, Billy."

"I'm willing," said Billy.

"Sam, he's too much like you. No decent woman would have him."

Later Sam signed the deed. "It's yourn, Billy." He turned to Brenda. "And tomorrow, you write Jim here into my papers. He's one of ours, sure as hell. Give him his share."

Jim grinned happily. "Course," added Sam, "we still got to teach 'im how to hold his likker."

††††††

It was after midnight when Billy drove Brenda home.

"You're easy to be with," he said softly. "That's an unusual quality. Tomorrow, would you go out with me? Just me, without Sam?"

"Yes." Brenda smiled. "But you'll have to protect me from Becky when she finds out."

"What in hell," asked Billy, "is Becky's last name?"

††††††

In Hogtown Jim was questioning Sam.

"Are the copperheads as bad as the papers say?"

"Boy," said Sam, "they're ever bit as bad, then some. But I can tell ye better tomorrow, when I ain't so woozy. Your Daddy ain't likely to git home before daybreak, but you and me can git some sleep."

"Do you think he likes me?" asked Jim.

"Billy?"

"Yes."

"Hell, Jimmy, he's yer daddy."

"He always was," said Jim. "But now he has to face up to it."

"Son," Sam said softly. "Billy ain't much for pretty words, but he's a hell of a sight more man than most. He loves you. He's worried over ye for twenty year."

The Corvette rumbled into the yard and Jim walked to the door. "Losing your touch?" he asked.

"Go to bed, boy," grinned Billy. "Or I'll cut off your allowance and take away your teddy bear."

CHAPTER 6

"FOR SHE IS THE CHOSEN ONE"

Skaggs Gap, and all of Cox County, buzzed.

"Sam, he give him over a hunnert acres," said Elmira Conn. "All legal and clear. That woman lawyer drawed it up. Billy, he's gonna fix up the old Cox homeplace and live in it. The boy, he's over twenty, he's Billy's. By Linda Cox, Jack's girl. He's stayin with Sam too. Law, Effie, I ain't never heard of sich goins on."

"I heerd," bragged Effie, "that Billy Cox and that lawyer woman was a livin together, too."

Elmira chuckled. "Then you sure don't know nothin about her. Brenda Higgens, she don't mess around with men."

"My Lord," gasped Effie. "She ain't one o'. . .one of *them*?"

"They say she is," Elmira said smugly.

"I never!" Effie was indignant. "Right here in Cox County."

"Billy, he buyed all the Bowle's farmin stuff," added Elmira. "Mules and all. Paid five thousand, cash money. He's movin it all right now. Jessie, he ain't speakin to Sam. Said he was gone foolish in his old age, takin in Billy and the boy. Says they're layin drunk, whorin, and actin like little boys."

"Law," sighed Effie. "That Billy Cox sure do liven up a place, don't he?"

††††††

Billy whistled happily as he dressed for his date with Brenda. Jim watched, sprawled across the bed with an open book. "I guess you'll really do it up," he laughed. "Take her to dinner at the Whip And Sip, go to the drive-in movie, then go necking up on the gap."

"There was a time, sonny," chuckled Billy, "when that would have been a first class evening." He combed at his shaggy hair. "Now, for tonight, what I got in mind is dim lights, some soft music, a few drinks, a little preliminary exploring on the sofa, and. . ." He shrugged. "You know."

"You do that," laughed Jim, "and you'll be back in an hour with a big thick law book stuck in your ear. Miss Higgens won't be so easy for you to push over."

"I don't think I want to," said Billy. "She's a pretty special woman. Besides, what makes you such an expert?"

Jim grinned. "It's one hell of a strange world when the son sends the father off on a date and gives him good advice on how to behave. Do you need some money? Want to use my car? Will you be home by eleven?"

Billy smiled as he buttoned his shirt. "Just do as the sitter tells you to, Jimmy, and if you're good I might bring you a present. But don't wait up for me."

The Corvette sparkled from a two hour cleanup, and the engine throbbed softly as he turned and swung out onto the highway. He punched in a cassette and Waylon Jennings flooded the speakers; Billy cruised at seventy, driving easily with one hand.

Brenda met him at the door, and he stepped back to let out a low wolf whistle. A green silk dress accented every curve, and the slit sides exposed lean, brown thighs.

She blushed. "You did plan to come in, didn't you?"

"I don't know." He grinned foolishly. "If I get inside with you I might not be able to leave."

Drinks were ready, and he studied her carefully as they sat in the cabin. "Am I that much of a shock?" asked Brenda. "You act like you've never seen a woman before."

"Not one like you. Not here in Cox County. I'll bet every woman in fifty miles of here hates you."

She giggled. "You're right. They're afraid I'll take their men. Single women don't fit in around here. The ones who've finally decided I'm no threat with their husbands have decided I'm gay."

"Are you?"

"Not that I've noticed."

He laughed and finished the drink. "What are we going to do? I didn't see any new supper clubs in Skaggs Gap."

"Do you feel like driving?"

"Always."

"Then there's a Holiday Inn in Huntington that I love." She blushed. "Their restaurant, I mean."

"Suits me. I haven't been to West Virginia in a long time. Is it safe?"

Billy sent the Corvette through the twists and turns of the narrow highway, caught the interstate highway, and drove easy toward the Ohio River. As he drove he pointed out familiar landmarks, and Brenda identified the progress. There were new state park lodges at Carter Caves and Greenbo Lake, large consolidated high schools in each county; tidy red brick houses and shiny mobile homes dotted the once isolated hillsides. "Damn," said Billy. "I never dreamed so much could happen in twenty years."

"It hasn't all been good," said Brenda. "Some of the programs—and the agencies—do more harm than the poverty. We now have third generation welfare recipients who actually can't afford to take a job."

Billy laughed. "Don't be ridiculous. How in the hell could a man not be able to afford to work?"

"It's the weird system," explained Brenda. "If a man takes temporary work he loses his benefits almost dollar for dollar. He figures he's working for nothing, and pretty soon he stops trying. A minimum wage job pays less than can be drawn from all the aid programs. Not working pays better than working. Given that choice, what would you do?"

"I see what you mean," said Billy. He drove quietly, then asked, "what will happen? We can't go on paying people to not work."

"I really don't know," sighed Brenda. "Maybe start over with a WPA type of program—something different, where a man earns more by working. Reduce the spending, get rid of the politics. It's already too late for lots of things. Most of the old ways are gone, for better or worse."

"What about the coal?" asked Billy. "We're supposed to be swimming in the damned stuff, and the whole world is eagerly waiting with planeloads of cash."

"It's better than it used to be," said Brenda. "At least the coal camps—like the one where I grew up—are gone. But so far coal is such an unpredictable industry—good wages for six months, then a market slump or a strike. When they work, miners make good wages, but they can never predict a steady income."

"Are they mining in Cox County?"

"Some. A few old deep mines and two new stripping operations." Brenda grinned. "Enough to where there are already disputes between the unions and the operators, and all the truckers are carrying pistols."

"Home sweet home," chuckled Billy. "I wish there was a coal seam right under Copperhead Mountain. Then, by god, I'd set and watch 'em cut away the copperheads."

"Fat chance," said Brenda. "All you've got is a big rock and thousands of snakes."

The restaurant in downtown Huntington was decorated with handmade quilts from West Virginia craft cooperatives, plus stoneware pottery, split oak baskets, and hand loomed tablecloths.

"Nice," said Billy. "I was expecting plastic flowers and coal figurines. Is the food good?"

It was. "One advantage of having all the managers and other administrators sent in," said Brenda, "is that we're getting some good restaurants. And, good roads to get you to them."

The meal, and the drive back, were relaxed and happy.

"The trouble with this car, laughed Billy, "is that there's no way I can slide you over close and drive with my arm around you."

"I might even volunteer to scoot over," said Brenda. "Too bad about these bucket seats."

"You," said Billy, "are a very special person. I've never met anyone like you. You're the best of both worlds–educated and sophisticated, but still you keep two big old hounds and a .30-.30 rifle. Why haven't you moved away?"

"Sometimes I wonder," said Brenda. "But, every time I go away from these hills for over a week, I get nervous. I *need* the mountains. They make me feel. . .oh, safe, I guess. I just don't fit in in flat places."

"I know." Billy slowed and turned onto Skaggs Ridge Road. "Since I came back I can sleep better, and I do feel safe."

Brenda giggled. "Even with Becky and the copperheads chasing you?"

He laughed. "Even with a new son and two year's worth of work to do in two months."

"Can you do it?" asked Brenda. "Can you really make a living from the land?"

"You mean will I stick it out?" He smiled. "I want to, and that's most of the battle won. I've got good help."

Brenda smiled and lay back in the padded seat. "I hope you do make it work, Billy."

"Could it be that you've decided to like me?"

"I sort of like you, Wild Bill Cox." Brenda grinned. "No matter if they all do say you're a sex maniac."

"What about you?" asked Billy. "Us maniacs need partners. Why is a woman like you still single?"

"I never met the right man." Brenda stared out the window. "Maybe I never will."

"Maybe you just have," grinned Billy.

"You?" She smiled.

"Hell fire," laughed Billy. "I'm civilized. I haven't tried to rape you."

Brenda stiffened and pulled back.

"Did I say something wrong?" Billy's hand was on her shoulder. "Brenda, I know I'm sort of crude sometimes, but—damnit—I *like* you. I don't want to scare you away. I guess I've always been around a different kind of woman."

"Obviously." Brenda turned, and smiled weakly. "You're funny, Billy, all bluff and little boy rolled into one." She relaxed, lifted his hand from her shoulder, and held it." Not a working man's," she murmered.

Billy chuckled. "Made to fit a basketball, they always said, or a bottle."

"Or a woman," added Brenda. "You're a legend in these parts."

"I never could quite live up to my reputation," laughed Billy. "Don't believe *all* of it, Brenda."

"You're making quite a stir, coming home," she said. "The hearts are fluttering."

"And the tongues are wagging," he added.

She giggled. "Yes. You've even enhanced my reputation."

"I wish it could sort of ease off," said Billy. "I could use a little less attention. Not everybody's happy to see me, and all the talk makes it worse."

"Who's unhappy?"

"Daddy. My big brother." He drove slowly, staring at the winding asphalt. "Old enemies, people that didn't approve of the way I was."

"Why does Jake Wilde dislike you so much?" asked Brenda.

"Who?"

"Jake. He owns the paper. You know."

"I don't even know the man," said Billy. "Are you sure he's mad at *me*?"

"Yes. At least that's the impression I get."

Billy laughed. "Is Jake one of your boyfriends?"

Brenda blushed. "A friend."

"Hell, lady, then I know why he's mad. I don't think I like him, either, if he's after you. I want you all to myself."

"Still," said Brenda, "there's more. He sort of. . .I don't know. Jake acts scared, or something, about you being here."

"Damned if I know," muttered Billy. "Maybe I ought to go see the man. Hell, he wasn't even around when I was growing up. I couldn't have done anything to him. He's just jealous, Brenda."

"Maybe so." She smiled. "You draw a lot of attention."

"I just want your attention," he said softly.

"Go slow, Billy. Just give me time." Brenda sat back and lit a cigarette. "I have to get used to you."

There was a soft, lingering kiss at her doorstep and she was gone.

††††††

Two weeks passed, busy days of hauling, clearing, and planning, and Billy's lean body was hard again.

He pumped the stiff clutch, cursed, and found reverse in a crunch of gears. He backed the smoking old Chevy closer to the house, shut off the engine, and jumped down from the cab. He pulled off the soft leather gloves and grinned ruefully. "My hands are still lookin like raw meat, Grandpap. Where's Jim?"

"Up toward the mountain," said Sam. "He said he wanted him a closer look. Said fer you to unload it yerself, that he was gonna git some rest." Sam chuckled as he pulled at the ropes holding the load in place. "Jim, he said he ain't no slave, and they was laws against child labor."

Billy grinned. "We have been going at it pretty hard. This finishes all the hauling except the mules, and we have to build some fence before we bring them in. Let's just stack these timbers until we need them."

He reached back into the truck. "But first let's drink a cold beer and wait for the baby to git all tuckered out and come back. Then we'll make him unload the truck." He tossed Sam the icy can and stretched out, his head laid against the dual rear wheels of the truck.

"Car comin," grunted Sam. "Must be Jess and Obe, comin to make fun of us."

"Let 'em laugh," said Billy. "Next summer we'll show 'em a thing or two about farming."

As the dust cloud drew nearer Billy recognized the gray BMW. "Brenda," he said. "The lady lawyer, Grandpap."

She stopped short of the house, waited for the dust to settle, and carried her briefcase to where the two men waited. "I've got your new will, Sam," she said. "Sign it, and Billy and I will be the witnesses."

"You're all business today," grinned Billy. "Do you have time for a beer? Or should I whip up a martini with a lemon peel?"

"Considering the heat, the dust, and the lack of social graces of my present company," said Brenda, "I'll have a beer."

"They're in the truck," said Billy.

Brenda tugged at the heavy door, reached in, screamed and jumped away.

"What in the hell?" yelled Sam. Billy came running.

"A snake," gasped Brenda. "On the seat. I think it's a copperhead."

Billy cautiously checked. A fat copperhead, nearly four feet long, was stretched across the hot plastic seat. "I'll be damned," he muttered. "I wonder if he's been riding with me all day."

"It's a biggun," said Sam. "You git Brenda outa the way, Billy, and I'll do the killin." Axe raised, he advanced, and tugged at the door.

The copperhead struck, slamming into the tin door. Sam dropped the axe and tumbled, tripped over thick grass, and the snake hit the ground close beside him. Tongue flickering, the copperhead moved in for another strike. Before Billy could react, a heavy walking staff flashed, crushed the flat head and pinned the squirming body.

Jim swung again, then cautiously prodded the dead copperhead. "Well, Grandpap," he said weakly. "Now we know for sure. The sons of bitches really do attack."

Billy blew out a deep breath and lay down the crowbar he'd grabbed. "Don't let go of your weapons just yet," warned Jim. "Let's make sure he was by himself." He moved slowly around the truck, then searched across the yard. Brenda clung to Billy. "Must have been a bachelor," grumbled Jim. "No more around."

"Shucks." Billy reluctantly released Brenda. "I was enjoying the search."

Brenda ran to Sam. "Are you okay?" she asked.

"I would be," he said shakily, "if somebody'd help me git up to where's I could defend myself."

Jim pulled him to the edge of the porch. "Feel better?" he asked. "That was close, Grandpap."

"I'm alright," said Sam. "He missed me."

"How about you, Brenda?" Jim asked.

"I'm fine," she said. "Except now I don't want any beer."

"Let's call it a day," said Billy, "and get the hell away from here."

"Suits me," said Jim. "I'm ready to quit."

Billy grinned. "Brenda? Want some supper? I have a reservation at the Burger Queen."

Brenda gagged. "You owe me at least a steak after trying to feed me to that copperhead."

"Why not do it up right?" asked Jim. "Let's go find a decent place and have some fun."

"We could go to Lexington," offered Billy.

"Why not?" said Brenda. "We can take my car and go to the Hyatt Regency. We can be there in two hours."

Billy shrugged. "Everybody ready?"

"You youngens go on," said Sam. "I'm gonna rest. Git ye a girl, Jimmy, and go on with 'em."

"I've already got a date for tonight," said Jim. "I met this girl named Beth Skaggs and. ."

"Becky's daughter!" exclaimed Brenda. "Great. Call her, Jim, and let's go."

By five-thirty they were on their way. Brenda drove. "Nobody," she said, "drives my car but me." She handled the curves expertly, and they were in Lexington in two hours.

In the restaurant Jim ordered prime rib. "No offense," he told Billy, "but I'm tired of pork chops. And for God's sake, while we're here let's buy some vodka. The bourbon is wearing thin, too."

"You're learning," laughed Brenda. "Stock up every time you're out. The bootleggers don't offer much choice, and Sam's moonshine is strong enough to use in your car."

"Couple of city slickers," scoffed Billy. "Me and Beth, we're real mountaineers. We could live on fatback and pure alcohol. Ain't that right, Beth?"

She blushed. "I guess so, Mr. Cox."

"It's Billy. You're makin me feel awful old."

"Okay. Billy." Beth smiled. "Now tell me who that man over there is who keeps staring at you."

Billy swung around, and groaned. "Hell, it's Ollie."

"By God." The fleshy, flashy man walked closer, and playfully slapped Billy's shoulder. "Wild Bill Cox! I heard you hung it up, old buddy."

"Yeah, Ollie, I quit," said Billy. "Ollie Wilson, meet Brenda Higgens, Beth Skaggs, and Jim Farley. Ollie's the lowest form of life. A gossipy sportswriter. He's hounded me for twenty years."

"You make a damn good story," grinned Wilson. "You old son of a gun, what are you up to? Did you really retire?"

"I'm a farmer, Ollie," said Billy. "Up in the mountains on

the family land."

"Bull!" Ollie chuckled. "Wild Bill Cox a farmer? You ain't foolin me none." He turned his attention to Jim. "Xavier, wasn't it? Fourth round pick, Celtics. Seventeen points, nine assists a game. Right?"

"Perfect," admitted Jim. "You know your basketball, Mr. Wilson."

Ollie backed away, cocked his head, and looked from Jim to Billy and back. "The two of you," he said, "could be brothers. You even played a lot alike, except Jim had sense and Billy could shoot better." He grinned. "No offense, son, but Wild Bill *was* one hell of a ball player."

"No offense taken," said Jim. "Even sportswriters are entitled to an opinion, even though they're almost always wrong."

"Damn, but the two of you sure do look alike." Wilson pursed his lips. "Are you related?"

Billy and Jim were silent. "Who cares, Mr. Wilson?" asked Brenda. "Neither of them play any more."

"Hey," laughed Wilson. "Brothers. Right?"

"Nope." Billy shook his head.

Wilson's eyes squinted. "Couldn't be. He's not–is he your son, Billy?"

"Sit down, Ollie," said Billy. "Look, I'll talk, if you promise it's totally off the record. Okay?"

"Sure, Billy." Wilson pulled over a chair. "No sweat."

Billy swiveled to face the writer. "Jim Farley is my son."

Wilson stared. "No kiddin?"

"I was fifteen when Jim was born," said Billy.

"Why's he go by Farley?" asked Wilson.

"I was adopted, Mr. Wilson," said Jim.

"You print a word of this, Ollie," growled Billy, "and I'll beat your precious few brains right out of your pointed head."

"Hell, I wouldn't do somethin like that, Billy," smiled Wilson. "Hey, you and me, we go back a long ways."

"My card, Mr. Wilson," said Brenda.

He blanched. "You travel with your lawyer now, Billy? Hell, I ain't gonna tell. But give me a story, for old times sake. What *are* you doin now?"

"Farming," grinned Billy. "Like I told you. In Cox County."

"The prodigal son, huh?" Wilson scribbled. "Let's see, you was All State in. . .?"

"Sixty and sixty-one," said Billy.

They talked for fifteen minutes. "I gotta be goin," Wilson finally said. "It's been nice meetin you folks."

"See you in court," said Brenda.

Wilson grimaced and trotted off.

"Damn." Billy watched him leave the building. "The squeaky bastard will print it all."

"Well, Pappy," laughed Jim, "that way my grandparents will learn all about me."

"Do you mean," protested Brenda, "that you still haven't met Jessie and Georgie?"

Jim smiled. "I guess Daddy—tough old hillbilly that he is—is still scared of his daddy."

"I'm not worried about him," said Billy. "Hell, every soul in Cox County knows all about you. But what will your mother do if all this hits the papers?"

"Which one?" laughed Jim. "My mother Farley will hide somewhere, and the other one will clip it all for her scrapbook."

"My God," whispered Beth. "My mommy told me you were all a little crazy."

Billy laughed. "Becky was right. Hell, all we can do anyway is wait and see."

They left at midnight, and were back in Skaggs Gap at two. Jim left with Beth, and Billy stayed for a drink with Brenda. He pulled her close.

"Forget it," she warned. "I'm tired, and I don't feel like a fight."

"Okay," said Billy. "But I'm persistent as hell. I'll keep right on trying."

Brenda smiled. "There's no law against trying."

††††††

She called at seven the next morning. "Want me to read it to you?" she asked. "Or would you prefer to see it while you're seated?"

"Read," grunted Billy.

"Here goes," she giggled. "The headline says 'WILD BILL IS BACK IN THE HILLS.' Subtle, isn't he?"

"Go on," said Billy.

Brenda read:

"Legendary basketball player Wild Bill Cox has hung up his sneakers and taken up the plow. The two time Kentucky All Stater and All American, a sixteen year NBA veteran, is back in Cox County to rebuild his ancestoral log cabin and farm the venerable hillsides."

"The newly retired Denver Nugget guard was in Lexington last night, accompanied by a lovely lady attorney—that's me—*and former Xavier University basketball standout Jim Farley."*

"Here comes the eerie part. Young Farley is a carbon copy of Wild Bill. Smaller, probably much more intelligent and definitely more urbane, Farley was an NBA pick four years ago. He could almost be Wild Bill's son. . .but we all know Billy Cox is not a father."

"A late fifties rumor attributed young Billy Cox with more than his share of success with the ladies of Cox County. Could Jim Farley somehow be a result of Wild Bill's wild oats?"

"I think so."

Brenda laughed. "Want me to sue him?"

"Naw." Billy chuckled. "Nothing like that. He'd have done a lot worse, except that I whipped him back in 1970, the last time he wrote about my personal life. Ollie's still scared. He doesn't know I've mellowed, and don't you dare tell him."

He groaned. "Where I need your help is with Becky. She's gonna be madder'n hell this morning. Jim came stumbling in, all worn out, about half an hour ago."

"My God," laughed Brenda. "Like father, like son."

"Nope," said Billy. "Like father used to be. If you'll remember, I didn't fare so well on my date last night."

"But," said Brenda, "you weren't out with a cheerleader."

"Thanks for calling, counselor," said Billy. "And, Brenda, thanks for last night. I had fun."

"Me too, Wild Bill." She hung up laughing.

He left the phone happy, poured coffee, then roused himself to answer the persistent pounding at the door. "Comin," he growled. "Don't break it." He swung the door open.

"I hear one of our famous copperbellies almost got you," a strong voice bellowed. "Howdy, I'm Jake Wilde, *Cox County News.*"

"Damn," grumbled Billy. "You scared me worse than the snake did."

"Sorry." Wilde laughed, a deep and rumbling chortle. "Sam told me I'd have to get here early to catch you before you went back to the hillside and the copperheads."

"Come on in. I'm Bill Cox."

"I figured so," said Wilde. "I saw you play, once, up in Chicago. You got twenty-eight points against Jerry Sloan."

"And he broke my nose to get even," said Billy. "What was the editor of the *Cox County News* doing in Chicago at an NBA game?"

Jake Wilde had been a Chicago newsman. "I got tired of always being cold," he said. "I saw the ad for this little paper, bought it, and moved in about ten years ago. Hell, Billy, I'm still an outsider. Sometimes Sam is the only person who'll speak to me." He poured coffee and sipped thoughtfully. "I guess," he said, "that you know a feller name of Ollie Wilson?"

"Sort of." Billy winced.

"He called me last night." Wilde stopped to light his pipe. "Said he knew you were here, wanted me to dig up some news about your son, Jim Farley." He struck a match and sucked the pipestem. "I don't print gossip, Billy. I know Ollie. I fired him once for irresponsible reporting."

"Jim *is* my son," said Billy.

"Hell, that's not news," grinned Wilde. "Not around here, anyway."

"Thanks," said Billy.

"I do want a story," continued Wilde.

"What about?"

Wilde tapped his pipe. "The farm. How you're rebuilding. Why you came back here."

"No problem," said Billy. "Except sometimes I'm not real sure why I'm here."

Wilde chuckled. "At least you're honest. Maybe if I watch you I can figure out why I came here."

"Okay. Feel free. Just don't call me Wild Bill."

"Fair enough," said Wilde.

Sam slammed the bedroom door and joined them, fuming.

"That damned boy of yourn," he told Billy, "can't take it. He says he ain't workin today 'cause he's too damned tired. I ain't so sure he's yourn." He noticed Wilde. "Howdy, Jake. I see you ain't been tarred and feathered yet, but they'll git ye before long. Billy, we got to move them mules today and start workin 'em to git 'em in shape."

He slapped a holstered revolver on the table. "We're takin this, and we got to git a shotgun. I'm a fightin them copperheads from a distance next time."

"Sam," asked Wilde, "did it really jump at you?"

"Damn near bit off the truck door," said Sam.

"That's right," added Billy. "Scared hell outa me. And Brenda."

"Brenda Higgens?" Wilde stirred. "She was there?"

"Yes," said Billy. "She found it first."

"Jake," said Sam, "we ain't got time to set and jaw with ye. You're welcome to come and talk to us whilst we're workin, but we got to go. Git that damn youngen outa bed, Billy."

Billy stood. "Some day, Mr. Wilde, we need to talk some. I hear you don't approve of me for some reason."

Wilde grinned. "Where'd you ever get that idea?" Their eyes met. "I don't even know you, Billy."

Jake Wilde frowned as he drove his battered pickup back toward his Skaggs Gap office.

At fifty-five, grizzled and brown, a dirty cap pushed high over his forehead, Wilde resembled the local farmers. To a degree he was one of them. On his eighty acres he grew a small tobacco crop and beef cattle, partners with a neighbor. But he was foremost a journalist, a once nationally respected and honored reporter who'd dropped out of the limelight. Few Cox Countians knew of Jake's background, and only Sam Cox knew anything of his personal life.

Young Jake Wilde had been a brawling, hard drinking writer, a rascal of sorts, a man who lived the saloon life he so vividly described for the Chicago newspaper and a series of national magazines. A brief respite from the crushing pace came when he married the daughter of a wealthy Chicago banker, a girl drawn to the strong passions she found in Jake. For two years he was sober, but restless. Then he drifted back to the streets and bar rooms, and his searing articles about the city's derelicts earned him a Press Club award.

After five years Jake's wife left, taking the two daughters. Jake, busy on an assignment, found out two weeks later. He shrugged, went back to drinking heavily and soon was immersed in a new series, a story about the Appalachian migrants to Chicago and the other northern cities.

He was intrigued by the snakehandlers, people who handled poisonous reptiles during religious ceremonies, a devout cult who fought in the courts to retain their right to worship with the rattlesnake and copperhead. Totally immersed, fascinated,

Jake longed to test his faith, to experience how the snake-handlers felt at the moment of danger.

He took a leave of absence, and spent the year exploring the mountain churches where the ancient rites were performed. He crossed West Virginia, Tennessee, and Kentucky; and finally, in an isolated Tennessee chapel, he was allowed to participate.

The first time, Jake had been terrified when the preacher approached with the fat copperhead.

In the silence, he had felt the eyes of the congregation bore in on him; he had gulped, afraid but entranced, and stepped forward. The skin of the snake was smooth and dry, always moving, and the copperhead curled slowly around Jake's trembling forearms. The quick tongue licked, the flat head swayed, and the lidless eyes gleamed.

Jake's terror vanished. He was taken by a sudden calm, an inner warmth which swelled and spread and sent its tingle to every inch of his body, through every pulsing vein, to the very core of his being.

As he peered at the swaying head, Jake's battered face softened. His leathery features loosened into a serene smile; his eyes glittered; his spirit soared, and his frame shook with spasms of pure emotion, of unknown joy. Tears streamed from his eyes, and he lifted the copperhead triumphantly above him. A hoarse, ragged yell cracked from his lips, the agonized scream of a tortured soul finding release.

The church was then absolutely silent, and every eye was glued to the big stranger.

Then, without a word, as a group, the men at the altar knelt before Jake Wilde, openly and humbly acknowledging his superior power.

The copperhead curled languidly down Jake's upraised forearm and poised, its forked tongue busy, one inch away from his radiant, joyful face.

††††††

Later, Jake heard of mysterious Copperhead Mountain and traveled to Cox County. He sought out Sam Cox, and they talked through the night. Sam's stories rang true, and Jake was fascinated. He returned often to talk more and climb near the mountain. When the newspaper was offered for sale, he was an eager buyer; he moved to Cox County in 1970. He carefully concealed his snake-handling worship, periodically attending ceremonies in the Tennessee church.

Jake's drinking sprees became less frequent, but more frightening. His week long binges included long walks, hours of aimless driving and dark periods he could not recall.

But most of the time Jake was an accepted, laughingly mocked figure in Cox County, a permanent resident who gradually blended into the affable culture.

He was, generally, at ease with his new life, content with himself and his surroundings. He studied his newly adopted home, learning all he could about the people, probing gently to get Sam Cox to tell more about his Copperhead Mountain experiences. He tried to buy the mountain and was cooly rebuffed. Sam Cox clung to a dream that his grandson Billy would someday come home, that he would build the old farm back to its former glory.

Jake had chuckled. "That's a likely story, Sam. Billy hasn't even come back for a visit since he was 17, and he sure won't ever want to live here again."

"Maybe not," Sam said stubbornly. "But I ain't givin up. That boy loved these old hills, and he always said this is where he was gonna live out his days."

"That's a dream, Sam," Wilde said softly. "I know it, and so do you. Sell me the mountain, at least. It's of no use to you, or to Billy if he ever does come back."

"Can't do it," answered Sam. He grinned. "Besides, Jake, that mountain ain't no fit place for anything but copperheads."

"What about the snake man?" asked Wilde. "The one people have seen up there?"

Sam stared off at the mountain. "People sees what they want

to," he finally said. "That's all part of the story, kids scarin theirselves at night. The snake man, that's just another old story, Jake."

"Not so old," countered Wilde. "Only goes back about 25 years. No more. Before then, nobody ever had said anything about seeing a man on Copperhead Mountain."

"Maybe so," grunted Sam. "Maybe it's just people makin talk."

"Sell it to me," pleaded Wilde. "I want to own Copperhead Mountain."

"Nope." Sam leaned to spit, and rocked back firmly. "Jake, that's part of what's been ourn fer 200 year. *I* own it now–not Jessie–and I'll give it to Billy if he comes back."

"What if he never comes?"

"Then it'll be Jess's, same as the rest."

Wilde had persisted, always with the same answer, and gradually had come to hate the absent Billy Cox, the man who stood between him and his goal of owning Copperhead Mountain. He had, in time, come to believe his own argument that Billy would never return to Cox County, and was content that the mountain would never be disturbed.

Now, what Jake had dreaded most was happening. The return of Billy Cox was complicating his world, frightening him, threatening to disrupt the orderly process of his life. There was the mountain–now Billy's–but there was an equally important problem, one Jake had not expected. Jake Wilde was hopelessly, foolishly, head over heels in love with Brenda Higgins, and Billy Cox–the first day he was home–had stepped between them.

††††††

Jim Farley stacked rough timbers, groaning and softly cursing as he worked.

"Your mamma'd die," laughed Billy, "If she could see the

way you're living."

"I got some catching up to do, on my living," grunted Jim. "Tonight—if I live through this—I've got a date to go see a baseball game in Paintsville."

"Beth?"

"Yep. And her mother." Jim grinned. "Want to join us?"

"Hell, no," growled Billy. "I ain't man enough to take on Becky Skaggs. I reckon you'll have to service both of them."

"Car comin," chirped Sam.

It was a dusty pickup, carrying Jessie and Obie. "Jim," said Billy, "it looks like you're gonna finally meet your granddaddy."

Jessie swung out, dragging a double barreled shotgun.

"Don't shoot," yelled Billy. "Hell, I didn't do it."

Jessie ignored him, and handed the weapon to Sam. "For the coppers," he said gruffly. His eyes were pinned on Jim, and he waited.

"Daddy," gulped Billy. "This here is Jim. Jim Farley. My. . . my son. Jim, this is your grandfather, and your Uncle Obe."

The men stood, quiet and nervous, awkwardly shifting.

Jessie spoke. "How's your mother?"

"She's fine, sir," said Jim.

"Good. Good." Jessie watched Jim closely. "You a city boy?"

"Yes, sir. Cincinnati. But I sure do like it here."

"Well," grunted Jessie. "I reckon you're welcome fer as long as ye want to stay. Pap, will ye bring this crew by the house fer supper tonight?"

Sam cackled. "We'll be there, Jess."

Billy smiled. "Thanks, Daddy," he said softly.

"Thanks fer what?" snapped Jessie. "I been wantin to meet my grandson—or nephew, or whatever the hell he is—fer two damn weeks. You never brung him, so I come lookin." He turned to Jim. "Your Grandma, she'll be proud to meet you, too."

"I'm looking forward to meeting her, sir," said Jim.

"Ye can stop the fancy talkin," growled Jessie. "Hell, call me Grandpa, like the rest of 'em."

"Okay." Jim grinned. "Grandpa."

Obie finally spoke. "Billy, Annie's wantin to see you again. She wants to see Jim."

"Bring em and come fer supper," said Jessie. "She's done cooked enough fer half the county again."

As he left, Jessie turned to stare again at Jim. "They sure as hell ain't no doubt who ye are," he said. "I jist hope you ain't half as crazy as yer daddy was when he was your age."

††††††

During the day Sam killed another copperhead near the barn. They unloaded the mules, ten year old sorrels, and draped the harness in the shed. "Tomorrow we start workin 'em," he told Jim. "They done gone and got fat."

Jim smiled happily. "I'll help. They look like they'd be a lot of fun."

"Fun, hell," grunted Sam. "Jist wait'll you've looked out over them rumps fer fifty years and you'll change your tune."

Over supper, after fussing at Billy for not bringing Jim sooner, Georgie planned a summer reunion for the family. "Sam," she said, "we'll git 'em all here. We ain't never done that before. You'll be stayin, won't you, Jim?"

"I wouldn't miss it," said Jim. "I'll be here unless Grandpap works me to death."

"Just stick with your daddy," advised Jessie. "That way you won't git hurt none by the work."

Obie, characteristically, said little. Annie was surprisingly quiet and nervous, afraid to meet Billy's eyes.

Afterwards, Jim and Billy took the children outside for basketball. "This old goal," Billy told them, "is where I used to practice. They used to ask me why I never banked in a shot, and

I told them. It's because I never had a backboard."

"You know," Jim said as they left, "old Ollie Wilson was right about one thing. You *are* better than me."

Billy grinned. "I told you that a long time ago."

††††††

Jake Wilde's constant companion was his journal, a worn leather notebook into which he poured his daily thoughts, ideas, and emotions. At home, that evening, a half empty bottle of vodka closeby, he wrote:

Today I finally met him. Billy Cox, the long lost son of Cox County, the man who owns my mountain.

I was prepared to hate him, but. . .

I find him reasonably literate, sophisticated, friendly, and sound. But he is dangerous. Already, his work at the Cox homeplace threatens. He is impulsive, likely to fight, and will require careful handling.

Surely, she does not find him attractive.

For Brenda, he is much too crude, too blunt and demanding, too coarse.

She is much too intelligent, too genteel, too kind and gentle to care for the likes of Billy Cox.

Or is she?

Some women, the inexperienced, find his kind attractive, and it is my duty to protect her.

For she is the chosen one, the goddess who will share my temple.

††††††

The heavy, restless man walked Copperhead Mountain until dawn, pacing and worrying, stopping occasionally to stare off into the darkness. He was uneasy, worried, and the prowling copperheads sensed the distress. Throughout the night, the slopes were alive with furtive movement.

CHAPTER 7

SOME FRIENDLY ADVICE

For two more weeks Billy, Jim, and Sam worked grueling, twelve hour days. "Fix up the farm first," ordered Sam. "The house'll keep 'till cold weather." They patched the barn and outbuildings, fitted new support beams, nailed on new siding and tin roof. They replaced posts, cleared brush, strung barbed wire fence, and bought the beginnings of a beef herd.

They cleared the hillsides of brush, cutting posts from the larger timbers and sawing the rest for winter use in the fireplace. Jim and Billy—and the mules—shed their layers of fat and became hardened workers.

Billy's years of drinking were sweated away; his face became the healthy, browned texture of the outdoorsman. Jim reveled in his endurance and new skills. He was now familiar with the use of the axe, crosscut saw, mowing sythe ("ig'nernt stick," according to Sam) and the mules, which he christened Linda and Bill.

Sam cleaned and greased the farm equipment, repaired and sharpened and painted, giving special care to the mule drawn implements. The tractor, a huge Ford, offended him, but he confessed a grudging admiration for its spinning post hole digger.

Billy, more careful now with money, swapped the Corvette to Jeff Bowles for $5,000 cash and a pickup truck, a high-wheeled, foglight equipped Chevy with roll bars and bellowing exhausts. "You're a real redneck now," laughed Jim. "Just git you a rifle for the gun rack, a fox tail for the radio aerial, and you'll be ready for Saturday night."

The work went on, and Jake Wilde provided a humorous running commentary in the *News*. Local farmers delighted at Jim's efforts to learn to fork hay; Sam finally taught him the slower but more productive old methods. The young man loved the old green John Deere mower pulled by the mules, and the longtoothed, highwheeled hay rake.

"It's like a chariot," he said. "Hell, I might decide to be a teamster. Get me four more fast mules and start running a freight line over the gap."

His love for the older ways, and especially the mules, drew Jim to Chester Bowles, Jeff's uncle, a champion mule breeder whose herd drew buyers from across the country and even from South America.

Jim learned that mules themselves are sterile, incapable of reproduction, and are the result of breeding a jack to a mare horse. Chester Bowle's jack was a Missouri champion, and he maintained thirty Belgian mares to carry the foals. The Bowles mules, with their precise bloodlines, were delicate, light red in color, with white manes and tails. Chester showed his best mules in competition, in shows which ranged from the four mule hitch to the World Championships in Sedalia, Missouri. A four year old, ready for sale, would bring from $1500 to $6,000. A champion jack, according to Chester, was worth over $20,000.

Jim toyed with the idea of becoming a mule breeder and spent many evening hours talking with Chester.

At the Bowles farm he also met Karen, eighteen years old, a shy and unpolished girl who blushed prettily whenever Jim appeared but who would not respond to his efforts at conversation.

Karen Bowles was slender but full breasted, soft spoken and given to fluttery femininity, almost too much so. Always, her dresses were modest and dated; her hair was long and silky and deep black. Her hands, Jim noticed, were red and calloused, and he assumed she worked the fields with Chester.

He learned, bit by bit, that Karen had attended high school but had no plans for further education; that she was a superb cook, and that her cedar chest was filled with delicately sewn linens for her eventual marriage. Karen seldom dated, and when she did, the young men were subject to Chester's direct scrutiny. Few returned a second time.

"Is she for real?" Jim asked Billy. "Or—under it all—is she a junkie, or a lesbian, or something?"

Billy laughed easily. "Son, I'd bet money she's just what you see. And I'm afraid she's a type I don't know very well. My reputation was so bad that no farmer in Cox County would let me closer than a hundred yards to his virgin daughters." He grinned. "Have you decided your mule farm also needs a good country wife?"

"Not yet," Jim said. "But, damn, these days a girl who can cook is a rarity."

"Before you start picking names for all the babies," said Billy, "you'd better figure out how to get through that layer of petticoats."

Jim persisted, finally caught Karen alone, and asked for a date. She smiled. "Yes. If Daddy says it's okay."

"Do I have to ask him?" groaned Jim.

"Yes," she said primly. "But it's not so bad. I think he likes you."

Chester honestly could not understand why Jim would be interested in Karen, but he shrugged, grinned, consented, and chuckled as Jim blushed.

Karen was dressed for the evening in a long print dress, buttoned to the throat, and flat heeled black shoes with plastic bows. "Have her home by eleven," ordered Chester.

"Did he mean that?" asked Jim.

"If he didn't like you," said Karen, "he would have said ten."

At the drive-in movie Karen affirmed that she loved the cooking, gardening, and housekeeping, and that she fully intended to be a housewife.

"Do you ever read?" asked Jim. "Can you drive?"

"I read magazines," said Karen. "I got my driver's license at school. Daddy won't let me drive on the highway, but I drive the truck in the fields."

At fifteen to eleven they drove back up the road to the Bowles house. "Stop here," said Karen. They were fifty yards from the porch. Puzzled, Jim twisted and found Karen pressed close, her face lifted.

"What's goin on?" he asked.

"Don't you want to kiss me?"

"Hell, yes." Her eagerness surprised Jim, and the kiss was hot and searching. Her breasts flattened against his chest, and his hand dropped to her hip. She jerked away.

"I'm sorry," blurted Jim. "I didn't mean to. . ."

"Yes you did." She was firm, but not angry.

"I just thought. . ." Jim stammered. "The way you kissed me I thought. . ."

"I wanted to." Karen smiled. "To kiss you. Like that. But that's all. You'd better walk me to the house."

He held her hand as they walked. "Karen, I'd like to see you again."

"Me too." She squeezed his hand. "Would you like to go to church with me Sunday?"

He stopped. "Well, I. . .yeah, Karen, I'd like that a lot."

"Okay." She slipped away and opened the door. "I had a good time," she said, and stepped quickly inside.

Jim ambled back to his car, aroused and puzzled. "God," he muttered, "I haven't been inside a church since I was twelve." He grinned. Karen was a new experience, a special challenge. He knew, from the kiss, that under the prim exterior there was a very ardent, real woman. "How the hell," he mumbled to himself, "do I get through to her?"

††††††

The copperheads continued to plague Cox County. Farmers carried weapons to the fields, and mothers kept the children under tight rein. A day of drizzle slowed the migration and gave Billy and Jim a day of rest.

"We ought to work on the house," grumbled Sam, but he agreed to take the day off and rest. Jim spent the day with Georgie Cox, deep in conversation. Sam rode off with Jake Wilde.

Billy, bored by early afternoon, drove to Skaggs Gap to visit Brenda and to ask for a date. He was quietly rebuffed. "I'm really sorry," she said, "but I already have plans. Jake called, and we. . ." Billy scowled and pointed the roaring truck toward Ashland.

Sam answered his phone at midnight. "Sam" laughed the sheriff, "I just caught me the wildest sumbitch ever to cross the county line. Says he's Wild Bill and to call you. Is he one of yourn?"

"Shit," growled Sam. "What all's he done, George?"

The sheriff guffawed. "Drove that damned black truck right up the courthouse steps, pissed on the statue, shot out a stop-light and throwed two of my deputies over a fence."

"Is that all?" asked Sam.

"All except he's haulin six cases of beer and most of a case of Jack Daniels. Is he bootleggin, Sam?"

"Hell, no. He'd a drunk it all if ye hadn't caught him."

"We got him locked up now. He's singin. Hear him?" The slurred cadence of "Amazing Grace" filtered through the wires.

"Leastways," grunted Sam, "he's singin hymns."

"Hell," said the sheriff, "this here's about the twentieth one. It's like all day meetin. He tried to get me to call Miss Higgens. Said she was his lawyer."

"Call her, then," growled Sam. "I'm goin back to sleep."

††††††

Billy woke to a cottony mouth, a throbbing head, and a black hound's tongue vigorously licking at his ear.

"You'll never get him clean, Buck," laughed Brenda Higgens. "And I don't think he's in the mood for playing."

"Lord," groaned Billy. "You must be old Carrie Nation. Where's your axe?"

"Out in the woodpile," snapped Brenda. "Which is where I should have left you."

He struggled to a sitting position and looked around. "How'd I get here?"

"Only with my expert assistance," she said. "The sheriff finally agreed to drop the charges."

"What charges?" asked Billy.

"Public drunkeness, indecent exposure, wreckless driving." She grinned. "Want me to go on, Wild Bill?"

"No." He rubbed his eyes. "I thought you had other plans."

"In the middle of the morning?" Brenda suddenly smiled. "Are you mad at me for going out with poor Jake Wilde?"

Billy stood and leaned weakly against a counter. "So he's the reason you keep putting me off."

"God!" Brenda stared, then giggled. "Are you insane, Billy Cox? Jake is . . . well, he's like the father I never had. And that's all there is to it."

"Maybe you think that's all," said Billy. "But you just explained why Jake watches over me so close. The old bastard's jealous of me."

"You're wrong," Brenda said firmly. "I'm flattered, Billy, that you care—and that you're jealous of Jake." She smiled. "I've never had two men after me. Really, Jake is just a friend, an old friend." She took his hand. "Come on, now, and drink some coffee. It won't cure you, but maybe it'll make you a little more human."

He suddenly remembered. "Where's my truck?"

"Outside," said Brenda. "The sheriff sent it over. He didn't want it parked in town with its cargo. Were you planning to drink *all* of that?"

"I don't remember." Billy blushed, and groaned.

The phone rang, and Brenda was busy for ten minutes. "That was Jake," she said when she returned. "There's been another death from the copperheads."

Billy grinned slowly. "And good old Jake called just to keep you posted on the latest news."

"Why . . . yes."

"Sometimes, Brenda, for an educated woman you sure are simple minded. Jake was calling about my truck being here."

"You really think so? Surely not, Billy."

"I think so," he said. "Your local reputation is shot all to hell—or made, depending on whose view you take. Either way, I'm sure the tongues are wagging again. Of course, since you're gonna be blamed for it, you might as well be guilty. I'm willing."

"Get the hell out of here," she said wearily. "Go sweat away last night. Sam will be waiting."

"Damn." He moaned, and moved slowly. "I don't know if I can take a whole day of keeping up with Grandpap."

"If you do," said Brenda, "come by and I'll feed you a hearty meal."

"Do you mean that?"

"I do."

"Then, by damn, I'll work old Sam Cox right down to the ground."

"You try that," laughed Brenda, "and you'll eat supper in a hospital bed."

††††††

Billy picked up Sam and they drove to the homeplace.

"Jimmy come out at daylight," said Sam. "Damn boy plumb loves them two old mules." As they got out, Sam tucked the pistol in his pocket. "Jim brung the shotgun," he said. "They got a little boy yesterday, about two miles from here. It's gittin worser."

In midafternoon, as Billy sweated and wrestled a cornerpost into place, Jake Wilde's old truck rattled up the road.

"You come to help?" asked Billy.

"Nope," Jake said solemnly. "I come to talk to you."

"Brenda?" Billy grinned, wiped his forehead, and squatted against the post.

"Yes. I had lunch with her."

"And?"

"Billy, Brenda is one hell of a woman. Smart, and tough. But she ain't ready to deal with a man like you."

"Just what in hell does that mean, Jake?"

"She's too good for you, Billy. Stay away from her. Starting now, I don't want you to ever go near her again."

"Well, now." Billy climbed slowly to his feet, his arms dangling, and a cold grin crossed his face. "Jake, I'm not going to get mad. Not yet. I'm gonna pretend you came out here to offer some friendly advice." The smile vanished. "But let me tell you something, Jake. Nobody—not ever—tells me what to do or where I can go. And I don't explain. To anybody."

He slouched on the iron digger. "Understand, Jake?"

"I hear you," said Wilde. "But don't you make the mistake of assuming I'm just an old fool. I'll be watchin you, Billy, and if you hurt Brenda . . . by God, you hurt her and I'll see you in hell." His breath was coming in choking gasps, and his big face was pale.

"That's big talk," Billy said softly. He smiled again. "Jake, I'm glad we finally understand each other. I sort of like you. And Grandpap thinks a lot of you. But, Jake, you cross me, and I'll walk all over you and never look down."

Wilde met his angry glare. "You'll need bigger boots, Billy."

"I hope we don't have to find out, Jake."

"You fellers is actin mighty serious," said Sam, walking closer. "You got some deal a goin?"

"Yeah," chuckled Billy. "We're talkin business. But we're finished."

"Good," said Sam. "Git back over here and help me string this here fence."

††††††

After dinner Billy told Brenda of Jake's visit. "He gave me my orders," he said. "Jake told me to stay away from you."

"I was afraid he'd do that," said Brenda. "We had a long talk, and Jake was pretty upset."

"He was mad enough to threaten to kill me."

"He wouldn't do that."

"Wouldn't threaten, or wouldn't kill me?"

"Jake was just hurt," said Brenda. "He'll be okay now that he's had his chance to yell at you."

"Maybe," grunted Billy. "But I damn well don't take to being talked to like that."

"You didn't hit him?"

"No." Billy laughed. "I didn't do that. I wanted to, but I figured you'd be mad if I did. All I did was tell Jake where I stand."

"Where's that, Billy?"

"I guess I'm a little crazy," he said. "But I don't bow down to any man." He stared bluntly at her face, looking for a reaction.

"Men." Brenda sighed, then smiled weakly. "You would have fit right in a hundred years ago."

"Probably," conceded Billy. "Brenda, I am just what I am. Just what you see. Sometimes I don't even like me, but there's not much I can do about it."

The silence was awkward. "There's hope for you," Brenda finally said. "At least you're not dumb. You can always learn, if you want to."

Billy chuckled. "You're somethin else, Brenda. I never met

anybody like you before."

"Of course you haven't," she laughed. "I'm like you. One of a kind."

Her warm kiss, as they lingered at the door, sent him home happily enchanted and content.

††††††

Jake Wilde wrote in his journal that same night:

Is it love? Or fear?

Which better controls the serpent?

The church ceremony is no longer enough. I must go beyond, past the mortal handling of the body, forward to a more total bond.

I feel, within me, a much greater power.

The serpents of the Lord, the serpents of the soul, they beckon, they invite me to come closer. They seek my presence and call for me from their very souls.

I must go.

I must go to the mountain, to the kingdom of the copperhead. They await me, trembling for my touch, longing for my guidance.

I, alone of all men, have the power.

I, selected of men, will lead.

I must go, now.

††††††

Billy slept little, twisting restlessly, vaguely aware that he was scared. He was up before dawn, staring off at the slopes of Copperhead Mountain.

Their first project on the homeplace cabin was the new roof. They ripped off the rusted tin, nailed on new plywood, and began placing the wooden shingles.

Sam had felled a red oak tree, sawed it into sections, quartered the pieces, and rived shingles with a froe and wooden mallet. Jim learned quickly, and the shingles now covered the slanted roof.

Billy inspected the interior. "Pretty sad," he reported. "We'll have to rip out the floor and walls and start over."

"She'll keep 'till Monday," said Sam. "We got us a reunion this weekend."

They locked the tools away, washed off the dust in the springhouse, and left content with a hard productive week's work.

CHAPTER 8

"OOH, PRETTY," COOED LOUVONNA

Saturday morning the preparations for the reunion began.

Jim and Billy dug a pit, killed a shoat, and buried the dressed pig in the glowing coals. "That'll be mighty good by morning," promised Billy.

Jessie brought in a ham from the smokehouse and gathered two bushels of fresh corn. Georgie fretted. "It's been so dry the corn ain't hardly fit to cook."

"Cook it anyhow," scowled Jessie. "I had to kill a damn copperhead to git it."

The men built a long table, resting stiff timbers across saw-horses, and gathered tubs to be filled with ice and watermelons. "And beer," added Billy. "Coxes sure ain't teetotalers." Jessie brought two quart jars from the crib.

"Pure corn," cackled Sam. "Cox drinkin whiskey. Reckon any of them boys will remember how to drink her?"

Obie staked out a horseshoe throwing pit and found the old croquet set. Jessie cleaned the .22 rifle and found extra shells. "They'll want to shoot some," he explained.

Georgie kept the kitchen hot, with Annie's expert help, and a dozen pies were cooling on the table. The house was squeaky clean, and the phone rang persistantly.

"Who is coming?" asked Jim.

"All of 'em," said Sam. "Even your mamma and your other granddaddy."

Billy chuckled. "Do you reckon Jack will want to whip my ass again?"

"Maybe so," drawled Sam. "Jim, did ye know that your

grandpa whupped old Billy's butt all over this ridge over you?"

"I had to miss two games, I was so sore and scraped," laughed Billy. "I told everybody I fell out of the barn."

By late afternoon, all was ready. Out-of-state relatives began to arrive, and a lively, crackling conversation carried well into the night.

††††††

A half mile away, at the homeplace, the copperheads stirred, crawled out slowly, and spread for their nightly hunt. The mules brayed and kicked angrily, but retreated to safety, high above their watering trough. By dawn the snakes had returned and were concealed in the cool darkness.

††††††

Sunday morning Jack Cox drove in at the wheel of a lime green Cadillac, dust billowing behind him.

"There's Mamma," whispered Jim. "Ed wouldn't come, so she came with Jack and brought Louvonna."

"She still looks good," said Billy.

"Don't get all excited," laughed Jim. "And, please, stay out of the damn barn loft."

"Don't worry," said Billy. "I ain't anxious to tangle with Jack again."

Linda Hamilton climbed out of the back seat, smiling. "Jimmy," she cried. "You come here!"

"Unca Jim!" A little girl screeched happily, burst past Linda and ran to Jim, hugging his legs until he could gather her in his arms. She kissed him soundly and grinned, then looked around. "Unca Jim," she asked, "is old Wild Bill here? Mommy said he was. Is he a cowboy? Is he gonna shoot at us?"

"No, sweety," laughed Billy. "I don't shoot much anymore." He walked to meet his uncle. "Been a long time, Jack."

"Not long enough." Jack warily shook his hand. "But I reckon it's good to see you again, Billy."

"You're not gonna hit me?"

Jack grinned. "I see you ain't changed a whole lot."

"Just a lot older," said Billy. "Half crippled, and some smarter."

"I sure as hell hope so," grunted Jack. He turned. "Linda, do you remember this feller?"

She blushed under Billy's intense stare. "My God," he whispered. "You are absolutely beautiful."

Linda, in a simple white dress, was slender and tanned, a mature but youthful thirty-eight year old woman, lean and trim and impeccably manicured. Billy stared at the vision of shimmering silk and firm brown flesh.

"Billy, this is my youngest. Louvonna. She's been looking forward to meeting you." Even Linda's voice was new, soft and husky.

"Are you Wild Bill?" demanded Louvonna.

"I used to be," said Billy. "But now I'm just your cousin Billy."

She shrugged. "You don't look so wild nohow."

Billy howled. "I reckon I don't," he said. But you, you look just like your mother. Beautiful."

"I know it," scoffed Louvonna. "Where's Sam?"

††††††

By noon the reunion was in full swing; over two hundred Cox relatives filled the yard and spilled over into the fields. Jake Wilde drove up slowly, his truck lurching, and sent for Billy.

"What now, Jake?"

"You sumbitch." Jake sagged to the steering wheel. "You son of a bitch." He could barely talk, and he grabbed the bottle for fortification. "I'm gonna kill you, Billy Cox. Deader'n hell, I am."

"Why?" asked Billy. "Brenda again?"

"Brenda, thash why. You bastard."

"Go home," said Billy. "Sleep it off, Jake."

"Oh, I'm goin," drawled Jake. "But I'm comin back after you, god damn you."

Jack Cox drifted closer, smiling. "Friend of yours, Billy?"

Billy grinned. "Sort of."

"Gonna kill 'im," said Jake.

"Good," beamed Jack. "You go right ahead, friend. You do us a favor."

Jake peered owlishly out the window. "Who'n hell are you?"

"Hell, feller, I'm on your side," laughed Jack. "I beat Billy damn near to death once, but the tough bastard was up and screwin in a week."

"When I git done with him," droned Jake, "he ain't gonna have nothin left to screw with."

Jack laughed and slapped Billy's back. Jake swallowed, straightened himself, and drove solemnly away.

"Who was that crazy bastard?" asked Jack.

"One of my new friends," said Billy. "You know how everybody just naturally falls in love with me. He's the editor of the newspaper now."

"Old fart sounded like he meant every word he said," mused Jack. "Who the hell is Brenda?"

"My lawyer," said Billy. He smiled. "That's the pure truth, Jack."

††††††

After eating, Billy and Linda walked in the field near the barn. "I didn't know about Jim," said Billy. "Not until he showed up that morning."

"I know," she said. She took his arm and they walked to a grove of pine trees. "I've got a good man now," she said.

"Jim told me," said Billy. "But he also said you keep a scrapbook about me."

She smiled. "Don't be too flattered. The scrapbook was for Jimmy."

"So much for my ego," grunted Billy. "It's been a shock, meeting Jim, and him full grown. All the work has made it go better. Jim seems to love it all, especially the mules and being outside all the time."

"I'm sure he's having fun," said Linda. "Just don't forget he's got a teaching job to come back to in September." She hesitated. "Billy, what was that man in the truck talking about? Why is he so mad? And who is Brenda?"

"Brenda's my attorney, and a friend. Jake owns the paper. He's a little upset that I've been seeing Brenda. He'll be fine when he sobers up."

"I don't think so, Billy. He sounded serious."

"Don't worry," laughed Billy. "We don't kill each other anymore. Not even in Cox County."

They walked on in silence.

"Your little girl is something else," said Billy. "She's as pretty as you, and all personality. She's charmed everybody."

"Louvonna never meets a stranger," said Linda. "She's everybody's favorite, and she always talks a mile a minute. She can ask more questions . . . she's a lot like you were, Billy, when you were little."

"I still ask questions," said Billy, "mostly, now, about me, and how any one man could have screwed up so much. I don't have a lot to show for the years."

"You had your basketball, Billy. And me, once. Now you've got a son."

"Remember that old barn?" Billy pointed, and Linda reddened. "Want to go take a look?"

"No thanks." She laughed. "I learned my lesson about goin up in there with you."

Billy smiled and drew her close. "I haven't forgotten," he

said. "You were beautiful. You still are." They kissed, and their bodies met in a gentle, lingering embrace. "And I still want you."

"Me too," she sighed. "I tried to hate you, Billy, but I couldn't."

"Then, let's, uh, let's go up to the loft."

She pulled quickly away. "Lord no. I've finally got a good marriage, a family, and a decent life. Ed—my husband—has already had to accept a lot. I can't hurt him anymore." Linda stared off at the mountain. "I used to wish that we weren't cousins so they'd have made us get married. That's what I wanted, then. How much did you ever hear, Billy?"

"Just that the baby—Jim—had been born and given away. Grandpap told me."

"It was awful," said Linda. "They made me stay in the house the whole time. Six months. I couldn't even go to the store. Then, after Jim came, it was like a prison. No dates, no movies—nothing. I went to college just to escape. Finding Jim, years later, helped. The Farleys are good people, and he loves them, but he was able to spare some love for me. And now, he's got you too."

She wiped her eyes. "We'd better get back, Billy." She smiled through the tears. "You don't want Daddy after you again."

"No," he agreed. "But the beating was worth it."

Back at the house the food was mostly gone and the quart jars sat empty. People were clustered around the yard, talking and gesturing and laughing.

"Where's Louvonna?" asked Linda.

"Why, she was right here jist a minute ago," said Jessie, "pullin at my britches and wantin to go see Jim's mules. She musta wandered off with some of the youngens, Linda. Here, I'll help ye find her."

††††††

Louvonna skipped and sang, working her way slowly along the dusty trail toward the homeplace. Her fat legs were dirty, and the shiny black sandals were missing. Her short yellow dress showed ruffled panties, and her golden hair was fast losing its curl.

She stopped to admire the poison ivy, the morning glory, and an empty tortoise shell, and called to Jessie's pup as he frisked around her. "You bad doggie. You stolded Grandma Georgie's apron, and she's gonna whup you." The awkward puppy cowered as she waggled her finger, and licked her dusty toes to make amends. Louvonna giggled and ran, stopping to inspect a shiny rock. The pup tugged at her hem and growled playfully.

"Over there is where Grandpa Sam lived," she told the pup. He whined and his tail flopped in the dirt. "Stop it," she ordered. "You're a dumb old puppy." He cowered and circled, wagging his hips, flopped to his belly and crawled to her.

"Unca Jim's mules is right up there," she said. "Come on, dog." She marched on toward the barn, the puppy loping at her heels. "There they are," sang Louvonna. "Them are old Bill and Linda, dog. Come here, you dumb mules."

Bill flicked one long ear and Linda watched impassively.

"Dumb dummy old mules." Louvonna stood with her hands on her hips, angry now, stubbornly insisting that the mules respond. The puppy ran barking, nipped at Bill's foot and drew a swift kick for his efforts. He tumbled, wailed, and ran whimpering to Louvonna. "Poor puppy," she crooned. "Old Bill hurted you. He's a mean old mule."

She crawled through the barbed wire fence and edged closer to the mules, who morosely watched the little girl and the anxious pup. She drew closer. "I'm gonna pet you, you dumb mule." She reached out. Bill's ears flattened and he bared long, yellowed teeth. "Ooh, mule, you don't brush your teeth good," laughed Louvonna.

The mules backed away and trotted to their water trough.

"Come back here," ordered Louvonna. "Come back, you dummies." Glaring, she tried to stare the mules into submission. Bill lowered his head to drink, then snorted and skittered sideways, sharp hooves flashing.

"Bill wants to play," Louvonna told the pup. "Let's go play with Bill, dog."

She ran to the trough. The mules huddled together and watched. The pup barked frantically, circled a clump of wiry grass, darted in snarling, then yelped with sudden pain and surprise. He ran for home, his tail tucked and his tongue rolling.

"You come back here!" screeched Louvonna. "You dumb puppy."

A slight movement in the grass caught her eye. The copperhead curled out slowly, its fat head lifted.

"Ooh, pretty," cooed Louvonna. She bent for a closer look. There was no one close enough to hear her scream; the mules snorted and backed away, then there was silence, broken only by a soft sobbing.

††††††

Billy, Jim, and Linda hurried down the roadway. "She kept asking me about the mules," said Jim. "I'll bet she came down for a closer look."

"She'll be fine," said Billy, glancing at Jim. "There's nothing to worry about, Linda."

"What's that?" shrieked Linda.

The black and tan pup lay limp in the dust. "Daddy's new pup," said Billy. "He's sick."

Jim bent to inspect the dog. "He's dead," he said dully.

"Oh God," gasped Linda. "Louvonna!"

Her screams brought a dozen men, led by Jessie and the rifle. He stopped and stared. "Damn, my pup."

"Come on," said Billy. "Somebody take Linda back to the house."

"No," she yelled. "I'm going."

Jim was already out of sight, running hard. Billy followed. They found the mules, still huddled close, nervously snorting and circling the water trough. Closeby was a flash of yellow. "They stomped her," groaned Jim. "I'll kill both of 'em." Billy charged the mules and sent them braying away. "Louvonna!" he yelled. "Are you okay?"

"Unca Bill," she said, "I'm so tired. That old snake, he bit me, but Bill and Linda kilt him. Please take me home."

"Copperhead," choked Jim. "The mules got him."

"We're too late," said Billy. "She's been bitten."

Jim gathered the small girl in his arms and ran, long loping strides that carried him quickly up the road. "Get Sam," he yelled. "Get Grandpap!"

††††††

On the picnic table Sam quickly slit the wound and sucked at the venom. "Git her to the hospital," he ordered. "Fast!"

Billy's truck was close, and Linda and Jim held the child as he powered the Chevy across the gravel and around the curves, lights flashing and throttle to the floor. He hit the paved road with a howl of rubber, wishing he still had the fast Corvette, praying as he wrestled the heavy truck through the curves. Two miles from Skaggs Gap Jim gently tapped his arm.

"You can slow down," he said softly. "She's dead."

††††††

"God damn you to hell, Billy Cox," wailed Jack. Tears streaked his weathered, anguished face. "First you ruin my girl and now you kill my grandbaby." He lunged, growling, and was restrained by Jessie and Obie.

"It weren't Billy's fault, son," said Sam. "Them copperheads is all over the place."

"Let him go," sobbed Billy. "Let him do it. Hell, let him kill me. It is my damned fault. There wouldn't have been a damn reunion except for me."

"Shut up, Billy," snapped Jessie. "It's damn bad enough without you carryin on. It ain't nobody's fault."

"It's that mountian," Jack whispered hoarsely. "First Uncle Obie, now Louvonna. It's that damn mountain of yours, Pap. It's their fuckin breedin grounds."

"Then, by damn," snarled an angry cousin, "let's burn it off."

"Yeah!" An angry muttering swept the crowd, and all agreed. Copperhead Mountain would burn.

"Ya'll can't do that." The voice was quiet and calm. Obie, his eyes swollen and his hands shaking, stepped forward. "If you start a fire now you'll burn the whole county. It's too dry."

"He's right," added Sam. "It's so dry we couldn't hold a fire."

"Maybe so," growled Jack. "But I'm tellin ye, Pap, that mountain is gonna burn, before another summer."

"That won't do any good," said Jim. "The—."

"Shut up!" Jack glared. "It's you and Billy and your goddamn playin that got that baby killed. I wish to hell I'd never laid eyes on you."

Jim backed away, stunned.

"Stop it, Daddy! Right now!" It was Linda, angry and anquished. "My baby is dead. Pickin on Jim won't bring her back. He's my son, Daddy. Like it or not, he is." She sobbed, and fell into Jim's arms. "Take me home, Jimmy, please take me home."

"Sure, Mamma." Glowering at Jack Cox, he led Linda away.

Billy wheeled, marched to his truck, searched under the seat and found a bottle. He took a long, searing drink. "Don't, Billy." It was Linda, close beside him. "It won't work. Drinking won't bring her back."

"Linda, I . . ."

She backed away. "Don't," she said. "Let's go, Jim."

Billy watched as Jim's car topped the hill and vanished.

"She was right, son," said Sam. "It don't make no sense, and it hurts, but it weren't your fault, Billy. Not this time. Don't go blamin yerself for somethin you couldn't a done nothin about."

Billy stared blankly. "It was my fault, Grandpap. It was me that caused it. Grandpap, I killed a little girl."

††††††

He drove for hours, aimlessly searching, haunted always by the looming presence of Copperhead Mountain. He traced the looping backroads, looking but not seeing, driving by blind instinct. At the new Cox County High School, he stopped, parked on the fringe of the parking lot and found a weathered basketball near the outdoor goal. He climbed out of the truck, shuffled to the ball, picked it up and palmed it, dribbled twice, and shot. The net twitched.

He loped to the bouncing ball, faked an imaginary opponent, drove to the left, spun, and arched a soft jump shot. He followed, grabbed the rebound, and slammed the ball viciously through the hoop. The metal rattled, and the rim snapped upward; the ball slapped hard on the asphalt.

He wheeled, ran down the ball, and launched a twenty foot shot. A lifetime of practice, instinct, and physical conditioning took over; he pushed off against the pavement, arched both arms and lifted the ball behind his head, released the shot at the peak of his jump and added a sweeping follow-up motion. The floating basketball barely disturbed the net.

The sweat began to flow.

He chased the ball, dribbled, shot, and rebounded, and pounded the ball through the worn net. The physical release, the instinctive concentration, the slap of leather on pavement and the rattle of the iron hoop transported Billy to another world, far removed from the reality of the baby girl who lay dead not three miles away.

He stopped, set, and dropped in a basket from thirty feet.

"You're still the best," she said softly. Billy spun and saw Brenda, ten feet away, smiling gently. "I've been looking for you," she said. "I finally realized where you'd be."

"Brenda, I–."

"Sam told me. He called. He was worried about you, Billy. So am I."

"Why?" He laughed coarsely. "Why the hell does anybody care about me?"

"Sam loves you," said Brenda. "And . . . and so do I, Billy."

He stopped halfway through the shot and tucked the ball under his arm. "You do?"

"I do, damnit. Don't ask me why." She walked to him, pulled his head down, and kissed him. "Now come on home with me, Wild Bill." She wrinkled her nose. "And take a bath."

He wheeled, dribbled once, and arched a shot.

"Maybe someday," said Brenda, "I'll be able to do as much for you as that basketball."

††††††

He dropped the empty bottle and watched closely as Brenda's car climbed the hill and snarled when he saw Billy's truck close behind. He reached for the rifle, carressed the cold steel, hefted the weapon and squinted through the scope. He saw them come together, near the cars, embracing, and his breath sucked in quickly. He followed them, his finger light on the trigger, the barrel steady against the rock. They stopped to kiss, and he took a deep breath. He sighted again, held his breath, and gently squeezed the trigger.

The firing pin clicked on the empty chamber.

He chuckled softly. "Would've been that simple," he grunted. He fumbled with the box of cartridges and loaded the magazine. "Next time is for real," he muttered. He levered a round into the chamber, rested the rifle on the rock, opened a new bottle and lay back to wait. Throughout the long and starless night, he kept watch over the small cabin on the hill.

CHAPTER 9

"THEY SHOT ME," HE GRUMBLED

Inside the cabin Billy gulped straight bourbon.

"You've had one hell of a day," Brenda said softly. "Would it help if you told me about it?"

"You've heard the most of it," he said wearily. "Except that while Louvonna—the little girl—was slipping away to be killed, her mother and I were down in the field talking over old times." He laughed bitterly. "Talking about our son." He stared off vacantly. "Right now Jim is taking care of his mother and getting ready to bury his little sister. If I hadn't—if *we* hadn't slipped off to talk, she'd still be alive." He shuddered. "At one reunion I father a son; and, at the next one, I kill his baby sister. God damn!" He poured more whiskey.

He chuckled. "Linda asked about you. Seemed a little jealous, too. And—damn, I nearly forgot. Jake was there, drunk as hell, threatening to kill me."

Brenda grimaced. "Was he drinking a lot?"

"Just gallons of vodka," said Billy. "Why?"

"Jake's a really bad alcoholic," said Brenda. "That's why he left Chicago. When he's drunk he has no idea what he's doing. He could—when he's drinking—really try to hurt you."

"Hell, what's one more after me?" He finished off the drink. "Where's that shower you promised?"

"This way." She pushed open the door.

"What?" He laughed. "No pantyhose?"

Brenda stopped him as he started to shut the door. "What does she mean to you, Billy?"

"Who?"

"Linda. Do you still love her?"

He did not hesitate. "No. I never did. Except for her body. She was beautiful. Still is. But, damn, I was afraid they'd make me marry her." He smiled. "No, I don't love her, Brenda."

She grinned. "Then you can use my shower."

For thirty minutes he soaked under the hot water.

"Where's my clothes?" he yelled.

"In the washer. There's an old robe in there. Wear it."

The robe came to mid-thigh. He shrugged and ambled to the living room. "I'm not used to mini-skirts," he grumbled. "My knees are too ugly."

"God!" Brenda stared. "They look like roadmaps. I never saw so many scars."

"Those are the stripes a professional athlete earns," he said. "Seven operations. Two while I was still in college. They may be ugly, but they still work. I just have to take a few minutes every morning to limber them up."

"What was it like?" asked Brenda. "Pro basketball?"

His wry grin startled her. "Hotel rooms and jets, mostly, and smelly locker rooms. Playing tired, popping pills, never sure just what city you're in today. Young studs out to earn a spot on the team. Old men trying to hang on one more season." He smiled. "The money's damn good, while it lasts, if anybody could hold onto any of it. Too much booze, cars and women. Three wives. Wild Bill. Hell, most of the time I was flat broke, and I played drunk half the time. It's a miracle I lasted as long as I did. But I *can* shoot, and I'm meaner'n hell, and I could never afford to quit."

"What did you do in the summers?" she asked.

"Very damned little," laughed Billy. "At first I just played around. Traveled and raised hell, spent all that money. I sold some shoes and beer, and worked at a few summer camps for kids. Helped with our rookies, as a shooting coach."

"Why didn't you ever come home?"

"Ashamed. Too damned proud to admit that I wasn't rich.

Too sorry to take the time."

"What about the wives?"

He burst out laughing. "Do you really want to know?"

"Yes. I have my reasons."

"The first one, while I was in college, was a cheerleader. I called home, halfway through my first pro season, and she was gone. That was a big relief. Two years later it was a stewardess. We got drunk after a flight, woke up married, and called it off a week later after we sobered up. The last one was high society. Rich, big name family–solid gold with all the trappings. She already had a yacht, a million dollar wardrobe, and a facelift, so she bought herself two racehorses and a ballplayer."

"I'm not much, but damned if I'll be a kept man. About the third time I came in drunk and dirty for one of her parties, she sent me packing. She was sweet, though–she gave me the house in Las Vegas as a goodbye present. I went straight out and borrowed a hundred thousand against it."

"You can see," he said quietly, "why I never spent a lot of time here. These people still see me as a hero, a good old boy who done good. I'm Wild Bill, the ballplayer, the swinger and hellraiser. I earned my reputation. I wrecked my first car, an old Mercury, rolled it halfway down Skaggs Gap. When I woke up, all they were worried about was whether or not I'd be able to play in the next game."

"Did you?"

"Yep. With one eye swollen shut and a leg taped together. Scored thirty points, got drunk after the game, forgot I didn't have a car and had to sleep in the gym."

Brenda laughed. "How did you wind up in school in Kansas? Did you really turn down an offer from Kentucky?"

"Hell, no." Billy drank deeply. "That's another lie. They didn't want me, for good reasons. Where I went, they were so glad to have me that I only had to practice when I felt like it, and the grateful alumni kept me supplied with cars and cash."

"What now, Billy?"

"Now I'm tired, and I want to be left alone. I want to live here, where I grew up. Sam's my closest friend—he's the only one who stuck up for me when I was little. Being with him again is good. And meeting you. . .that's the best part."

"I told you I'd never met a man I wanted," she said. "Now I have."

"If you mean that," said Billy, "scoot over here and sit by me." He pulled her close as she moved to the overstuffed chair, and their embrace was long and gentle.

††††††

Outside, the moon rose over Copperhead Mountain and the hounds howled mournfully. The rifleman dozed, and he never saw the copperhead which curled itself comfortably in his blanket.

††††††

"Do your hounds howl like this every night?" asked Billy.

"No." She snuggled closer. "Only if they think I'm in danger."

"What are they worried about tonight?"

"They saw you come in." Brenda giggled. "Billy?"

"Yeah?"

"Take me to bed."

"Are you sure?"

"Yes, damn you, I'm sure."

They climbed the stairs to her bedroom loft. One wall, all glass, overlooked the sweeping ridge, dominated by the dark mountain.

"Beautiful," whispered Billy.

"The view?"

"That too." She turned off the lamp and was silhouetted against the moonlight as she undressed. The skirt dropped to the floor, and she shook her hair loose from the pins. She removed her bra in a graceful shrug, stepped out of silky panties, and came to him.

He was trembling.

Neither spoke. He drew her closer, and was surprised when she pulled away. "What's wrong?" he asked.

"The robe."

He had forgotten, and laughed nervously. "I'm acting like a schoolboy."

"That's the way I like you," she said.

Their lovemaking was slow and intense, almost fumbling, and afterwards she clung to him. "I didn't know about this," said Billy.

"Don't talk," said Brenda, pulling closer. They explored each other, a deliberate and sensual discovery, and this time she cried with pleasure. Then, pressed snugly together, they slept.

Billy woke, two hours later, and she was gone.

"Brenda!" He was almost scared.

"Down here!" The smell of frying ham wafted up from the kitchen. "I woke up starved."

"Me too. Put on some more." He found the old robe and joined her. "What time is it?"

"Midnight." She wore an old shirt, and below it her long legs flowed gracefully.

"Damn," he sighed. "You look good enough to eat."

"And I feel even better," she grinned. "Just hungry."

"I love you, lady lawyer."

"And I love you, Wild Bill."

"Then come here."

"No way. First I eat."

From behind he attacked, slipping his hands under the shirt to caress her breasts, pulling her tight against him. She twisted for a kiss, then dropped the fork and clung to him. His hands slipped down to clasp her slim buttocks, and she nuzzled his robe open. He lifted her easily, and her legs opened to wrap around his waist. He rested her against the countertop, and they moved slowly together. She shivered and arched, trembled violently and broke out laughing, tears streaming, and pulled her upper body away.

"What's so damn funny?" asked Billy.

"Us. Me. If I'd known it could be like this I'd have raped you in my office the day we met."

"I was willing," said Billy.

"Let me down," she suddenly shrieked. "The stove's on fire!"

She twisted and ran. Billy leaned against the counter and howled with laughter as Brenda jerked her shirt off to smother the greasy flame.

"Damnit!" she yelled. "You could help."

"Okay." He slipped his hand between her legs. "Is that better?"

She swung and missed, and he grabbed her arched body. "Let go, damn you," she sputtered. "My house is on fire and you want to play."

They ate, later, plates piled high with ham and eggs and potatoes. "Jesus," grinned Billy. "You eat like a man."

"Only," said Brenda, "when I've been working hard."

Billy smiled serenely as he watched her. "I want to marry you," he said suddenly.

"You'd better be careful," snapped Brenda. "I'm an attorney, and I know all about breach of promise."

"I mean it," said Billy. "Damn. I surprised myself. I really do want to marry you. I never thought I'd hear myself saying that."

"I believe you, Billy," said Brenda. "I really do. I love you. But. . .marriage. . .that's too much to think about right now. Do you understand?"

"Not altogether," he said. "Lord knows I'm not a very good prospect. I've got one hell of a bad track record. But I *do* have my forty acres and a mule."

"Billy, right now it's not you. It's me. I don't know if I could be a decent wife. I've made my own way for a long time, and marriage would be a big change. Besides, I'd have to buy all new business cards and signs."

He chuckled and took her hand. "I do love you," he said. "The offer stands. Let me know if you ever decide to be a farmer's wife." He yawned. "Let's go back to bed."

"To sleep?"

"Hell, no," said Billy. "There's still an inch or so of you that I haven't explored."

"Let's go," said Brenda. "I like being investigated."

An hour later they slept again.

††††††

The rising sun woke the rifleman.

For a second he forgot, then he felt the cold steel of the rifle barrel and looked quickly to the cabin. "Truck's still there," he muttered. "The bastard stayed all night." He reached for his bottle, swallowed heavily, and gritted his teeth. The warmth returned to his insides, and the headache subsided.

He studied the terrain carefully. Three hundred yards east the Skaggs Ridge Road circled back close to his perch, and Billy Cox would drive that direction. He would slow for the sharp curve, and. . .he adjusted the scope for the distance and sat back to wait.

The copperhead lay unmoving in the blanket.

††††††

The alarm blared and Billy jerked.

"Monday morning," said Brenda. "Remember me?"

Propped on one elbow, breasts jutting, hair tangled, she smiled. He reached, and she came eagerly.

She called the office to tell Becky she'd be late, and came

back giggling. "She had already canceled all my morning appointments," said Brenda. "She saw your truck." Brenda tossed his clothes across the bed. "You'll be needing these." She laughed. "Nobody will ever believe that I had to hide your pants to make you spend the night."

He came down the steps to the smell of morning bacon. "Feed the dogs for me," said Brenda, pointing to a hundred pound bag of dry dog food. "Their dishes are on the porch."

The rifleman watched as Billy stepped outside, yawned and stretched, then fed the hounds. "You son of a bitch." The crosshairs centered on Billy's back as he bent to pet the dogs, and his finger tightened on the trigger. "No," he mumbled. "Not while she's here."

Brenda was very serious. "Before we go any further," she said, "there's something I have to tell you."

"I knew it," said Billy. "You're gay."

"I'm damned serious," snapped Brenda, glaring angrily.

"Go ahead," said Billy.

"A long time ago—I was thirteen—my uncle raped me."

"So?" Billy's eyebrows lifted.

"So that's why—I guess—that I've avoided men. Up 'till now. You're the first."

"And the last," he said quietly. "Is the son of a bitch still alive?"

"No. No, he. .he died five years ago."

"Good," growled Billy.

"You don't quite understand," said Brenda. Her fists were tightly clenched and her lip trembled. "He didn't just die. He was drunk, singing in the bathtub, and I. . .I drowned him. I hit him, Billy, and I held him under until he was dead." She ran from the table.

"I'll be damned," Billy said softly. He followed, and found her huddled in the kitchen. "Brenda, I—hell, don't stab me!"

She stared vacantly at the knife in her hand, then let it slip through her fingers and clatter to the floor. He pulled her close and let her cry into his shoulder.

"Look at it this way, Brenda," he said. "Now you don't have to defend me in a murder trial."

She looked up at him. "What?"

His voice was harsh. "If you hadn't already done it, I'd have to kill the bastard."

She peeked up through tearstreaked eyes. "You don't hate me?"

"Hate you?" he held her shoulders firmly. "I love you even more. What would I want with a woman who couldn't take care of herself?"

"Billy, you're crazy."

"I know." He grinned. "So are you."

††††††

He walked Brenda to her car, then went back inside to call Sam. "You at the lawyer woman's house?" the old man asked.

"How did you know?"

"Son, I picked her out fer you four years ago. I figgered I'd git them hounds back into the family."

"You will, Grandpap," laughed Billy. "You sure as hell will."

††††††

He watched Brenda leave, then followed Billy through the scope as he turned the truck and drove down the hill. He grunted, swung his aim to the highway, and waited. He heard the truck accelerate, and took a deep breath. He rested the long barrel against the rock and tightened his finger on the trigger.

††††††

Billy leaned forward to rewind the cassette tape, causing the first shot to miss and slam into the dashboard. The second bullet smashed the windshield. Billy jammed the brake and skidded, all four tires screaming as he wrestled the truck for control. The third shot, through the rear window, clipped Billy's head and shattered the rear view mirror.

The truck wailed, sped head-on for the steep cut, climbed up the sheer wall then rolled, from the front, over and back. It hit upside down, horn blaring and the engine roaring. In a second the engine blew, and smoke poured out from around the grill and wheels.

Except for the clicking exhaust and the gurgle of leaking gasoline there was silence.

††††††

He watched the truck roll, saw the smoke, and waited. He levered in another round and watched intently for any sign of movement. In ten minutes the gas tank blew and flames belched up from the wreckage. "That'll do it," he said.

He lowered the rifle and reached for the blanket. The copperhead tumbled out, still stiff and slow from the morning coolness. "I'll be damned." He smiled. "I had company all night and didn't even know it." He shoved the snake gently away and vanished quickly through the trees.

††††††

Billy, dazed, sat on the low guardrail and watched his truck burn. Thrown halfway out the window by the impact, he had instinctively scrambled away. The explosion had slammed him hard against the rail, taking his breath, searing the hair from his arms and pushing him into unconsciousness.

He woke, blinded and frantic, screaming and clawing at his eyes. When he wiped the blood away he could see, and he dragged himself to his perch on the rail. He sat, muttering under his breath, as the black smoke poured from the truck.

The roar of a diesel Mack, laboring up the hill with its payload of coal, roused him. The red semi, in a hiss of air brakes, stopped just short of the flames. A wiry, stetson topped man dropped nimbly from the cab and came running. "You alright, feller?"

Billy grinned weakly. "Some son of a bitch," he said, "just shot me." He collapsed and slid down the railing and onto the hot pavement.

††††††

He regained consciousness at the hospital door. "Take it easy, bud," said the attendant. "You got a nasty little cut there."

"Cut, hell." Billy tried to reach for his head, but his arms were strapped. "It's a damned bullet hole."

"Yeah, sure it is. Just lay still and let us get you inside."

A doctor checked him quickly. "Nothing broken," he said. "The blood is from that head cut."

"Was a goddamn bullet," mumbled Billy. He strained against the straps. "Son of a bitch shot me."

"Give him another shot," ordered the doctor, "before he jumps right off the table."

††††††

He saw Brenda, dozing, slumped in the chair beside his bed.

"Damn, you look good," he croaked.

"Billy!" She was up quickly, at his side. "You're awake."

"I sure am." He grinned feebly. "My head hurts like hell."

"Oh, Billy." She snuggled close, and kissed him.

"Take off your clothes," he whispered.

"Oh, no!" She jerked away, smiling. "Is that all you ever think about?"

"Just about," he said. "Where's Grandpap?"

"Outside. Walking the hall. Madder than a wet hen."

Billy laughed. Then, remembering, he struggled to sit up in the bed. "Somebody shot me!"

"Easy," cautioned Brenda. "Lay back down, Billy."

"Where's Jim?"

"In Cincinnati." She shoved him gently back against the pillow. "I like being able to push you around."

"Who shot me?" he demanded. "Did they catch him?"

"Nobody shot you," said Brenda. "You wrecked your truck."

"No!" he said angrily. "Somebody shot, two or three times, and busted out the windows and hit me in the back of the head."

The door opened. "Is he awake?" asked the doctor.

"Yes," said Brenda. "Awake and swearing he was shot. If he was, it's no problem. All they hit was his hard head."

The doctor laughed. "He just needs more rest. There's a slight concussion, and he lost some blood." Billy felt the needle.

"They shot me," he grumbled.

"I know," said Brenda. She bent to kiss him. "I love you, you wild hillbilly."

She lifted her head and smiled. Billy was fast asleep.

††††††

Brenda drove a worried Sam Cox back to Hogtown. "Don't worry," she said. "He's not hurt very bad, Sam."

"I done quit worryin about him," sniffed Sam. "Now I'm wonderin what we're gonna do fer a truck."

She laughed. "He's just like you, Sam. I love you both."

"I figgered you would," said Sam. "If I was fifty years younger, though, I'd take ye away from him."

"Not even you could do that," said Brenda.

He cackled. "You mind me of Lily. Did I ever tell you

about the time she took a shotgun to the Waggoners?"

"Twenty times, Sam."

She left him and drove home, physically exhausted and emotionally drained. Buck met the car, sullen and subdued. "Where's Sam?" asked Brenda. Buck whined and ran to the porch. Brenda followed, running now.

"Sam!" She screamed, ran to the hound, and lifted his head. He was already stiff, stretched awkwardly across the steps. Sobbing, she held him close. Buck's cold snarl opened her eyes. The copperhead slithered across the porch, its fat body sliding easily. Brenda froze, half standing, as the snake drew closer.

She was thrown aside by ninety pounds of growling, charging hound, and Buck's claws hit the wooden floor in a tearing, desperate skid. "No!" screamed Brenda.

Buck already had the snake, his big jaws clamped behind its head, shaking savagely. He quietened, the growl rumbling deep in his throat, and Brenda sagged to her knees and wept.

††††††

Kentucky State Policeman Larry Blake sat in the hospital room, notebook in hand, scowling. "You say you were–."

"Look," growled Billy. "If you don't believe me just say so. I was shot. That's why I wrecked the truck. That's where I got this." He pointed to his bandaged head. "I'm tired of being treated like a criminal. Forget it. I want to go home. I don't care anymore."

Blake laughed. "As I was trying to say, before the sermon, what about Jake Wilde? You say he threatened you?"

"Twice. He said he'd kill me if I didn't stay away from Brenda Higgens."

"Any witnesses?"

"Not the first time. But he came to the reunion, in front of fifty people, the second time."

"Why's he so mad?"

"Don't you know Brenda?"

Blake snapped his notebook shut. "Yep." He grinned. "I'll talk to Jake. They're still checking your truck. It's mostly melted, but maybe we'll turn up something."

"Thanks," said Billy. "Thanks for believing me."

Blake reached into his pocket. "There's just one more thing."

"What now?" asked Billy.

"Would you autograph this for my son?" He handed Billy a wrinkled, faded NBA game program.

††††††

Jake Wilde scribbled in his journal:

Somehow he still lives.

I failed.

I will not, the next time.

Billy Cox will die.

He shut the worn book, sighed, and stared out at the pale moonlight. By some miracle Billy had lived through the fires; the big hound's death had been an angry, thoughtless retaliation.

The next time he would not strike alone. They would help rid the land of the man who dared interfere; Billy Cox would die as had his uncle before him. Jake grinned. The copperheads would do it. He reached for the bottle, drank gratefully, tugged his cap down over his bushy hair and left for the mountain.

††††††

Brenda arrived early the following morning, her eyes swollen, her face downcast.

"Hey," Billy said gently. "There's no need to be so upset. I'm fine."

She raised her head. "It's Sam."

"Sam? Is he hurt?"

"No. Not your grandfather. Sam, my dog. He's dead, Billy. And there was a big snake on my porch." Sobbing, she told him all that had happened. She had buried the big hound, and shoved the dead copperhead over the steep cliff.

"It was Jake," swore Billy. "He put that snake there. And killed the dog. Cox hounds are born snake killers, Brenda. First Jake tried to kill me, then he warned you. Wait 'till I get my hands on that son of a bitch!"

"No, Billy, she said wearily. "You don't know any of that. Don't go off half cocked. Jake wouldn't harm me."

He held her until the tears stopped. They left the hospital together and drove to Brenda's office.

"God!" said Becky. "Both of you look like hell warmed over."

††††††

In her office Billy sat with his feet propped on the corner of the desk. "Are you going to be alright?" he asked.

"Sure." Brenda blew her nose. "I'm more worried about you."

"Why?" he asked. "It's all in a day's work. My head's too hard for me to get hurt bad." He smiled sadly. "You're the only reason I can keep going, though."

"Take some time off, Billy," she urged. "Stay away from the farm for a few days. You'll feel better."

"Maybe." He rubbed his sore head. "Anyway, tomorrow I have to go to Cincinnati for the funeral."

"Should you?"

"Probably not. But Jim called last night and said Linda asked me to be there."

He met her worried eyes. "I guess I owe her that much," he said lamely.

"That's all you owe her," said Brenda.

"What does that mean?"

"Billy, if you do love me, there can't be any other women. None at all. Not even old girlfriends." She frowned. "Especially not her."

"It's a funeral," said Billy. "Not a party."

"You know what I'm talking about."

"Yeah." He grinned. "I know. I like it. See you tonight?"

"You'd better."

"I'll be there. Right now I need to find me some wheels."

"You can use my car."

"Oh, no. Nobody drives your BMW."

She blushed. "That changed. Two nights ago."

"Everything changed," said Billy. "I love you, counselor." He kissed her quickly and walked to the door. "See you for supper."

††††††

After an hour of haggling and checking on the insurance on the burned truck, Billy ordered a new 4WD pickup from the Chevrolet dealer. "Now," he said, "for that much money you ought to throw in a Chevette."

"I can't do that," chuckled the dealer. "But I do have just the car for you. Out back I've got the hottest piece of machinery ever to hit Cox County."

A dull gray, four door Nova was the only vehicle there.

"Where's this hot car?" asked Billy.

The dealer raised the hood. "Moonshiner special," he said. "Look here." A fuel injected 350, with headers and sparkling chrome trim, was tucked into the engine compartment. "The sheriff finally caught him two months ago. This has got a racing suspension, disc brakes all around, even an extra eighty gallon fuel tank." He chuckled. "We ran a gas line from it, to make it legal."

"How'd they catch him?" asked Billy.

"He was parked."

Billy eased the Nova out into the traffic, and smiled. The harsh suspension and heavy steering made city driving difficult, but on the winding Ridge Road he punched the throttle. The Nova swept forward, nimble and tight in the curves, accelerating with a sudden rush and slowing with a touch of the brake. He powered it through a tight curve and then saw the flashing blue lights behind him. "Oh, hell," he groaned. He slowed and eased off to the side.

Larry Blake grinned when he saw Billy. "I might have known," he said. "Like it?"

"I'm not sure," said Billy. "But it sure gets there in a hurry."

"Yeah," said Blake. "The old Ridgerunner is plenty fast."

"Ridgerunner?"

"That's the car's name. Earl Williams is at Eddyville Prison right now, but he and this Chevy gave us all a rough time for six months. Every law officer in fifteen counties knows this car."

"I appreciate the warning," said Billy. "I'll be careful. Did you find anything in my truck?"

"It's hard to say. They found what looks like a bullet hole in the dash, but no slug. Lead would have burned at those temperatures."

"I know. So would I, if I hadn't jumped."

Back in Skaggs Gap the dealer was waiting. "Fast, ain't she?"

"Fast enough to draw the attention of every policeman in eastern Kentucky," said Billy. "I think they've got it bugged."

"They stop ye?"

"Just for a warning. How much do you want? It's a '68, isn't it?"

"Sixty-nine. But it's all new, Billy. I could let it go for twenty-five hundred. That's rock bottom."

"Then keep it," grinned Billy. "Paint it green and try to sell it to some old maid."

"Two thousand?"

"I'd go fifteen."

"Eighteen?" The dealer pursed his lips.

"Sold," said Billy. "Could you throw in a good bail bondsman?"

††††††

"I should have guessed," laughed Brenda, "that you'd go and find the Ridgerunner."

"Does everybody know it?"

"Just about. Earl bragged a lot and claimed he'd spent over six thousand fixing it up. About a month before he was caught he put in a new motor." She smiled. "Now you and Sam can go back into the whiskey business."

"We may just have to," said Billy. "That'd be one way of putting gas in the Ridgerunner. Or I may just convert the engine to run on alcohol."

"Oh, Billy, will you ever grow up?"

"I hope not," he said.

††††††

Wednesday morning he stopped by the hospital to have the dressing changed, then pointed the Nova north toward Cincinnati. He asked the second trooper to radio ahead. "Tell them I'm not hauling anything," he said. "Ask 'em to not stop me just to look at the car."

At eleven-thirty he crossed the Ohio and arrived at the funeral home at noon. Jim was waiting, and they went for lunch in a nearby restaurant. "How's the head?" asked Jim.

"Sore," said Billy. "It's just a crease. I know it was old Jake. I was lucky to live."

Jim smiled. "You were due a little luck."

"How is Linda?"

"As good as you could expect. Ed is pretty bad. He's ready to kill somebody."

"Me," sighed Billy.

"Or me. Or any other Cox. At best he's always just barely tolerated the idea of my existence. I can't say as I blame him."

"I don't either. Jim, should I skip the service and go on home?"

"No. You're here, and you're staying. Mamma wants you here. The hell with Ed Hamilton."

The service was simple and brief.

Outside the chapel Billy approached the parents, awkwardly accepting Linda's hug, offering his hand to Ed Hamilton.

"Ed," said Linda, "this is Billy Cox."

The blow caught Billy off guard and he stumbled; blood spurted from his mouth and pain stabbed his temples. Hamilton's icy voice cut through the dull roar which hammered at Billy's brain. "You bastard," choked Hamilton. "You no good, hillbilly son of a bitch!" He lept forward, grabbing for Billy's throat, redfaced and grim in his murderous rage. The two men met, swayed, and toppled over the rail. They hit a thick shrub, and rolled to the sidewalk. Jim grabbed for Hamilton's arm, and was sent staggering by a wild left hook.

Billy's head rang, and he felt new blood seep through the dressing. "Lord," he gasped. "I'm sorry. I just wanted to—."

A pointed oxford cracked into Billy's ribs; he gagged and rolled, choking for air. Hamilton stood over him, poised to kick again. He swore, spat, and his shoulders slumped. "You're not worth it," he said. "You don't deserve my attention." He wheeled and stalked away, and Linda followed timidly.

Jim stooped and helped Billy to his feet. His nose was red, and blood dripped down on his shirt. "Daddy," said Jim. "How did you like your cousin Ed?"

Billy swayed, caught onto the railing, and spat blood. "All things considered," he gasped, "I'd rather take my chances back home with the copperheads and bushwhackers."

Jim insisted they visit a closeby clinic, where a fussing nurse changed Billy's dressing and wheeled him in for x-rays of the ribs. Two were cracked. The doctor wrote out a prescription for pain pills and cautioned Billy against driving.

"Stay with me tonight," said Jim.

"No." Billy was stubbornly adamant. "I'm going home. I won't spend a night in this damned place."

He wheeled up Brenda's driveway at midnight. "My god," she gasped. She inspected his swollen nose and lip. "You wrecked that car."

"Worse than that." He smiled feebly. "I broke all of Ed Hamilton's knuckles and toes. Get me some water so I can swallow some more of these pills."

Four tablets, two sandwiches, and two drinks later, he slept restlessly.

††††††

For the rest of the week Billy rested, spending the days reading or taking long walks with the hound Buck, rebuilding his strength and letting his grated emotions settle. On Saturday he rode with Sam and Brenda to the farm. Sam, fussing from the back seat, was worried about the mules and impatient to get back to work. "Come Monday," he said, "we'll rip out them floors and git some work done."

"Over there," Billy said quietly. "Over by the pond. That's where we found her." The mules raised their heads to stare cooly at the car. "See, Grandpap, they're still alive." He pointed, and winced as his side burned. "I feel like one of them kicked me in the ribs."

Brenda turned the car and drove slowly back out the lane. "Have you talked to Jessie and Georgie? Were they at the funeral?"

"They were there," said Billy. "I don't think they saw me. Or what happened afterwards. I'm just not ready to talk to them yet."

"You have to, someday," said Brenda. She blew the horn and waved at Obie, who was walking beside the road. He frowned, then nodded in acknowledgement as they rolled past.

"He's goin up to walk on the ridge," said Sam. "It's a wonder to me that they ain't kilt him by now."

"Who'd kill him?" asked Billy.

"Why, the copperbellies," said Sam. "Who else?"

††††††

Jim was waiting at Sam's house in Hogtown. "I see you lived," he said to Billy. "Ready to get back to work, Grandpap?"

"Time's a wastin," said Sam. "Monday mornin we're goin to rip out them floors and git started. Billy, he's too damn crippled to help much, but he can drive the truck."

Billy groaned. "I don't know if it's safe to have me around, but I'll give it a try. Now, if you fellers don't mind, I have to see this young lady home."

They stayed inside Brenda's cabin until Monday morning, interrupted from their lovemaking only by Buck's braying demands for food and water.

††††††

On Sunday night the dark man walked to the Cox homeplace in the moonlight and bent low to enter the crawl space under the floor.

"I have come," he whispered tonelessly.

The copperheads slithered over his feet and curled around his shoulders, writhing close to him in the darkness.

"Tomorrow," he said. "Stop them."

He vanished at daybreak, moving easily with the stealth and ease of the serpent.

††††††

The University of Kentucky specialist arrived early Monday.

"You're a what?" Jessie was baffled.

"A herpetologist." Dan Webber grinned. "I study snakes."

"Fer a livin?"

"They pay me, Mr. Cox. I usually work in the laboratory, so I'm happy to be out in the field for a change."

"By damn," said Jessie. "You orta like it here."

Webber chuckled. "In town they tell me these copperheads are some new breed. All full of vinegar and ready to fight it out with anybody who comes close."

"Don't laugh." Obie spoke for the first time, slow and ponderous and sullen.

"I didn't mean to insult you," said Webber. "I'm sorry. Where could I find James Farley?"

"Jim's up the road there," said Jessie. "They're workin on an old house, about a mile straight ahead."

"Thanks. I'll find him."

"He don't know nothin about these copperheads," scoffed Obie. "Jim ain't even from here."

"Who does know?" shrugged Webber. "From what I hear, these snakes don't do anything they're supposed to do. They break all patterns."

"These ain't reglar copperheads." said Obie. "They come from the mountain."

"That fact," grinned Webber, "doesn't tell me a thing. See you fellows around."

As he drove away Obie grumbled. "I don't like it, Daddy. All these damned experts comin in here. It ain't right."

"Obe," sighed Jessie, "after sixty years of watchin them copperheads kill us off, I'd let the Russians come here if I thought they could git rid of 'em."

"It still ain't right," insisted Obie.

††††††

Jim and Sam had unloaded the wrecking bars and hammers, and Billy was struggling to turn the big truck around, cursing as he fought the wheel. Webber parked his state car up close. "Howdy," he yelled. "I'm Dan Webber, University of Kentucky."

"You with the taxes?" asked Sam.

"No," laughed Webber. "The county health department asked me to come here. I'm the herpetologist."

"The snake expert," said Jim. "I'm Jim Farley. They told me you'd be here today. This is Sam Cox, my grandfather, and the hungover man over there cussing at the truck is my father, Billy Cox." Billy shut off the engine and joined them. "Daddy, this is Dan Webber."

"Hello," said Billy. "What can you do to help us?"

"I really don't know," said Webber. "I guess we can start by reviewing all the information they sent me. Some of this stuff is hard to believe."

Billy nodded. "I'll bet it is."

"Son," said Sam. "We'll be proud to tell ye all we know, but could ye see your way clear to do your talkin while we're doin our workin?"

"Sure," said Dan. "I'll even help." He rolled up his sleeves and picked up a crowbar.

"Watch out fer the damned copperheads," warned Sam.

"Thanks for the warning," said Dan. "I'm scared to death of snakes." He walked with Billy. "Aren't you the basketball player?"

"I was," said Billy. "Right now I'm a little too crippled to play anything. Cracked ribs." He saw Dan's smile and remembered the bandage. "I keep forgetting. I got shot, too. That was the day before my ribs were kicked in. So far it's been a dull summer."

Dan stared, then guffawed loudly. "They *said* you people

up here do things a little differently."

Inside the homeplace Sam pointed. "Start over there, and we can rip her both directions."

Jim and Dan wedged crowbars into the cracks and pulled together. Creaking, rusty square nails released their grip and the rotted board flew loose.

Jim stopped, frozen, and peered down into the opening.

"My god," he whispered. "Oh, my god."

CHAPTER 10

"HURRY, DADDY, THERE'S AN AWFUL, DREADFUL SNA-A-AKE"

Under the floor, in the musty darkness, there was a rustling movement. Then came a faint rubbing sound, and from the squirming mass a flat head reared. A thick copperhead poked upward, swaying and searching, tongue flicking.

"I don't believe it." Dan Webber's voice trembled, and the crowbar hung loose at his side. "It's impossible. That can't be." He staggered back slowly. "That just can't be."

The first copperhead struck, aiming at Jim's foot, and Sam's lashing pry bar crushed its head. Jim swung angrily and killed a second snake. "Run, you fools!" yelled Billy. The trance broke, and they retreated out the open door. Sam slashed again with the long iron rod. "Come outa there, Webber," he yelled.

Outside, Webber hesitated, staring. "Come on, you idiot," snorted Sam. "Git away from there." The copperheads streamed out, a liquid, lethal mass movement. Jim grabbed Webber's arm and yanked him clear.

"Up on the truck!" ordered Billy. He ignored the stabbing pain from his ribs, pulled Sam up, and fell back gasping. He scrambled to his feet and reached into the cab to get the shotgun.

"No!" squalled Webber. "Don't shoot."

"What?" Billy lowered the barrel, unbelieving.

"Don't shoot. Let's see what they do."

The mass of copperheads stopped at the porch's edge, and searching sentries fanned out across the grass. "It's. ." Webber's voice cracked. "They're like an army."

Billy watched closely and suddenly slapped the shotgun

barrels at the flat head which wedged through a crack in the truck bed. "Son of a bitch!" he growled. He swung the gun up and jerked both triggers. Buckshot splattered against the house, and twisting bodies squirmed. He held his breath and watched; beside him Dan Webber's breath was a rusty bellows.

Slowly, as if by signal, the copperheads retreated back in the house and out of sight. "If you boys smell somethin," whispered Sam, "I jist filled my britches."

"Somebody comin." said Jim. They stayed on the truck bed and waited. Jake Wilde's old pickup stopped short, and he stepped out confidently. "You fellers playin?" he asked. "Or does it take all four of you to hold down that old truck?" He swung up his camera and the shutter clicked.

"Don't move, mister," said Dan Webber.

Wilde stood, his finger poised on the shutter button.

"Why not?"

"You're standing in the middle of a thousand copperheads," said Dan. "Just stay real still."

"You don't say?" Wilde, amused, relaxed. "How come I can't see them?" He twisted the focusing ring. "Smile for the birdie, Sam." He snapped the photo, lowered the Nikon, and walked closer. "You can crawl out now, Billy. I didn't bring my rifle."

"Mister, you're crazy," swore Jim. Billy glared.

"Lord help me," choked Sam. "I'm gonna burn that damn house to the ground. Right now."

Wilde chuckled at their story, walked into the house, stuck his head down under the floor, and came back grinning. "Where is it?" he asked. He peered under the truck.

"What are you looking for?" asked Dan.

"The moonshine. You all gotta be drunk. I didn't see a thing except those three dead copperheads there. Your count is off about 997 snakes, friend." He grinned happily. "Of course, I don't imagine Billy can count except by the thousands."

Sam crawled off the truck bed and unscrewed the gas cap to

insert a hose. "What are you doin now, Sam?" asked Wilde. "Drinking gasoline?"

"Siphonin" grunted Sam. "I intend to burn them bastards right in their den."

Billy watched as Sam filled a five gallon can, then reloaded the shotgun, cocked both hammers, and walked slowly to the house. "Hold it right there," called Wilde. The camera clicked. "Okay. Go ahead."

Billy eased into the house. "Bring me a flashlight, Jim," he ordered. The flare showed only worn bare dirt under the floor. He walked back out swearing. "The son of a bitches are gone."

"One more shot," said Wilde, swinging the camera. "Could you hold the shotgun a little higher, Billy? Try to look fierce, now."

A quick flicker darkened Billy's eyes. He looked down at the shotgun and he smiled slowly. "Jim," he asked solemly, "did you ever see me shoot any film?"

"Why no. Why?"

"Just watch." He moved quickly, yanked Wilde's camera loose and swung it by its colorful strap. He danced away from Wilde's lunges, laughing. "Watch close, Jim. I'm going to shoot a whole roll in one shot."

"No!" screamed Wilde. "You can't do that." He ran, but a flying tackle by Dan Webber sent him sprawling. Billy laughed, swung the camera round and around, sent it flying off, and whipped up the shotgun. Both barrels spewed buckshot and the camera stopped in midair and disintegrated. There was an unbelieving silence, then Billy chuckled softly. "I do believe I exposed an entire roll," he said. "Nice tackle, Dan."

"Excellent focus," giggled Webber. "Fine control."

"F-12 at fifteen yards, double exposure," howled Billy. "Real action photography." He slapped his legs and waved the shotgun.

"You're fuckin insane," whispered Wilde. "I don't believe

this is happening."

"I prefer the twin lens Browning," continued Billy. "Though I have used the .38 Smith & Wesson."

Dan Webber laughed away his tears of laughter. "Have you tried the Remington .410?" he asked. "It's a good all around caliber for your type of photography."

"What in the hell is goin on?" asked Sam. He stood watching, puzzled and anxious. "You shot Jake's picture box, Billy. What are you two laughin at?"

"Let me borrow your pistol," said Billy. Sam hobbled to the truck and returned with the .32. "Now," said Billy. "Mr Wilde, you have exactly thirty seconds to haul your ass out of here." He thumbed the hammer and started counting, grinning happily. Jake looked to Sam, saw no help, looked back to Billy and started running.

Billy's soft voice followed him. ". . .47, 48, 49. . ."

Jake found the starter, gunned the engine, and swung across the field. The front wheels left the ground as he topped a low rise, and he fought the steering wheel as the pickup skidded and bounced. Billy aimed carefully, squeezed the trigger, and laughed as the truck swerved. The bullet splattered harmlessly off a rock on the hillside.

Dan Webber lay exhausted, gasping for breath, his eyes wet as he laughed.

Billy turned to stare at Jim and Sam. "Jim," he said calmly, "go to town and get us some more gasoline. And get some whiskey from the house. Might as well bring some wieners because we're about to have us one hell of a hot dog roast."

Jim grinned hesitantly. "You okay?"

"Fine." Billy smiled broadly. "You go on. And bring some more shotgun shells. Stop and tell Daddy and Obe to not call the fire department. Will you be needing anything, Mr. Webber?"

"A roll of film," giggled Dan.

"Get moving, Jim." Billy reached under the seat and found a

pint. "Drink, Grandpap? Dan?"

Sam chuckled softly. "Billy," he said admiringly. "You the craziest sumbitch I ever seen."

Jim was back in a half hour with two five gallon drums of gas, three fifths of bourbon, and a box of shotgun shells. The four men drank formally, then Billy dropped the bottle and yelled.

"Frying time, damnit!" He sloshed gasoline across the porch and into the first room. Moving cautiously, Dan Webber poured the second drum, and Sam soaked a torch. They all drank again, then Webber stuck a match to the pine burr. Sam swung and threw.

The explosion lifted the roof off the frame, sent glass spraying, and toppled all four men backwards. They lay, watching the smoke climb higher, grinning. Billy reached for the bottle, drank, passed it on, and happily watched the flames consume the wreckage. "Ain't none of 'em gonna live through that," he said with satisfaction. He took the bottle again. "To our success, gentlemen." He swallowed heavily and handed the bottle to Webber.

Dan Webber drank, blinked, found the shotgun and staggered to his feet. "I'll make damn sure they ain't none still alive," he yelled. He fired from the hip and neatly clipped the top out of a pine tree twenty yards to the left of the house. "Close enough." he said seriously. "Where's that bottle?"

"I'll show ye how," grunted Sam. He took the revolver, aimed deliberately into the flames and methodically squeezed off two rounds. Grinning, he emptied the pistol and started reloading.

Jim stood still not believing. "You've all gone mad," he whispered.

Webber tossed him the shotgun. "Your turn," he grinned. "Here's the bullets." He threw the shells and one bounced into the fire. Jim dived to avoid the ricocheting buckshot as the shell exploded. "Hit the dirt!" screamed Webber. "The sons of bitches are shooting back!"

Billy was scowling as he poured gasoline into an empty bourbon bottle. He finished, tucked a handkerchief into the neck, and held it high. "Here's to you, Mr. Webber," he yelled, "and the great University of Kentucky." He hefted the bottle and threw, then yelled. "Three point play!" The blast sent burning timber soaring.

Sam sat up and fired six more shots. Jim shrugged, reached for a bottle, and gulped down the brown liquid.

Jessie and Obie heard the first explosion and hurried toward the homeplace. "God holy damn," muttered Obie.

"They've set the whole county on fire," gasped Jessie.

They ran closer to investigate, and Webber saw them coming.

"Revenooers!" he yelled. He lifted the shotgun and sent shot tearing through the brush. "Get 'em, men!"

"Maybe we'd just better go home," Jessie said wearily. "Let 'em kill each other off."

Sam carefully drew a bead on a glowing ash, and the pistol bucked. "Just like the war," he said happily.

Billy found the box of shotgun shells and grinned. "Hit the dirt!" he yelled. "Bombers comin!" He heaved the shells into the flames and dived behind the truck. The impact of the explosion flattened the remaining walls and sent hot coals spewing. A large, smoking chunk landed close to Sam. He aimed, fired, and chuckled. "Kilt the sumbitch!"

Webber peered out from behind the truck's dual wheels, grinned, and passed out. "Help me move him," grunted Billy. "I got to use the truck." He dragged Webber's limp body aside, reached in the truck and shifted the gears to neutral. He shoved hard, and the truck started rolling backwards.

Jim dropped his bottle and ran. "Don't do that."

He was too late. Billy staggered and stopped as the old truck rumbled sedately down the bank and toward the flames. Sam aimed again and fired, and a slug spun off the front bumper. Jim swore and ran for cover.

The old Chevy, in slow motion, rolled into the glowing embers. The explosion rattled windows in Hogtown.

††††††

When Brenda arrived, in midafternoon, she found Sam snoring against the cellar wall. Jim was high on the hillside with the mules, singing loudly. The stranger, cradling a shotgun, was propped against an apple tree muttering softly.

Billy Cox, a copperhead curled neatly in his armpit, was asleep in the middle of the road.

Carefully, Brenda took the .32 from Sam's limp hand and walked back to Billy. The snake reared, licking angrily. She aimed, took a deep breath, and fired.

Man and copperhead soared into midair, then separated.

Billy's eyes, slits in his scorched face, opened.

He stared at Brenda's feet, looked up at her knees, worked up her thighs, then fell back giggling.

"I thought you was two copperheads," he mumbled. "Standin on their heads." He giggled again and slumped back to the dirt.

She threw the revolver and bounced it off his shoulder.

"You bastard!" she screeched. "You miserable, stinking, drunken, insane bastard!"

Billy moved. "Yessum."

"Revenooer!" moaned Webber, clawing drunkenly for the shotgun. He lifted both barrels and fired straight up as Brenda flattened behind Billy's prone body. "Got her," said Webber.

"Get up, Billy," ordered Brenda, "and walk between me and that fool until I can get clear."

"Yessum," he mumbled, "anything you say. Just watch out for the damned copperheads." He pointed solemnly. "A million of 'em, right over there."

"Walk," ordered Brenda. In the car Billy sang, warbling an off key rendition of a song she'd never heard:

"I heard the screams of my little girl, far away.
Hurry, Daddy, there's an awful, dreadful sna-a-ake.
I ran as fast as I could,
through the dark and dreary wood,
but I reached our darlin girl, too late."

"God." Brenda shivered and stopped him. "What happened back there?"

"Million damn copperheads," said Billy. "All a chasin us. We burnt 'em, and I shot me a camera. Nearly got old Jake, too."

"Jake Wilde?"

"That's him. I shot his damn camera."

"Lord." Brenda wiped her face. "Who's the other idiot? The one with the shotgun?"

"That's old Dan Webber. Snake doctor." He giggled. "Don't shoot too good, but he's a damn fine tackler."

Brenda opened the car door. "Get out," she snapped.

"Okay." Billy staggered, and fell in the gravel. "Gotta go save Jim and Grandpap," he mumbled. "Gotta go."

"Oh, hell." Brenda climbed out. "I'll help you."

Jessie and Obie returned, and Obie was furious.

"D-damn crazy fools coulda burnt the whole county."

"It's a little safer now," said Jessie. "I took their guns." He stared. "Damn, they burnt the big truck."

"The truck?" The charred outline of the frame was visible in the smoking ruins. "Why?"

"C-crazy," sputtered Obie. "All t-three of 'em."

"Billy, he shot Jake Wilde's camera, then took the pistol and run him off." Jessie sighed. "Jake went for the sheriff, but he ain't come yet. Fraid to, likely."

"I'll take them home, Jessie," said Brenda. "I caught Billy. Would somebody go up on the hill and run down Jim?"

Obie left, walking carefully.

"I'll load Pap fer ye," said Jessie. "All the fight's gone out of him. The little one, though, he's different. Webber, his name is. He's still wild as hell."

"Watch for snakes, Jessie," warned Brenda. "One was asleep with Billy when I got here. I shot it." She picked her way to where Dan Webber sat groaning. "Mr. Webber, do you surrender? The war is over now."

His browless face was soot covered and his lips were cracked. "I give up," he croaked. He moaned. "I didn't try to shoot you too, did I?"

"You did. But when you shoot, the only danger is to innocent trees over on the hillside. Come on. I'll take you home."

"Where to?"

"To Sam's. You can all finish your playing over there."

"Ma'am," insisted Webber. "We wasn't playing. They was a million copperheads."

"I know. Billy already told me. I know there was at least one."

Brenda snapped the car into second gear, jerking hard.

Billy lurched against her. "What's the matter?" he mumbled. "They chasin us?"

"Damn you," said Brenda. "When you sober up you had better have a good explanation for all this. Do you hear me, Billy?" She smacked the wheel. He was snoring, his jaw slack.

She drove across Sam's yard and up to the door. "Out!" she yelled. She jerked the doors open and pulled, leaving them scattered across the grass. Hands on her hips, she stopped to survey the scene. "What have I done?" she said to herself. She prodded Billy's leg and he smiled happily, snoring.

The BMW spun across the yard, and she whirled onto the highway in a howl of tires. Jake Wilde was waiting at her cabin.

"I heard all about what happened, she snapped. "He'll replace your camera, Jake."

"That's nothing," he said. "Brenda, that man is insane. Stay away from him."

"We've been through all this before, Jake."

"Brenda, he actually thinks I tried to kill him."

"And he thinks you killed my dog, and left that copperhead

on the porch."

Jake's face quivered. "No copperhead will ever harm you."

Brenda frowned. "Go home, Jake. I'm tired. I'm mad. I don't ever want to see another man. You're *all* insane!"

She marched past him and slammed the door.

††††††

The moon softly lit the hillside, the ashes smelled of wood smoke, and the embers still snapped and crackled.

At midnight, from the mountain, the dark figure came. He moved restlessly, searching through the ruins, gliding across the flickering light.

He stared at the flames, distraught. "Go back," he whispered hoarsely. "Go back to the mountain." He turned and vanished in the darkness.

Jessie, asleep in Billy's car, woke and rubbed his eyes.

"Must have been the wind," he muttered. He went back to sleep.

††††††

From the journal:

Disaster!

The fool! He endangered the family with the flames; he endangered my life.

I, of all, must survive.

For I am the leader, the chosen one.

CHAPTER 11

". . .COME HELL OR HIGH WATER OR COPPERHEADS. . ."

At daybreak Jake Wilde's booming kicks at the front door roused Sam. He struggled to his feet, cursing, pulled up the straps of his overalls and wobbled to the door. "Comin, damnit," he growled. "I'm comin."

Jake, brighteyed, stepped quickly inside. "Where's Billy?" he asked. He carried a burlap sack under his arm.

"Sleepin," yawned Sam. "Dangit, Jake, ain't you had about enough?"

Jake strode past him, found Billy in the sun porch bed and swiftly kicked him in the ribs. Billy roared with pain, clutched his side, and swung to his feet, naked and enraged. "Don't push your luck, old man," he snarled. "I'm about to forget you're old and foolish."

Jake smiled. "Here, Billy." He tossed the sack into the bed. "Be seein you." The sack twitched.

"Hell fire!" wailed Billy. He scrambled free from the sheets and slammed into the wall, clawing frantically. The copperhead crawled slowly out of the bag as Jake's wild laughter echoed throughout the little house. Billy slammed the door and shook Dan Webber awake. "Get up! There's a copperhead in my bed."

"Go 'way," mumbled Webber. Jake's truck roared off down the road. The phone rang, and Sam answered.

"It's fer you, Billy," he said.

It was Brenda. "I can't talk right now," he said. "I seem to have a copperhead sleeping with me."

"Billy, are you still drunk?"

"Hell, no. Your buddy Jake walked in and threw a live snake in with me."

"I'm coming over there," said Brenda.

"Bring the rifle," yelled Billy.

He ran back to Webber. "Dan, damn you, roll out of there. You're the expert. Come and catch that snake."

"Billy," groaned Dan, "go sleep it off."

Sam came in with his axe. "Here. It's yore bed. You do it."

Jim yelled weakly from the couch. "Just burn down the house, Daddy. Gets 'em ever time."

"Webber! Wake up, you bastard!" Billy rolled him off onto the floor.

"Hey," giggled Dan. "You better put on some britches."

"Damnit to hell! Give me that axe, Grandpap." Billy cracked the door and poised himself for the attack. "The fucker is hid," he growled. Webber pushed past him carrying a long handled, pronged instrument.

"I'll catch it," he said sleepily. "I need a sample anyway."

After ten minutes he came out carrying the sluggish copperhead. "It acts drugged, or something. Strange. What can I put him in? My cages are in the car."

Sam found a heavy box and Dan carefully deposited the copperhead. "Back in the lab I'll milk him," he said. "Then we'll find out just how potent these Cox copperheads really are."

Billy, pulling on his jeans, watched from a distance. "Jake just got even with me for the camera. Make us some coffee, Grandpap. Lots of it, strong."

Brenda knocked, and peeked in the door. "Ugh." She wrinkled her nose. "Smells like an old locker room in there."

Webber grabbed his pants and blushed furiously. "I'm sorry," he stammered. "I was–."

"That's okay. Just don't take another shot at me." Brenda stepped inside. "Did you kill the copperhead?"

"Caught him alive," cackled Sam. "This feller, he's a snake doctor. He put him in that box over there."

"I'm a herpetologist," explained Dan. "I'm Dan Webber, from the University of Kentucky."

"Really? Then tell me, Mr. Webber, did you actually burn a million snakes, or were you all just wild drunk?"

"I didn't count the copperheads," said Dan, "but the whole floor—under the floor—was crawling with them."

"And you—you geniuses—decided to fry them." She wheeled to face Billy. "This is too much. You are dangerously insane, Billy."

"I never said I wasn't," grinned Billy. "But I guess we did get a little wild, didn't we?"

"A little wild? Don't you remember burning the big truck?"

"The big one?"

"Yes. It's on top of the ashes."

"I'll be damned." Billy moaned and rubbed his head. "Aw, hell, it was needing new tires anyway."

"That is the last straw!" yelled Brenda. She stomped to the door. "*If* you ever sober up, call me. I have to be in court. *I* work for a living." She slammed the screen door angrily.

"Billy," drawled Sam, "she is one fine woman, that one. Don't you mess around and let her git away from ye."

"I won't, Grandpap," said Billy. "But right now I got to have some coffee. I don't even feel good enough to chase after a pretty woman."

††††††

They poked furtively at the smoldering ruins.

"What now?" asked Jim.

"Get a bulldozer, clean it up, and start over," said Billy. "Right here is where I'm gonna live, come hell or high water or copperheads."

Webber was cautiously searching, probing the weeds, shrubs, and debris. "Nothing," he said finally. "No copperheads. I'd better go over to the health department and check out their records, and ship your friend in the box back to the lab." He grinned. "Did you hear the one about the nearsighted snake? He raped a rope."

"Funny," growled Billy. "You're a real comedian, Dan." He turned to Jim. "Take Grandpap home and put him to bed. He's walking around asleep. You rest up too. I'll go to town and get a dozer out here, and we'll start building again."

Jim nodded agreement and grinned. "I guess while you're in town you'll need to see your attorney, too."

††††††

"What happened to you?" Becky Skaggs pulled her glasses down and stared. "Were you boiled or roasted?"

Billy's smile hurt. "I just decided I didn't need any eyebrows, and that I wanted a quick tan. Is your boss here?"

"Yep." Becky grinned. "But she ain't none too happy about it. She just told me to go fuck myself."

"Becky," smiled Billy, "*if* that could be done, I'm sure you're the one who could do it." He knocked, and eased into Brenda's office.

She glared. "Well, it's old Wild Bill. Burned any trucks today? Shot any film? Blown up any houses?"

"Brenda, I'm sorry," he said lamely.

"Sorry?" Brenda slammed the ledger book shut. "Why should you be sorry? Wild Bill Cox isn't sorry. Not the great American hero. You just have to grin and act sheepish and everything's fine. Go away and leave me alone."

"Brenda," he started, "I'm going to–."

"I don't give a damn!" She spun her chair and faced away. "Billy, you're a spoiled, insensitive immature redneck."

"But I–."

"What are you planning to use for money? Your new truck is in. Ed called." She shook her head. "You're going to build a new house. You're going to farm. You're going to marry me.

God damn you, Billy Cox! Will you ever grow up?" She glared, then continued. "Yesterday you burned over $6,000 worth of new building materials. You shoved a truck into the fire for fun. You bought a moonshiner's hotrod. You bought a $9,000 truck. You blow a hundred a week on booze. You buy tractors, and mules, and sawmills, and every other thing you see and want. A new $9,000 truck! Why, Billy?"

"I need it." He stared at the floor.

"Bull!" Brenda stood and stalked around the office. "Any old five hundred dollar truck would serve the purpose. Toys! That's what it all is. Big toys for a forty year old boy." She slumped to her desk, sobbing. "Billy, I can't raise a forty year old child."

"I'm no child," he said shakily. "I know what I'm doing."

"I guess that applies to Obie's wife?"

"What?"

"Annie." She laughed bitterly. "Annie." She shook her head. "You forgot to tell me about her, Billy. No wonder he hates you." She turned, eyes glistening. "Just go, Billy. Please."

He spun and left, kicking the door shut and stopped at Becky's desk. "Thanks. I ought to break your damned neck. You just *had* to tell her, didn't you?"

"Well, it was true." Becky cringed. "You and Annie–."

"Twenty years ago, Becky."

She met his eyes boldly. "And last month."

Billy left.

At the bank he checked his checking balance–$9,140.

There was $7,500 still owed on the truck. He walked into the president's office and signed an application for a fifty thousand dollar mortgage.

Sam, when he heard, raged. "They ain't never been no Cox land mortgaged," he spat. "It ain't right. That land, it won't never pay off that loan, Billy." He stomped away.

"Well, Jimmy," Billy said softly. "It's your turn. Anything you want to yell at me about?"

"Nope. Not today."

"Then come with me. I have to pick up a new truck."

††††††

Dan Webber nursed his throbbing head, sipped black coffee, and chuckled softly at the memory of the previous day. He felt a strange closeness to the Coxes. In one day they had given him acceptance he did not feel at the university after nine years as a student and employee, and he relished the easy familiarity.

Scrawny Dan Webber was a loner, a slightly eccentric and openly sarcastic individual, more at home with reptiles than with people. He was small—five nine and 135 pounds—and his thick lenses and acne scarred face were complimented by the baggy, ill fitting clothes he selected.

The Webbers, an old Owensboro family, were florists. Webber Floral, with branches in Bowling Green, Paducah, and Madisonville, was Jonathan Webber's consuming passion, leaving little time for a frail and studious son. Dan turned to plants and animals for companionship and for a career. At the university he studied horticulture, then went more into the study of reptiles. After a Masters Degree in Zoology he was employed by the university's extension program, and his work made for easy access to a continuing study of snakes. In time he became the resident herpetologist, an active researcher and field worker. Dan had few close friends, and viewed the female scientists he met with distaste. They were, he felt, overly antiseptic and clinical, and sex resembled a laboratory dissemination.

He first read of the Cox County copperhead problem in the newspapers; he was already familiar with the Copperhead Mountain legends. He had welcomed his new assignment and now was even more pleased with his new friends. He grinned when Jim Farley staggered into the kitchen, rubbing his eyes and whimpering. "You look snakebit, Jim. Want some coffee?"

"A gallon," grunted Jim. "How do Sam and Daddy do it?

They're both up and gone."

"They've both got a lot of years of practice over you," said Dan. "You've never had to be so totally immersed."

Jim grinned feebly. "What about you?"

"First time I've been drunk in over five years."

"First time you ever used a shotgun?"

Dan groaned. "You ought to see my shoulder."

"You ought to see those poor dead trees."

"I guess I never was around guns much," apologized Dan.

"That was obvious," laughed Jim. "I'm sure glad you missed Jessie and Brenda. And–damn, Dan–that was a fine tackle you laid on Jake Wilde."

"I'm off to a great start," said Dan. "The county will probably send me home with a recommendation that I be locked up." He grinned broadly. "But nobody–and I mean nobody–would ever believe what we did yesterday."

After the visit to the smoldering homeplace, they came back to Sam's house and sat quietly over more coffee. "I'd better find a motel," said Dan. "I kind of forgot, yesterday."

"No you won't," smiled Jim. "Stay here with the rest of us fools. No decent motel would accept you anyway."

"Okay." Dan grinned happily. "You got a boarder. But I still have to go in to the health department. What are you up to today?"

"With a whole day free? What else? A girl, some cold beer, and some soft blankets."

"You got two?"

"Find your own," laughed Jim. "Pickings are slim in these parts. Except–I got it–you could go with me. My date's mother–."

"Mother? Damnation, Jim."

"Don't say no 'till you see her. Becky is. . .well, she's a lot younger than the calendar says."

Dan stared, skeptical. "You wouldn't set me up?"

"Trust me," said Jim. "Have I ever lied to you?"

††††††

Brenda reluctantly allowed Billy back into her office, then sat cooly at her desk as he searched awkwardly for words.

"I came to say I'm sorry," he said softly. "For yesterday. For making a fool out of myself."

"You certainly did do that," Brenda said firmly. "Over and over, you keep doing things to convince me that there could never be a solid relationship between us."

"Old Becky just *had* to tell you, didn't she?"

"Better her than someone else," snapped Brenda. "*You* would have been the logical one to explain it to me."

"Explain?" Billy fished for a cigarette and sucked in the hot smoke. "You don't want any explanation, Brenda. You've already made up your mind. You believe what you want to, and it won't make any difference what I say."

"Is that the way you see me?" Brenda stiffened. "Billy, I don't think this conversation is getting anywhere. You'd better go on home to your toys and booze."

He stubbed the cigarette, angry eyes locked to hers. He shrugged. "And you'll go back to a hound, a cold nose, and some cold memories, all by yourself in that cabin."

"Not necessarily," she said softly. "I have friends."

"Jake? Old Jake, the snake worshipping newspaperman?"

"The *what*?"

Billy smiled. "You've got Becky to bring you gossip, but I've got Sam. He told me. Jake Wilde goes to some church down in Tennessee where they handle snakes."

"Don't be a nasty little boy, Billy, making up tales. Jake doesn't–."

"He does, Brenda. About once a month, sometimes more often. He came here, originally, because of the mountain and the old stories about the copperheads. For ten years he's been tracking around the hills, studying the snake handlers–."

"He studies them, like you said. Lots of writers do. That

doesn't make him some sort of voodoo practitioner."

"Suit yourself," grunted Billy. "It's the truth. I just wanted you to know that I ain't the only one with problems." He stood. "We're not gettin anywhere. Call me when you're ready to talk sense."

"Me? Talk sense? Billy, it's time you realized just *who* caused the problems here. *I* didn't wreck a house and a truck and endanger the lives of innocent people. *I* didn't burn $10,000 for drunken entertainment."

He chuckled softly. "And you didn't sleep with Annie. Just with an over-the-hill writer who plays around with copperheads."

"You're wrong," snapped Brenda. "But I don't expect you to understand anything except promiscuity."

Becky's knock interrupted them. She poked her head around the doorjamb. "I got to go. Got a date."

"Anybody I know?" asked Billy. "I'd hate to see some innocent person get eaten alive."

"You don't *know* any innocent people," said Becky. She blanched. "Sorry, boss."

Brenda laughed. "Go on, Becky. You're absolutely right, including me among the lost souls. Have fun."

"I hope you catch something," snarled Billy. "Something incurable."

Becky wiggled her hips and tossed her hair as she left, slamming the door with a wide grin.

"Hard woman to stay mad at," muttered Billy.

"Becky's a survivor," said Brenda. "I am, too." She stood. "It's time I went home to the cold nose."

"We can't be friends? More than friends?" Billy waited.

"Not now. It's too much, Billy. Maybe, sometime, I'll calm down and see things differently, but right now I can't." She snapped her briefcase shut and switched off the lights. "I'm sorry."

"That's it?"

"That's it, Billy."

††††††

That evening at seven, Jim and Dan drove to Becky Skaggs' trailer and waited for Beth to finish dressing. Becky mixed drinks. "Your daddy is mighty mad at me," she told Jim. "Did he tell you?"

"Sort of," said Jim. "He'll get over it."

Dan stared openly at Becky. Her warm personality and raw sexuality intrigued him, and her solid body was fully displayed in snug pants and a low cut blouse.

"You do *what*?" had been her response to the introduction. "Snakes? Why in hell would anybody want to hang around with a cage full of copperheads?"

The drink led to a second, and a third, dim lights and slow, up close dancing. Jim and Beth slipped quietly out.

"You remind me of my first husband," said Becky.

"My hair?" asked Dan.

"No." She ground against him.

Dan blushed and backed away. "I–I'm sorry," he stammered. "I didn't mean to. . ."

"Sorry? Hell, honey, I wouldn't like you any other way." She snuggled closer, and their dance slowed to a swaying, grinding standstill.

Becky smiled and pulled her blouse over her head. She unhooked the lacy bra, dangled it in one hand, and dropped it, staring hard at Dan. Her breasts jutted, ending in brown, swelling nipples. She took his hands and pressed them to her. "Do you like us older women?" She smiled again.

Dan's rasping breath was her only answer.

Becky slid her pants down over firm hips. "I never did like to wear underclothes," she said softly. Dan stared, and licked his lips. Becky swayed to him, smiled as their bodies touched, and worked loose the buttons of his shirt. "Oh, my," gasped

Becky. "I'm gonna like you a lot."

Her arms clenched his shoulders, caressing and tugging, and her hands slid down to draw him closer.

Later, breathless, still connected and sweating, they clung together. Becky sighed. "Don't move. Just stay like this."

In time it was her hips that arched and started them anew. Their pounding, thrusting bodies filled the dark room with whimpering urgency.

††††††

"I never met a woman who had so much fun," said Dan. He clung limply to the headboard, smoking.

Becky laughed, deep in her throat. "Them city women don't," she said. "They got too much schoolin to ever let go. Like Brenda Higgins is."

Dan grinned. "Then don't you ever go back to school."

"Don't you worry, honey. I know everthing I'll ever need to know."

"Amen," said Dan.

The door slammed and Beth came running through. "I'm home, Mamma." She stopped at the bedroom entrance. Dan curled under the sheets. Becky stretched and smiled, arching her breasts.

"Have a good time, sweetie?"

"Yes, Mamma, I did." She licked her lips. "Hi, Dan."

"Uh, hello, Beth. I was just leaving."

"I saw." She giggled. Becky reached, jerked the sheet away from Dan, and grinned at Beth. "Join us?"

Beth smiled faintly and dropped her dress. She was nude underneath, a curved young version of Becky. The pink nipples were erect.

So was Dan.

††††††

Jim missed Dan when he returned to the house, grinned and shrugged his shoulders, and slept. The next morning he heard a car and crawled to the window; a disheveled Dan Webber was staring after Beth Skaggs' dusty Chevelle. Jim chuckled as Dan trudged to the house. "Mornin," he said.

Dan blushed. "Jim, I, uh. . .last night I. . ."

"Well, hell," laughed Jim. "Did you or did you not get the family special?"

"You mean they. . ." Dan turned redder.

"Only if they like you."

"But, Jim, you and Beth are—."

"Buddies," said Jim.

Dan stood awkwardly, still redfaced. "Did you—Jim, did you plan that?"

"Anything for a friend." Jim smiled broadly.

Dan sat down heavily and slapped Jim's shoulder. He shook his head happily, and grinned. "What a place."

††††††

The dry weather held, and construction of the new house went quickly. Billy worked with the crew, driving them stubbornly, coming back after supper to work until dark, working Saturdays and Sundays. He stayed coldly sober, spoke little, and shunned visits to Skaggs Gap. Brenda did not call; he made no attempt to contact her. The stalemate continued in stony silence.

Almost by miracle, the copperheads vanished. No attacks, bites, or discoveries were reported for two weeks, and Dan was at a loss. "Same exact conditions," he said. "Where in the hell have they gone?"

"They're up on the mountain," said Sam. "But they'll be back."

"Then so will I," said Dan. He reluctantly returned to Lexington.

By late August the plumbers were making the final hookups in the house. Billy himself dug the trenches and a new, larger cistern. His new truck, dusty and dented now, served as work-horse, tractor, and transportation; the gray Nova sat unused beside Sam's house. Jim and Sam finished the fences, erected a new pole barn, and hauled rock for the fireplace. They worked the mules, hitched to a low work sled or a wagon, and Jim's skills were soon obvious. "He's gonna start growin his own," chuckled Sam. "The Farley-Cox Mule Farm."

Billy only grunted.

"By damn," growled Sam. "Leastways that might bring in some cash money. Have you figgered out jist how we're gonna live? It'll be next year before we git a penny in offa this land."

"And me with a $50,000 mortgage," Billy chuckled. "Looks hopeless, don't it?"

Sam nodded his dour agreement.

"It's not as bad as it looks," said Billy. "I'm going to finish the house for $30,000 by us doing so much of the work, and that gives us a cushion; I have some cash coming in from old contracts, and my agent is scheduling a speaking tour for this winter. If I have to, I can sell some more basketball shoes. We'll make it. I'm not nearly as footloose and foolish as some people think."

"Meanin Brenda?" asked Sam.

"For one." Billy plucked a blade of grass and chewed. "If things get too tight I could even play another season. I don't want to, but I would if it was necessary."

"I told 'em you'd done growed up," smiled Sam. "I know you can do it, Billy."

"Thanks for the confidence, Grandpap. Right now I need to hear somebody caring."

"Brenda, she'll come around."

"I don't know," sighed Billy. Wearily, he stood and tied on his nail apron. "Let's hang some more doors." He stopped, looked at the house, and chuckled. "Grandpap, this time a year ago I was stretched by a pool in Las Vegas, watching the girls and sipping a cold drink, with not a worry in the world."

"Do ye miss it all, Billy?"

"That's the funny part. I'd rather be here."

Brenda had mailed the mortgage papers, with a cooly efficient letter addressed to "Dear Mr. Cox," and had inserted a bill for $900. Billy had mailed the check promptly, stubbed "For Personal Services." But he also made a furtive stop at Brenda's cabin and left Sam's best new puppy tied to the doorknob.

††††††

The courtship of Karen Bowles was a new experience for Jim Farley. In time her gentle personality emerged, along with a lively sense of humor, but mostly she evoked warmth–visions of strong, deep passions, loyalty, and stability. Jim went to church often, just to be with her, and was relieved to find that her beliefs were strong but not rigid. The actual attendance at the little chapel was as much social as spiritual.

Karen was, clearly, a passionate woman. She was equally determined to save sex for marriage.

Billy was concerned. "Jim," he said, "I can understand your interest. Karen is so different from anybody you've ever been around, and any man's ego would love a woman who makes it so clear that he's the most important thing in the world. But I also think you've gotten serious about her, and she loves you."

"We're serious," said Jim.

"Then I'd better lay it on the line. Can you–with your background and education–ever be really happy with Karen? What about conversation? Entertainment? Could she ever understand your work? Do you *want* a marriage like my father and mother?"

"I want a woman like Georgie," Jim said quickly. "But–unlike Jessie–I don't need a slave. Karen is not stupid. Neither is Georgie, for that matter."

"What about your Cincinnati friends? Your parents? What will they think of Karen?"

"They'll love her," said Jim. "But it may not matter what they think. I might not go back to Cincinnati."

"Jim, don't get mad at me." Billy blew smoke from the cigarette, and sighed. "Right now, you're all wrapped up in some romantic fascination with summertime, farming, and a beautiful country girl. Just be damned sure, before you quit your job and move here, that the attraction is a lot deeper."

"Look at you," said Jim. "You'd be much better off if you'd stayed here."

Billy roared. "I'd be a drunk, Jimmy, or dead. I had to leave." He stared off, pensive and reflecting. "That's not a valid comparison, anyway. I came back here knowing the good and the bad, and there's a hell of a lot of bad you haven't seen yet. This can be a hard, cold place, Jim." He suddenly grinned. "But if you decide to drop Karen, I'd appreciate an introduction and a recommendation."

"You have the woman you need. You and Brenda belong together."

"Easier said than done," Billy said grimly.

"Let me know if I can help," said Jim.

"You've helped already, Jim. Just being here this summer; you've made my life a lot more complete." Billy grinned shyly. "Getting to know you, seeing that you're a fine young man. . .that's meant a lot to me."

"You waited long enough to start finding out," laughed Jim. "Didn't you ever wonder about me?"

"I wondered. I never knew what had happened to you, and nobody would tell me. I guess I could have found Linda and asked her, but. . .Grandpap was the only one here speaking to me, and he didn't know where you were. I'm sorry, Jim, for being such an ass."

"I never knew I was adopted until I was twelve," smiled Jim. "I found out because Dad got so mad over my basketball.

Once I got over the shock, I tried harder; so, in a funny way, you're responsible for my athletic career. I felt sort of obligated to be good out of some weird feeling—partly spite—to show you up and partly hoping that somehow you'd find out about me and be proud. . .maybe even come to see me play."

"I. .I would have. . ."

"I wasn't as good as you," said Jim.

Billy shrugged. "I wasted it all. The talent, the money, and the chance to get somewhere. My trademark was being a flake. Once in a while it was different. Sometimes I'd make a great play, win a game—just enough to keep me going and keep the contracts coming. I just never did put together a full season. I'm a young has-been."

"My god," laughed Jim. "You talk like your life is over."

"No," grinned Billy. "It's not hopeless. I found you. And Sam, again."

"And Brenda," added Jim.

"You're the youngest wise man I ever saw, Jim. If I hadn't already seen you act human, I'd worry. There's enough of me in you to keep you from being too perfect."

"You always took the blame," laughed Jim. "Every time I took a drink or screeched a tire, Dad went into his lecture about my shiftless father."

"I'd like to meet the Farleys sometime. To thank them."

"Not just yet. Right now you're the last person on earth they want around. You're leading their only son astray."

"I can't blame them for worrying. I wouldn't want *my* son hanging out with me and Sam Cox."

Jim's laugh rang out. "Just remember that you're a newcomer to the father business. And, for the record, I'm not engaged, or whatever they call it these days. I'm just friends with a fine woman, one who hasn't been in every bed in six counties."

"I guess you know about little Beth," chuckled Billy, "and the mother-daughter act."

"All too well," grinned Jim. "I sicked 'em on Dan."
"Good," chuckled Billy. "They'll cure his pimples."

CHAPTER 12

"HE'S THE DEVIL!"

That night Jim parked under the trees and reached for Karen. She came eagerly, clinging close and trembling. Her body arched to him as they pressed together, and his hand slid to her knee and worked upward. Karen moaned, pulled away slightly, then shivered and melted to him. Her dress was up to her waist and Jim's trembling hand searched the soft buttocks and found the elastic of her underwear.

Suddenly the door was open, a light glared, and a strong hand jerked Jim out the door and slammed him to the gravel. He hit hard and lay addled, confused and afraid.

"Stop!" screamed Karen.

Chester Bowles' heavy boot hung over Jim's chest. Karen scrambled across the seat, tugging her dress down, and was out the door. "Nothin happened, Daddy. Please! Don't hit him." She clung to Chester until he relaxed, unclenched his stiff muscles, and stood glaring down at Jim.

"I mighta knowed," Chester said quietly, "what would come of lettin you see Karen." He shoved her away roughly. "Whore! You little tramp!"

Jim stumbled to his feet and grabbed Karen, hugging her close. "That's enough, Chester," he snapped. "Nobody talks about my future wife that way."

"Your what?" Chester hesitated.

"We're going to be married. "Jim grinned down at her. "Right?"

She paled. "Y-yes." She blinked, and stumbled closer. "Yes, yes, yes."

Chester frowned and fumbled with his big hands as he grinned broadly. "Damn." He coughed to clear his throat, and shuffled nervously. "Good. I reckon. I mean. . .hell, Jim, congratulations. But let me tell you somethin." He offered his hand as he spoke. "That stuff–" he pointed to the car– "that can wait 'till after the weddin." Chester coughed again. "I guess I better git inside and git some sleep." He backed away, smiling. "Jim?"

"Yeah, Chester?"

"Don't git it in yore head that this'll git you your mules any cheaper."

Jim drove home, shook Billy awake, and told him.

"Do you have to?" asked Billy. "Is Karen pregnant?"

"Damn you!" Jim punched at Billy's shoulder. "No. I'm not that good a son to you." He reddened. "Chester did catch us–necking–but we'd already decided."

"Congratulations," said Billy. "Do you need a best man?"

The phone rang, and Billy grumbled as he walked to answer. "Hell, she's calling you already to back out. "He looked at the clock. "It's two in the mornin."

He lifted the receiver. "Hello?"

"Billy? Wild Bill?"

Billy frowned. "Who the hell is this?"

"Hells bells, Billy, it's me. Walter. Walt King, who still has you under contract for another two years."

"At two o'clock? Walt, you crazy bastard, call me back in the morning."

"I've tried, Billy, but you're never there. This is not a social call, hoss. I'm talkin money."

Billy was awake. "A commercial?"

"Hell, no. I wouldn't call for somethin as petty as that. We got an offer, Billy. To play."

"Play?"

"Basketball, damnit! The NBA. Remember? You and the black dudes, little round ball, glass backboards?"

"Forget it," growled Billy. "I quit, Walt."

King chortled. "How does $300,000 sound to you?"

"For what? A ten year contract?"

"One season."

"For who?"

"Dallas. They're a new team."

"Why? Do they need a clown?"

"Nope. They need a shooting guard."

Billy laughed. "I'm flattered, Walt. But you know I can't play full time anymore. Remember my knees?"

"That's the best part. They see you as a third guard. Twenty, twenty-five minutes a game. To shoot that jump shot, Billy, and open up the defense. What you do best, old buddy."

Billy yawned. "When?"

"Summer camp starts in three days."

"Forget it."

"How about September 1? They'll let you skip camp. They really want you, Billy. You shoot good, and you're good box office."

"So they're looking for a white flake."

"Maybe," said King. "You always had style, Billy. Any way you look at it, you can't walk away from $300,000. You never made that much. Hell, fake it. I've seen you go through the motions before, times when you were so soused you could barely walk."

Billy said nothing.

"You still there?" asked Walt.

"Yeah. I'm still here."

"Then how about it? Deal?"

"I'll have to think about it."

"Think? Damnit, Billy, you couldn't make this much off them hillsides in fifty years."

"Look, Walt," snapped Billy. "I know you don't understand, but it's not the money, it's. . .forget it. Just give me some time."

"Tell you what. I'll mail you a contract. Look it over."

"Okay. But, Walt, could you send it to my attorney?"

"Sure. Who is he?"

Billy gave Brenda's name and address.

"A broad?"

"A woman, Walt."

"Now I understand. She a hot number?"

"Knock it off, Walt. This one's special."

"Sure, kid. So were about twenty others."

"Walt," said Billy, "you go right straight to hell." He slammed the receiver down and waited. It rang again in two minutes. "Hello again, Walt."

"Okay, Billy, I'm putting the contract in the mail. That's a lot of money."

"And you want your cut. Could you figure out a way to take ten percent of the cuts and bruises?"

"Hell, no. That's what you jocks get paid for. I earn my money with my brains." He hung up.

Billy sat grinning as Sam, coughing and snorting, opened the door. "Who was that, callin in the middle of the night?"

"My agent," said Billy. "From California. I've got an offer of $300,000 to play one more season."

Sam's face drooped. "But you quit, Billy."

"I know it, Grandpap. But—damn—that's a lot of money. More than I ever made, even when I was good. We sure could make good use of it."

"Why they wantin to pay you so much, Billy?"

He grimaced. "To be a clown. Raise hell, draw the press and the crowds. Shoot long shots, sometimes."

"Ye'd be made fun of, Billy."

"I know, Grandpap. But $300,000. . ."

"I ain't ever pushed you none," said Sam. "But this time. . . you said you was home to stay, Billy. If you go back for another year, you'll stay gone again. I'm seventy-nine, son. We got to do it now or I won't be around when we do."

"You're healthy as a mule," grinned Billy. "You'll live forever."

"I'm a old man," Sam said quietly. "I'm tired, and I'm livin fer one last good thing. You and me and the farm."

"Well," said Billy. "I didn't say yes."

"Ye never said no, neither," grunted Sam.

Brenda called three days later. "I have your new contract," she said cooly. "I've looked it over, and it's legitimate. A base salary of fifty thousand and—."

"Fifty thousand? Walt said $300,000."

"He'd be right, *if* you averaged twenty-five points a game, played in the All Star game, and made All Pro. *If* your team won a division title."

"One of those," muttered Billy. "Performance clauses that are impossible. That greedy bastard."

"At least it's a job offer," said Brenda, "and fifty thousand is a lot more than you'll ever make from farming."

"What do you think I should do?"

Why should that matter to you?" she asked. "It's your business. You always do what you want, anyway."

"Do you care? At all? About what I do?"

"Yes," she finally said. "I do care, Billy. That's why I won't help you decide."

"Could we get together, Brenda? I miss you."

"Don't push me, Billy. Maybe. When you've made up your mind—about everything—we can talk."

"Okay." He waited. "Thanks, I guess."

"What do you want me to do with this contract?"

"Hang onto it," he said. "I'll let you know."

"Billy, I. . ." She sighed. "Nothing. Forget it."

"Look Brenda," he said. "You're the only woman I've ever really loved. I want you, more than I ever wanted anything."

"But?" she waited.

"But I'm no trained seal, I do things a little differently." Her dry chuckle cut in. "I came back here," continued Billy, "to change my life. To accomplish something, for a change. And, damnit, I'm doing pretty good."

"Yes," she snapped, "even with Annie."

"Hell yes!" he yelled. "That happened. I never said it didn't. The first day I was here, she crawled into my bed naked." She did not respond. "Brenda, since I met you there's been nobody–nothing–and. . .ever since you told me where to go I haven't gone anywhere."

"So now you're a penitent monk? Don't try that on me, Billy. I'm not Annie."

"No. You're not," growled Billy. "That's why I'm trying to tell you the truth. Now it's up to you. I don't beg anybody for anything. Ever." He paused. "But–Brenda–I do care. I love you. And. . .and I need you."

"Burn the damned contract," he snapped. "I should have never let you see it."

"Billy?" Her voice was soft.

"Yeah?"

"Thank you. For the puppy. Little Sam."

He laughed sharply. "You're welcome. I hope he's a good replacement."

"For Sam?"

"No. For me." Billy slammed down the receiver, kicked the chair across the room, and took a full bottle from the cabinet. An hour later Sam heard the muffled sobs from the bedroom, and gently closed the door.

††††††

A delegation from the Skaggs Gap Rotary Club located Billy, shirtless and grimey, mixing mortar and helping Sam lay the rock fireplace. The president asked Billy to be the parade marshall and speaker for the annual Labor Day homecoming; his response was a bitter laugh. "Why?"

"Because you're the best known man in this county," said

the club president. "You're a legend."

"Do it," grunted Sam.

"Oh, hell," said Billy. "I'll try. But don't be too surprised if I'm less popular than you expect."

Brenda read Jake Wilde's report of Billy's selection:

Illustrious Billy Cox, Hogtown's most prominent ex-athlete and gentleman farmer, will grace Skaggs Gap with his presence for the Homecoming Celebration. He has agreed (for free, we presume) to lead the parade and speak at the picnic.

Unfortunately, Mr. Cox was forced to sell the bronze convertible he drove home to Cox County, so he'll be reduced to riding in the mayor's old Ford.

Since his recent return to Cox County, Mr. Cox has made admirable contributions to our economy. He has spent thousands rebuilding the Cox homeplace, and he has sacrificed at least two trucks to the fire gods. His housing renewal project has definitely been a 'glowing' success.

Our 1980 Homecoming will be one to remember; we will celebrate the return of Wild Bill Cox and the end of the Copperhead Summer.

Brenda stared out the window, absently fondling the floppy eared pup, remembering the plans she and Billy had made for a Labor Day wedding. "Get off, Little Sam," she said. "You'd better go outside and play with Uncle Buck."

††††††

He watched from the ledge as Brenda romped with the hounds, then sadly climbed to his feet and walked wearily across the crest of the ridge. He reached the mountain at dusk and climbed quickly, reached the top and sat immobile until after midnight.

††††††

Jim nervously signed the register, took the key, and returned to the car. "You're sure?"

Karen smiled. "I'm sure."

In the room she slipped into the bathroom and emerged wearing a gown which covered every inch of her except her head and hands. Her eyes were sparkling, and the long hair was brushed to a dull sheen. "Turn off the light," she whispered.

Through the cotton he could feel her warm, strong body, and her heavy breasts swung to him. Gently he untied the ribbons and opened the gown. He drew it from her shoulders, stopping to nuzzle her slender neck, then pulled the cloth away. He kissed her softly, a lingering and questioning moment. She came to him, wet and trembling, and they did not speak.

††††††

She was silent as he drove her home. When Karen did speak, her voice was dull and mechanical. "I guess now you got what you wanted you'll be goin."

Jim's tongue was thick and dry. "No." He was nervous, hesitant. "It's no different, now."

"Yes it is."

They rode in uneasy silence.

"It's okay," she finally said.

"What is?"

"What we did. You don't have to pretend to love me. I wanted to do it. I wanted to know what it would be like with somebody . . somebody like you."

"What in hell are you talking about?"

"I know you can't marry me," said Karen. "And it's all right. You don't have to."

"But, Karen, I do love you." Perplexed, he eased the car to the side of the road.

"Just keep drivin," she said. "We've done all we're goin to

do tonight."

"Damnit!" Jim shifted, and sent the VW roaring toward the Bowles farm. "Karen, you drive me crazy."

"Thank you," she said softly. "You finally told me the truth."

He swore, locked the brake, slid in a circle, and accelerated. At the intersection he swung right and gunned the engine past the redline. "You can call Chester from Jellico," he growled.

"From where? Why?"

"From Tennessee. To tell him we're married."

Karen leaned over, jerked the key from the ignition, and was out the door as soon as the car swerved to a stop. She flung the keys into the darkness. "When I get married," she yelled, "it won't be from pity. Goodbye, Jim." She slammed the door, rocking the car, and walked briskly away.

For ten minutes Jim sat stunned, staring blankly. Then he grinned, found his flashlight, and searched for his keys. As he tramped through the high grass, light flickering, he whistled happily.

From thirty yards away Karen listened, and her heart sunk as his happy song filled the night air. She slipped silently away, headed home, walking blindly. She lept for the ditch as headlights flashed and tires screamed. She fell, tumbling down the thick grass of the road cut, and lay dazed. Jim's body pressed her even deeper into the grass.

Karen screamed, scratched and kicked, then was suddenly still. Jim's pealing laughter filled her ears. She jerked her knee, but was stopped by a firm hand clamped to her calf.

"Let me go!" she yelled. She twisted and fought, getting nowhere. Jim pinned her flat, held both hands, and pressed hard down on her.

"Now," he whispered. "Are you ready to listen to me?"

"Not to you, you—you—you bastard!" Karen shrieked. She arched, then gasped as Jim slid between her legs.

"Just lay still, damnit," he said. "At least until you hear what

I have to say."

"Just go ahead and do it," she spat. "Get it over with. Take what you want. I don't care anymore." Jim bent closer, and suddenly she reached up and bit his nose.

"Yeow!" He tore loose, recovered, and pinned her again. Blood dripped from his face. "Stop it!" he yelled. "Hold still and let me talk. I love you, you wild woman!"

She spat in his face and kicked, pulling her dress higher, and both feet pounded at his back. He laughed, swore, let her go and jumped clear, then sat down to wipe blood from his face. Karen scrambled after a heavy limb and advanced, ready to do battle. She saw his face, stopped, and burst into tears. "Oh, Jim, are you hurt?"

"Just don't hit me again." He held up his hands. "I give up."

She wiped her tears. "You were whistling," she screeched. "You were happy! You don't love me, Jim Farley!"

"I was happy." He grinned. "I still am. Just shut up and listen to me, Karen." He grabbed her shoulders. "I do love you. Back there, I was happy because you fought back."

She stopped twisting and stared. "What?"

"Until a few minutes ago I didn't know if. . .I was scared you were so nice you'd never take up for yourself. I didn't want a weak woman, Karen."

She watched, eyes wide.

"I wanted you to fight back, damnit. Do you understand?"

She relaxed and smiled through tears. "Your nose tasted salty," she grinned.

He hugged her close, and they snuggled deep in the damp grass. "Do you believe me now?" asked Jim.

"Yes. This time." Their lips met.

She relaxed, closed her eyes, and pressed to him.

"Here?" Jim chuckled.

"Yes." She giggled. "If you can stop bleedin on me."

Afterwards she found her shoes and underwear and sat in the car cleaning Jim's face. "I can't go home like this," she said. "Daddy'd kill me."

"We can be in Tennessee in five hours."

She waited, then smiled weakly. "Do you have enough gas?"

Jim grinned and started the motor. "If we run out we'll walk. I'm not gonna give you any more chances to get away."

††††††

Jake Wilde sat at his desk at dawn. His bottle was beside him, and he wrote:

He is still here, still close to her, always nearby, always pressing. She says no, but she wavers. She will take him back. I will not fail again. He will die.

He shoved the journal away angrily, left the house, and drove to the base of Copperhead Mountain.

††††††

As Jake Wilde was climbing, Billy's phone rang. He groaned, crawled out of bed, and answered. "You want to talk to my wife?" asked Jim.

Billy chuckled. "Where are you?"

"On my honeymoon," laughed Jim. "In the Great Smoky Mountains."

"Congratulations. Did you kidnap her?"

"Almost." Jim laughed. "But she's decided to stay with me now."

"Good. Take all the time you want."

"I intend to," laughed Jim. "Tell Sam where I am."

"Okay. See you whenever you wear down."

Jim hung up the phone and reached for Karen.

††††††

"Gonna be a hot one," said Sam. "Mountain is all hazy."

"Maybe it'll choke the snakes," chuckled Billy. He looked up at the clouded slopes. "They're all up there, Grandpap."

"Not for long," Sam said grimly. "Not for long."

††††††

Jake made the familiar trip south to Tennessee, joined the worshippers on the mountain, and nervously waited for the comforting ceremony to peak. He was calm amidst the chanting and wailing, grimly expectant, aware of the contents of the battered suitcase near the pulpit.

Then it was time, and Jake Wilde's bulky presence overshadowed the others as he approached to receive the serpent. The copperhead looped around his brawny forearm, but there was a change, a new agitation, and the snake struggled to rear its darting head.

It struck, twisting and chewing, fangs sinking in the heavy cotton of Jake's shirt-sleeves, thrashing its thick body in sudden anger.

Jake bellowed, slung the writhing body away, swung his arm and sent the copperhead flying. The snake landed in the crowd, striking frantically, squirming and darting as the screaming crowd fought for safety from the savage fangs.

"He's the devil!" screamed a toothless old woman. She pointed a trembling finger at Jake. "Him! It's him!" She wailed, slumped in a faint, and Jake wasted no time.

He bolted through the startled crowd, burst out the open door, and was in his truck before they could follow. Slashing, steering desperately, he sent the pickup careening off the mountainside.

At Cumberland Gap he stopped, inspected his trembling arm and found no broken skin, then drove on in a brooding trance. At midnight he reached Copperhead Mountain and sat in the truck, watching and wondering until daybreak.

He wrote, finally:

It was him.
He does have powers, strange powers, almost equal to mine.
He is a formidable opponent.
We must be more careful.

CHAPTER 13

"ANYBODY WHO ISN'T SCARED IS A DAMN FOOL"

A low keyed, intense terror gradually spread across Cox County, fueled by the superstitious awe of the copperhead and of the mountain. Old timers recalled tales of hunters killed by a strike to the base of the skull, cunning attacks by copperheads who magically climbed trees, and a flurry of protective remedies were noted.

"A cowsnake, that's the best," argued Elbert Simms. "He'll swaller a copperhead whole and keep the varmints run off forever. Cowsnakes is death to copperbellies."

Others advocated hogs—"stomp 'em and eat the bastards, by damn!"—and others recommended dogs or even cats as protection.

Detecting the copperhead presence was simple, argued some. "They smell jist like cucumbers, and things gits real still when they's a copperhead closeby. Birds don't sing, and nothin moves. Horses, they know, too; git nervous and go to runnin and snortin."

Pentacostal preachers gloried in the fear, and took to the pulpits to announce the second coming. "Hit's the Lord's will," they cried. "He's a testin us, brothers and sisters, a weedin out the pure of heart. If you believe, and trust yourself to the Lord, you're safe."

"He's usin the copperhead, sendin 'em down amongst us, findin out the sinners and the evil, puttin us all to the test. You better repent now, brothers, 'cause it's gonna be too late if ye wait fer the copperheads."

No one was free from the apprehension, and every man

carried a weapon—a shotgun or hoe or axe, closeby and ready for immediate use. Nervous citizens killed hundreds of harmless snakes; even grapevines and ropes were blasted and chopped by edgy Cox Countians.

Tired deputies took hundreds of calls, made wary investigations, shot first and questioned later, and life was suddenly dangerous for any animal which moved in the underbrush.

Then, on a muggy afternoon, the copperheads killed a small boy near Hogtown. He had gone to the spring to dip water for his pony, and the snakes struck as he bent, sinking fangs deep in his neck. The mother found him, two hours later, a copperhead huddled close to the body. She killed the snake with a slashing hoe, and ambulance drivers killed two more as they rescued the body and fled back to the safety of Skaggs Gap.

More attacks were reported. "They're here," grunted Sam. He called Dan Webber. "Time fer you to git back here." Webber agreed.

Billy, when he came in from working, was tired and angry.

"A goddamn copperhead bit one of the electricians. We got him to the hospital in time. Grandpap, I'm tired of fighting snakes."

"You ain't seen nothin yit," warned Sam. "I got a feelin. It's different, this time. Start carryin that shotgun again, Billy. Them snakes mean business."

"I'll watch out," said Billy. "At least this time Jim is safe."

"He'll be comin home," grunted Sam.

Webber arrived after supper with a report from county officials. "One dead, a dozen more bites." He shook his head. "What really scares me is. . .damn, I can't explain it, but that copperhead I took last time was perfectly normal. No strange venom, nothing. But this morning he was crazy. Striking at the cage, all agitated and mad. He was trying to get at me. I swear."

"He was," said Sam. "If he could have got out he'd have headed for home, too. This time it ain't water they're lookin fer, boys. It's us. They come to kill, this time."

"I can't explain," shivered Dan. "But I tend to agree with Sam. In the morning, first thing, I want to go where we burned them before."

"Why?" asked Billy. "I've got a new house built in the very spot."

"It's just. . ." Dan shook his head. "I don't know, Billy, but I have this weird feeling that. . .that's where they'll be."

"Damnation," said Billy. "Are you serious?"

Webber nodded.

"Dan, you're a scientist. You don't believe all this. Give me a logical explanation."

"I can't," Webber said softly. "I can't say why, Billy. But I know–I just know–the copperheads will be there."

He was right.

They were there at daybreak, and Billy turned away the work crew. "Come and take a look," he said. "I don't think you'd want to work in there today."

The copperheads, during the night, had moved in. They were stretched across the porch, draped over the low, sloping roof, and they blocked every entrance. Dan Webber was busy with a telephoto lens, photographing from every angle, carefully picking his way through the construction debris. He grinned as Billy approached. "Don't shoot my film."

Billy's laugh was half-hearted. "Dan, is it revenge?"

"Hell, I don't know, Billy." Dan sat back on his haunches. "I really can't accept that as a fact, but. . ." He shrugged. "I just don't know. All I'm sure of is that nothing like this has ever happened before. I think Sam can give you a better answer."

Sam was quiet. "I knowed they'd come."

"Why?" asked Billy. "What's going on, Grandpap?"

"It's you. And me. They come fer us, Billy."

Billy laughed. "That's a little too far fetched, Grandpap. Not even I believe you this time."

"You will," murmered Sam. "Before the day's over, you'll

believe me."

The following hours brought reports of copperhead bites, near misses, evacuations, and a rising terror. A crowd gathered around Billy's house to stare, and the copperheads rested languidly under the warm afternoon sun. Jessie took Sam home to rest shortly before the state police cruiser arrived at three.

"Clear out, folks," squawked the bullhorn. "Go on home." Larry Blake found Billy. "Orders," he explained.

"Hell," Billy said dully. "Order the copperheads out too."

Blake stared. "I didn't believe it when it came over the radio." He fingered the handle of his revolver. "You got more company on the way. TV crew out of Lexington. It'll make things worse. We plan a roadblock." He shivered. "If those devils started moving. . ."

"Moving?" Billy paled. "Webber! Where are you?" The young man came running. "Dan, you said they'd be here, and you were right. What about Brenda? She's about two miles that way." He pointed. "See that big rock?"

"I don't see why they would," said Webber. "Unless they really *are* after you."

Billy stared and was gone, running hard, and his truck tore the earth as he left the roadway to get around the parked cars of the onlookers.

"Where the hell is he going?" asked Dan.

"I don't know," mused Blake. "But if I was on patrol I'd sure have to arrest him."

Billy hunched over the wheel and drove as fast as he could hold the lumbering truck. After ten minutes he slammed up the drive to Brenda's cabin, braking hard to miss the frantic dogs. He swore angrily, loaded both hounds into the cab, spun off in a circle, and roared toward Skaggs Gap. He led the panting dogs into Brenda's office.

"What are you doing?" she protested. "Are you drunk?"

"Don't go home," ordered Billy. "Your cabin is swarming with copperheads. Like mine."

"I heard about yours," she said, "but I. . ."

"Don't ask questions. I've got to check on Sam."

She caught up at the outer door. "I'm going with you," she said. In the truck she showed him a pearl handled automatic. "I keep it in my desk."

"Hang on to it," he said. "I've got an axe." He steered precisely, slinging the truck through the curves. "Brenda, I know this sounds strange, but it's me they're after. The copperheads. Me and anybody who means anything to me."

"Billy, are you serious?"

"Yes. Even Webber is beginning to agree."

"I'm scared, Billy."

His eyes were fixed on the roadway. "Right now," he muttered, "anybody who isn't scared is a damn fool."

At Hogtown he drove the truck through the picket fence and slid to a stop at Sam's doorstep. He was out, axe ready, in seconds. Brenda was close behind, swinging the little pistol. Billy froze at the step as her shot rang out; a copperhead slid to the ground. "It was on the doorjamb," she said. "Where's Sam?"

The house was jumbled, and two dead snakes were stretched across the floor. The back door was open. "The pups," said Billy. "He's out back with the puppies."

He jumped from the top step, over the waiting copperhead, turned and slashed with the axe. "Come on," he told Brenda. "Stay close behind me."

The dog pen gate was open, and a dead pup lay at the entrance. Billy swore, his hair rising on the back of his neck. "Grandpap! Are you out here?" He poised, axe lifted, ready to move.

"Sam!" screamed Brenda. "Where are you?"

"In here," came the feeble reply. "Watch yourself, Billy."

"He's in the shed," said Billy. "Cover me." He approached cautiously. A dead snake lay limp in the doorway. He edged closer.

"Two more in here," croaked Sam. "Jist inside of the door." He lay in the corner, his arms around the dying hound. "Hurry, Billy." His breathing was ragged, his voice weak.

"Comin through," growled Billy. He jumped past the entrance, spinning as he landed, striking with the axe. The copperhead's fangs bounced off his high boot, and he slashed quickly. The window glass shattered and Brenda's automatic barked twice. Billy stood stiffly, sucking for air.

"That's all of them," said Sam. Billy bent, lifted Sam easily off the floor, and stooped as he went out the door. The blur caught him off guard; he felt the sudden sting. Brenda shot three times and the snake lay twitching.

"Get the truck," gasped Billy. She ran, and Billy hobbled quickly forward. He was waiting when she backed close, and he sat Sam gently between them in the seat. "Get us to the hospital," he said. "Hurry."

"It got you, didn't it?"

"Just once. In the leg. Keep moving, Brenda. I'm fine, but Sam is sick." The old man's incoherent murmerings began, and Brenda listened as she pushed the truck to its limit. They were in Skaggs Gap in fifteen minutes.

"Him first," Billy told the attendants. "I don't know how many bites he has." He turned to Brenda. "Somehow you have to intercept Jim. Don't let him go home."

Brenda's linen suit was torn and dirty, and tears streaked her face. "Hurry up," Billy urged. "Sam and I will be fine." She smiled and turned to leave. "Hey," called Billy. Brenda stopped. "You come back, when you're through. We'll be waiting for you."

"You fool," she laughed. "Not even the damned copperheads can keep me away from you." She was gone, running, her hair flowing behind her.

Billy's stretcher was wheeled into the treatment room. He lay quietly amidst the bustle, listening to Sam's labored breath. "Your grandfather's tough," said the doctor. "He should be dead, by all medical principles. He was bitten four times. Any one should have killed him."

"He was fighting," said Billy. "By the time I got there he'd already killed six or seven of them."

"He may not pull through," cautioned the doctor. "It all depends on how strong his heart is."

"Then he'll make it," Billy said quickly. "Sam Cox has got the biggest, strongest heart in the whole state of Kentucky."

††††††

Brenda was back in an hour, huddled close to Sam, fussing and worrying. "What about me?" asked Billy.

"You'll live," she said. "Nothing as simple as a copperhead bite would hurt anybody with skin as thick as yours. What about Sam? What did the doctor say?"

Billy shrugged. "We'll know by morning. All we can do is wait. You'd better go and get some rest."

"I'm staying right here," she said, "until Sam is up and walking." Her face was determined. "Oh, I found Jim and Karen, still in Tennessee. They're on their way back now."

"Good. Hey, do you still have that little pistol with you?"

"Old habits are hard to break. I've had it in my desk for years, and today's the first time I needed it." She shivered. "I'm glad I kept it."

"You're glad? You saved my life with that shiny little Saturday night special."

She moved closer and took his hand. "Easy," he warned. "The doc said the poison spreads when you get excited."

"You fool." Brenda giggled. "You'll be thinking about sex on your deathbed."

"I hope so," he grinned. He stared as she pulled away. "Did you know you've got blood all over your face and that you're dirty as hell?"

"I know it." She smiled and tugged at her hair. "But I don't look as bad as you did the last time I saw you."

He frowned. "About that, Brenda, I—."

"Forget it, Billy. I have. I gave up. You'll always be a little insane. That's part of what I like about you. But there's one thing you'd better always remember."

"What's that?"

"If I ever catch you with another woman, I'll use that pistol on *you.*"

"You would, wouldn't you?" He grinned and lay back.

"There's one more thing, too."

"Oh, no," he groaned. "What is it?"

Brenda smiled. "I like driving that dirty old truck of yours."

She stayed all night, pressing wet cloths to Sam's forehead, soothing him as he raved in his delerium, watching over Billy. At dawn Sam finally rested, breathing easy, and Brenda slept. Jim, Karen, and Dan Webber burst through the door at seven.

Sam stirred. "By damn," he croaked. "It's the snake doctor. Have ye ketched 'em all, son?"

"Grandpap!" Jim smiled happily. "Last night they were ready to bury you."

"They would have done it, too, if it wasn't fer her and yer daddy." Sam lifted his head. "Somebody git me some breakfast."

The doctor poked his head in the door an hour later. "Sounds like a family reunion," he chuckled. "Sam, I'm glad to see you alive again. Billy, you can go on home if you'll promise to take it easy for a day or two."

"I'm goin too," growled Sam.

"No you're not," grinned the doctor. "We want you right here for two or three more days. I promise we'll be good to you."

"Then git me some goddamn real food," spat Sam. "I'm about to starve to death eatin this slop."

Billy dressed quickly. "Let's go," he said. "Let Grandpap get some sleep."

As they walked outside Brenda gasped. "Those hounds," she wailed. "Buck and Little Sam are still in my office."

††††††

From his pickup, parked across the street from the hospital, Jake Wilde watched Billy and Brenda step out into the open. He reached for the bottle and drank, almost growling in his anger.

Jake had been awake for four days; three empty bottles rattled around in the floor of the truck. A stubble of beard covered his sagging chin; and his eyes were red, sunk deep into his forehead.

He petted the box on the seat beside him and gingerly lifted the lid. The copperhead stirred. He shut the box, grinned, and drank again. As they opened the door to Brenda's office Jake started the truck and drove across town, caught the Cox Ridge Road and vanished.

††††††

Buck howled and lunged to meet them at the door.

"Oh, no," moaned Brenda.

Papers were torn and scattered across the office, and Little Sam yawned greetings from the remains of what once had been a foam seat cushion. The smell was overwhelming. The younger hound came leaping to Brenda, and she hugged him as he licked her face.

"Let's leave 'em a little longer," chuckled Billy. "This clean-up is going to have to be done on a full stomach." They walked to a restaurant, ignoring Little Sam's plaintive howls, and sat around a large table.

"The dogs reminded me," said Jim. "We found two of Grandpap's pups alive. They were out in the field, scared half to death. We left them with Minerva, next door."

"What else did you find?" asked Brenda.

"Nothing. Just dead copperheads."

"No live ones?"

"None," said Dan. "They're gone. We searched all over. It's almost like they've—retreated, maybe? After the battle. It's weird, Billy. We didn't find any at Brenda's, either."

"They sure were there yesterday," said Billy. "All over, just like they were at my place."

"I believe you," said Dan. "I'm just telling you they're gone. Vanished. Poof! Just like that."

"Mine too?"

"I don't know yet, but I'll go take a look."

"You go with him, Jim," said Billy. "Hell, I'd forgotten. Congratulations, you two."

Karen blushed, and Dan stared. "What for?" he asked.

"Didn't Jim tell you? They got married."

Dan grinned and sat smugly back in his chair. "I'm glad," he said. "Uh, I mean for Jim and Karen. Congratulations."

Jim winked. "I know what you mean," he chuckled. "Ready to go?"

"I'll stay in town," said Karen. "I'll help clean up your office, Miss Higgens."

"It's Brenda. I sure would appreciate some help, Karen. Billy and I will take those crazy hounds back where they belong."

They loaded the dogs and drove to the cabin. Billy got out slowly, hefting the axe. He searched, finding nothing. "Let Buck loose," he said. "He'll help me make sure we're alone." The big hound circled nervously, then returned carrying his food dish. "It's clean," laughed Billy. "I'll feed them."

He lifted the bag, tilted it to pour, and a squirming copperhead slid into Buck's dish. "Damn!" He jumped back, and Buck shoved past in a snarling attack. He shook the snake fiercely after it was dead, and growled proudly. Billy wiped his brow. "By god," he whispered, "that'll teach 'em to try and eat old

Buck's food." He released his breath, and Buck's tail thumped happily.

Brenda lowered the rifle. "Enough is enough." She tossed the carbine to Billy. "Guard me while I gather up some clothes. I'm not staying here."

††††††

Dan and Jim parked beside the state trooper who'd spent the night at the homeplace to ward away the sightseers. "Not a sound," he yawned, "all night. I didn't see a thing. How's Sam and Billy?"

"Daddy was released this morning," said Jim, "and Sam will be out in a couple of days. You say you didn't have any visitors?"

"None walking." The trooper grinned. "Now, to tell you the truth, I wasn't out there searchin around. I stayed in the car, with the windows rolled up good and tight, and used the spotlight."

"I don't blame you," muttered Webber. He moved closer. "I don't see a thing, Jim." He opened the door. "They're gone. I knew it." They searched the house and the nearby piles of rubble.

"Call it in," Jim told the trooper. "Tell them the tourists would be wasting their time. Let's go back to town, Dan."

"Okay," said Webber. "I need to talk to Sam and Billy. You can go help your new wife clean up the doggy mess."

††††††

Her leg was thrown over his waist as he lay on his back and smoked.

Brenda giggled. "Just think what they'll say. Us in a motel, in the middle of Skaggs Gap, in broad daylight."

He traced the line of her thigh with a finger. "It's *your*

reputation that's ruined. Mine was shot to hell twenty-five years ago." He stubbed the cigarette and pulled her over on top of him.

They had left the dogs with the vet, then driven to the Skaggs Gap Motel. As Brenda checked in the clerk stared over her shoulder at Billy's truck. "How long will you be staying, Miss Higgens?" she asked.

"Until the copperheads get away from my house," smiled Brenda, "or decide to follow me here."

In the musty room Brenda slid away and sat crosslegged on the bed. "We need to talk, Billy. We can't live forever on sex—or maybe we could, at that—but we did an awful lot of yelling the last time, and I don't want that to ever happen again."

"Part of the yelling won't stop," grinned Billy. "We're both too hardheaded. But I think I can help us get some stuff settled."

"Please do." She nibbled his ear and snuggled close.

"Stop that or I'll lose my voice." He grinned again. "Don't give me an excuse to change the subject. You know how bad I hate to talk about serious stuff." She nodded her agreement and he pinched a nipple.

"Ouch!" Brenda jerked away. "Go on. Be serious."

"Brenda, what I've been trying to say is that I love you so much that I've changed. I really have. You're the first woman I ever respected, as a person. Most women are empty headed, whiney, and phoney."

"God," she laughed. "Wouldn't the Women's Rights people love to get their hands on you."

"You know what I mean. Women are always talking about parties and diapers and cooking and stuff. You're different. You talk like. . .like a man, almost."

She laughed. "Not like a man, Billy. Just a woman. A modern woman. Obviously you've never associated much with that particular type."

"No," he chuckled. "But it's more than that. It's your

hounds, and that car, and your work. I always figured smart women were all old dried up prunes. Damnit, you're smart, and sexy too."

Brenda smiled. "In a lot of ways, Billy Cox, you've led a sheltered life. And, you've only needed women around for one thing."

"Two," he blurted. "I like home cooking."

"You're not *all* wrong. But a lot of what you say about women applies to men. I've always had a choice of crude, horny rednecks or dry intellectuals. You're both. When you ever get over being a tough guy, you're a very gentle and sensitive person."

"Don't go and tell anybody," he warned. "I like my image."

"Some things will never change, Billy. I've conceded that you'll always love cars, basketball, whiskey, physical labor, and–."

"Don't forget sex."

"And sex. For which, I might add, I will be eternally grateful. But if that was all there was to you, I wouldn't be here. Or, rather, *you* wouldn't." She grinned. "It's *my* room."

"Anyway," she continued. "I love you just the way you are. An intelligent redneck."

He chuckled. "And an elegant hillbilly lady."

Brenda smiled gently.

"I'm not much," said Billy. "A good old boy that could play basketball. Now, I'm trying to be a farmer of sorts."

"And snake hunter, father, carpenter, businessman, and maybe in a year a grandfather." She was now serious. "I meant what I said, Billy. To love me–enough–means you never even want another woman, or take one who's just available. And, damn you, you have to start sharing things with me, for real, even the bad stuff. I'm tough, but I'm a woman. I want you to need me."

"I need you." He kissed her gently. "But, Lord have mercy, don't tell anybody I said that."

"As your potential wife," said Brenda, "I think I do need to know one more thing. Just how do you plan to support us?"

"I'm not as bad off as people think. I still draw some royalties from sporting goods companies, and this winter I'll make some speeches. The farm *will* make money, in time. Ten thousand pounds of tobacco is over $15,000. We plan to sell timber—about forty acres. If worse comes to worse, I can coach or go back to selling shoes. I don't owe any money—except the mortgage—and I can borrow more if I need it. And then, if you're thinking way ahead, professional sports organizations have great pension plans. I'll be well paid, when I'm old."

"That's a relief," grinned Brenda. "I figured I'd have to support you. Anyway, when you're broke I'll buy you beer and groceries. I'll even give you an allowance when you're good." She smirked. "Which had better be all the time."

"Just a minute," said Billy, pointing his finger. "We might as well get some more stuff settled. You'll have to buy your own dogfood, and makeup, and pantyhose, hairspray, and gas for your ugly old car."

"And you," answered Brenda, "you'll damn well pay for any more junk cars and trucks you find and drag home, and any more mules or pigs or cows. And you'll have to wash my car when your dusty old road gets it dirty."

"Fair enough. You do the washing."

"You cut the firewood."

"You cook." Billy chuckled.

Brenda frowned. "You clean the bathroom."

He groaned. "I'll do it. But only because I love you so much." He smiled. "And I'll rub your back if you'll trim the hair out of my nose."

"Verbal contracts are binding," she warned.

"I'll make you happy," he said softly.

"It's a deal, Billy. Now, do you want your hair trimmed before or after?"

"After what?"

"After you've rubbed my back." She rolled over onto her stomach.

"After," said Billy. He reached for her.

"Hey, my back doesn't go down that low."

"So sue me," he mumbled.

"I will," said Brenda, "but only if you stop rubbing."

††††††

From Jake Wilde's journal:

I am confused.

During my blackness the family raged, fell upon them, but returned to the mountain.

I did not call them back.

Who is the other, the one who threatens my control? Does he watch me, and slip around me to talk to the family?

I must find him, stop him.

Other things I cannot remember.

Did I, in the blackness, direct that she be harmed? Or did he—the other one—send them to Brenda?

I must know. I must stop him.

The blackness. I must not drink.

I will deal with Billy Cox; I will deal with whoever threatens my presence.

CHAPTER 14

"...HE WAS FREE TO WALK UNHARMED AMONG THE COPPERHEADS..."

Brenda came out from the steaming shower wrapped in a white towel and bent to search through her suitcase. She squealed as Billy yanked the towel away, then smiled and moved with him to the bed. Two hours later she stretched, yawned, and stood. "Time for another bath," she said. "You sure ruined the last one. For a man who was almost dead yesterday you sure do good."

"If I wasn't snakebit," grinned Billy, "you wouldn't be able to walk. Hurry up. I'm starved."

They dressed and walked to the restaurant across the street. Dan Webber, surrounded by empty coffee cups, was waiting. Brenda blushed. "I didn't know where you'd gone," said Dan. "But I..."

"Go on, Dan," laughed Billy. "It's okay. We're adults."

"Jim took Karen out to the Bowles place. I've been talking to Sam. Billy, we want to burn Copperhead Mountain."

"How do you know they're back up there?" asked Brenda.

Webber paled. "They are. I know, and Sam agrees. They go back there after every...after every attack."

"Attack?" Billy smiled. "Do you really think a bunch of copperheads is that organized? That they hunt as a unit, and then retreat on command?"

"Sort of," admitted Webber. "You got any better ideas?"

"Just one. Find Jake Wilde, and–."

"No, Billy," protested Brenda. "Jake had nothing to do with any of this."

"Wait," Webber interrupted. "I know it sounds foolish, and

my boss would fire me, but. . .Sam told me about a man, one who goes up on the mountain. He says he's seen him. A big, heavy-set fellow, light on his feet."

"Jake," said Billy. "He's half copperhead."

"You've both gone crazy," said Brenda. "That old tale about the man on the mountain is just another old legend." She laughed. "You're both arsonists. You just want an excuse to build another fire."

"Sam agrees?" asked Billy. "He wants to burn it?"

"Yes."

"Then scorch the damn thing." Billy pushed back his chair. "Let's go take a look. Brenda, do you want to go for a ride with your fiance in his dirty old truck?"

"Fiance?" Webber grinned. "Since when?"

"We drew up the contract this morning," laughed Brenda. "The wedding is Labor Day, *if* the two of you don't burn the county away before then."

Jake Wilde stared coldly after the laughing couple. From the corner booth he'd listened; he left angrily through the back door. He cursed, a dull monotone, as he drove the old logging trail near the mountain, parked and began the steep climb to the top.

††††††

Obie raged. "Hell, no," he argued. "You ain't b-burnin no damn mountain."

"It's mine, Obe," said Billy. The others watched, uncomfortable as the brothers squared off. "We've already decided, Obie. I just came to tell you. Not to ask."

Obie glared, and spoke in a trembling voice. "It's you," he growled. "You caused all the trouble. They wasn't no p-problem 'till you come back. You b-bastard." He almost hissed. "You ain't gonna burn the mountain."

"Stay out of our way, Obie." Billy smiled cooly. "We don't

want to hurt you."

Obie's only answer was an angry glare.

††††††

Billy parked at the restaurant. "Isn't that Jake's truck?"

"I think so," said Brenda. "Maybe he's inside."

It was well after dark, almost eleven, and there were no other customers. They ordered and ate, leaving as the restaurant closed. Jake's truck was gone.

"Let's just walk over," said Billy, "to settle the supper. Anything else I do today I want to do lying down."

Arm in arm they crossed the vacant street to the motel.

The thick copperhead curled slowly around the gearshift, probed at the door, searched for an escape route. He climbed, and lay stretched flat across the back seat. He reached the width of Billy's truck, silent and lethal, waiting.

Jake watched until the motel room lights went out, then walked furtively to Billy's truck. When he closed the door and crept away, there was no one to see the small box he carried tucked close to his body.

††††††

The fools!
They would burn our mountain.

And I, am I losing control?
Who? Who argues against my commands, disrupts my orders?

It must be him. He, who took the woman.
He will die, this time, and his death will prevent the fires.

I will succeed. I must.

††††††

The work at Copperhead Mountain started early. Jim, Dan, and a group of volunteers used Billy's truck and six more to haul wood scraps, tires, and tins of kerosene to the base. They scattered the supplies at twenty yard intervals, working quickly and cautiously. Billy, driving the Nova for the first time in nearly a month, first visited Sam at the hospital—promising he'd get him out before the fire was lit—and then drove to the state police headquarters to tell them of the plans to burn Copperhead Mountain.

"Under the circumstances," said the commander, "I have to agree with you. I'll send over every available man, first thing in the morning."

"With shotguns?" asked Billy, grinning.

"Shotguns, cannons, hand grenades—anything we can find."

As he returned Billy followed the old road, which climbed to a high bluff opposite Copperhead Mountain, and he parked to watch the activity below. Trucks and men scurried frantically. Volunteers were plentiful, and more men arrived every hour.

The back side of the mountain, to the east, was circled at the base by a narrow highway. Vehicles jammed the grassy strips on both sides of the road, and as Billy watched, Jake Wilde's old truck threaded through the congestion. The journalist parked, ran to one small group and gestured wildly, obviously angry, then tried another clump of workers. He waved his arms and ran back to the truck, and the slam of the door echoed off the mountain.

Billy chuckled.

Most of the men at the mountain were armed with shotguns and pistols and short axes. Cool heads would be needed to control the mob; Billy sighed and began to plan work crews.

His eyes swung back to the steep slopes. The thick underbrush was dry, and would burn quickly. A sudden movement distracted his thoughts, and he squinted to stare.

A man, moving rapidly, crossed over an open area and slipped behind the trees. He reappeared, fifty yards upslope, and stopped to look back down at the men swarming at the base. Billy blinked and looked again. Something was familiar—the shoulders, the movements, the easy gait—and his stomach sunk.

It was Obie.

Billy watched as he slipped away from his lookout post and came down the mountain. He lost him, then saw Obie's broad shoulders emerge from a thicket near the highway. Obie circled, joined a clump of workers, and stayed close to the mountain.

Billy somberly drove off the ridge and down to the worksite, and found Brenda and Karen watching the preparations. "It's like an army," said Brenda, "getting ready for a battle."

Jim, sweaty and weary, drove up in the truck.

"Afternoon, general," grinned Billy. "Looks like the troops are hard at it."

"It's almost ready," said Jim. "Tonight we'll light small fires and post guards, and try to keep them up there. Are the state police coming tomorrow?"

"First thing in the morning," said Billy. "I'll feel a lot better when they get here. This mob could go wild."

"Speaking of wild," laughed Jim. "Your friend Jake was here. I ran him off. He was wild drunk, preaching and yelling, carrying a live copperhead with him."

"A live copperhead?"

"About four feet long," said Jim. "He was so soused the snake would have died if it had bitten him, though." He started the engine. "Come on, Karen. We have to go feed Dan."

"Let's go too," said Brenda. "All this makes me nervous."

As they drove, Billy told her about seeing Obie. "But what was he doing up there?" she asked. "I don't understand."

"Neither do I," said Billy. "Maybe it's been him, all along, instead of Jake. You said once that Obie hated me."

She was silent. "Maybe," she finally said. "But he wouldn't harm you. Not his own brother. I know that much for sure."

"I wish I were as sure as you. Obe is weird, Brenda."

"Weird, but not evil. Maybe he. .I don't know, Billy. Could Obie be trying to save the copperheads?"

"He sure doesn't want us to burn the mountain." Billy rubbed his jaw. "Hell, how would anybody know what Obie is thinking? I just wish this was all over."

After supper Billy could not rest. He paced the floor of the motel room, peeked out the curtains, and chainsmoked, puffing quickly and stubbing half used cigarettes. "Okay," Brenda finally said. "Let's drive over there."

They took the same road Billy had used earlier and climbed to the overlook opposite the mountain. Below, flickering fires ringed the base, and periodic yelling drifted up to them. "They're getting drunk," said Billy. "I was afraid of that."

"Two hundred drunk men with shotguns." Brenda shivered. "I'd rather be up with the copperheads. Before the night's over they'll be shooting each other. There won't be anybody there able to walk in the morning."

"Let's go on down. Maybe I can slow them down a little."

He backed out on the pavement and drove slowly off the ridge. Halfway down he heard the screaming tires behind them, and saw a pair of glaring headlights coming up fast. "Somebody," he grunted, "is coming down off this mountain like a loose freight train." He monitored the lights as they drew closer, and listened to the straining engine. "Fool!" He was tensed, ready to make room for the thundering vehicle. The lights bore down relentlessly.

At the last second he slammed the throttle. "Hold on!" he yelled. "He's gonna hit us!" The Nova lept forward, seconds before the truck crashed into the rear bumper and skidded sideways with the impact. Brenda's scream was drowned in the howl of tires and the roar of the engines.

The Nova jumped ahead and a hard right turn was on them. Billy jerked the wheel, accelerated, and came out of the turn sideways, fighting for control. The truck was close behind, its motor wailing. Billy straightened the Nova and sped toward the next curve. He did not brake. He hung the little car in a four wheel drift and slid around, rear tires clawing, engine screaming.

A half mile down, Billy remembered, was the old Bishop Grocery, with a small paved parking lot. The truck was gaining now, and deliberately he let it close to where the bumpers were almost touching.

Then he accelerated, locked the brake with his left foot, and flicked the wheel hard. The Nova spun and the truck whipped past, missing them by inches. Sliding backwards, tires digging, throttle open, Billy wrestled for control. The rear fender slammed into a concrete wall, the storefront shuddered, and they stopped. Smoke drifted up from the tires, and dust rolled. Billy took a deep, long breath and shut off the ignition.

"If he could drive like that sober," he said softly, "Jake Wilde could give Richard Petty a run for his money." He collapsed back against the seat. "You alright?"

"Yes. I think so. Help me out."

He looked. Brenda was curled under the dash, her feet up on the seat. "Did you get down there on purpose?"

"No, damnit!" she spat. "You put me under here with that last little trick you tried. Now get me out!"

Doors slammed and lights flashed on and a man came running.

"Anybody hurt?" he asked. He was still pulling overall straps over his shoulders. He helped Billy pry the fender away from the tire and mount the spare. Brenda sat trembling on the bench as they worked. "What happened?" asked Al Bishop.

"Somebody tried to shove us over the ledge," said Billy. "He almost got us, too."

"Was it Jake?" asked Brenda.

"It was his truck."

She was silent.

Billy grinned. "You can thank old Earl Williams we're still alive. No ordinary car would have pulled it off."

"No ordinary driver, either," she shivered.

At the mountain, Dan was content. "The copperheads are not trying to break through. The fires have got them scared. In the morning we'll finish them, Billy."

"I hope so," Billy said glumly. "I'm afraid this project is about to get out of hand. I'm as nervous as a cat in a roomful of rocking chairs, and I'm damned paranoid about Jake Wilde." He told them about the attempt on the hillside to shove them over.

"Go get some sleep," said Jim.

At the motel Brenda clung desperately to him. "Lock the door and stuff towels under the crack. I'm beginning to see copperheads in my sleep."

"Better them than Jake," grunted Billy.

Jake was awake, busy with the truck, using a crowbar to bend the bumper and fender clear of the front tire. The old truck clicked and steamed, wheezing after the hard run. Jake stopped to drink, then tested the steering. Satisfied he could safely drive the truck, he moved on. At the Skaggs Gap Motel he parked, and for half an hour glared at the darkened window. Then he drove on, mumbling darkly, a vodka bottle cuddled close.

††††††

Throughout the hot night Obie Cox prowled restlessly, eyeing the fires, crisscrossing the slopes of Copperhead Mountain. Finally he rested, crouched on a ledge overlooking the valley, the lookout he'd used for thirty years, and waited for dawn.

††††††

Young Obie Cox had been a loner, given to long walks across the Cox County hills, a brooding and withdrawn teenager. From his earliest memory he had been drawn to Copperhead Mountain; the thickets and rocks intrigued his imagination. At first he studied from a distance, and then he came closer, gradually working his way higher up the slopes.

Obie did not fear the copperhead. Instead, he delighted in the flat, copperish heads and flicking tongues which greeted his closeup studies, and he would not harm the plentiful reptiles. In time he was free to walk unharmed among the copperheads, a natural ally, accepted as kin. He was safe to watch closely as the snakes hunted, slept, sunned themselves, and lived their life secure on the mountain.

He was thirteen when he discovered the ledge, his lookout, and from the lofty perch he looked down over the looping ridge and silently observed the comings and goings of the human population. The copperheads shared his resting place; they nestled with him to bask in the sun, and sought the coolness of the big rock on hot summer evenings.

As Copperhead Mountain welcomed Obie, the rest of the world shunned him.

He watched with mixed emotions, proud but resentful, as Billy's athletic ability and glib personality charmed the entire county. At sixteen Obie quit school to work on the farm, away from the strange outside world and closer to his copperhead friends. Jessie welcomed the help and the companionship, and they became partners, talking little but living in close harmony.

At twenty-five Obie had been heavy, already balding, still reluctant to venture out but pressed by physical needs to seek the company of women. Annie Clark, then twenty-two, first serviced Obie for a pint of bourbon and a crumpled twenty dollar bill.

Annie was, by Cox County standards, a tramp. Full breasted, free with her favors, short of intelligence, she lived with the hope that Billy Cox would come back for her. He had been the first, when she was twelve and he was thirteen, and for five more years Billy had sought her out, come to her furtively, used her generous body as he wanted and needed.

Annie grieved when Billy left for college, and she waited for him for five years. Instead, the offer came from Obie. He told her, bluntly, that he did not love her. He did want sex, and children, and in return Annie would get security, a new home, her own car, and the Cox name.

The deal was consumated.

Obie did not protest, was even pleased, when she named the first son after Billy. He loved Billy, in his strange way, and was happy to have sired the first grandson for Jessie.

Obie's life was wrapped up in the farm, and in Copperhead Mountain, leaving no room for old angers.

Over the years he was a proud godfather to generations of copperhead young; the snakes thrived and accepted Obie even more completely. Obie came often during the winter months to insure that his sleeping family was undisturbed; each hatching season was a time of joy and pride. He carried stray copperheads from the farm to the mountain, releasing them unharmed, shielding them from the dangers of men.

Annie wondered, and asked about Obie's night visits to the mountain. He offered no explanation. He provided only food and shelter; he did not object when Annie turned to other men for warmth and friendship.

The dry spring season had alarmed Obie. He waited and worried, watching the water level drop steadily, and tried to confine the copperheads to the immediate vicinity of the mountain. They were safe, he decided, at the old Cox homeplace. Billy's sudden return, and Sam's gift of the land, threw Obie's life into a turmoil. His agonized rage at the burning of the old house was vented on the mountain in fierce, shaking sobs.

Obie was torn, wanting vengance but bound to Billy by

the strong sense of family, and he was surprised when the copperheads attacked. He called them back to the mountain, calmed the rage, and was stunned when again the copperheads moved against Billy. Finally, he had discovered the reason for his loss of control.

Concealed in the underbrush, heart pounding, he had watched Jake Wilde's primitive ceremonies with the copperheads. The snakes responded to Jake, yielded to his dark urgings, let him walk safely on the mountain. He saw Jake carry copperheads from the mountain, for ceremony or evil, and he wept.

Torn between his anger at Billy and his love for Copperhead Mountain, Obie was tormented. He fought against Jake's powers. Anguished as his own control slipped away, he wailed his frustrations against the harsh rocks.

Now, as dawn broke, fire threatened Obie's mountain, his very source of life.

From his lookout he raged at the unfairness. Billy and Jake Wilde had destroyed his world, his life, killing his only friends. Around him the copperheads stirred; Obie was afraid with them.

He whimpered as the men gathered, and sobbed as the flames spread relentlessly.

CHAPTER 15

"FORGIVE ME, LORD"

The morning sun was still cool when Dan signaled and the ring of fire roared to life. A cheer shattered the groggy quiet as flames nibbled at the mountain's underbrush and spread quickly, racing upwards.

††††††

Obie Cox watched the swirling smoke and sobbed. The tears streaked his face, and his eyes darted nervously.

A hundred yards away Jake Wilde was also on the mountain. He drained another bottle, reached for his rifle, wiped the scope, and scanned the valley and hillsides. He was searching, angry and relentless, looking for the tall target Billy Cox would present.

The copperheads stirred. Those on the lower levels climbed higher, away from the smoke and noise, and the ones on top crawled aimlessly, circling and regrouping, unsure.

††††††

Sam, still pale from his days in the hospital, sat in Jessie's pickup and watched expressionlessly. Jessie chewed solemnly, then spoke with a catch in his voice. "I reckon Obie is up yonder, Pap. Annie said he ain't been home all night."

"I was wonderin about him," said Sam. "He'll come down off from there, Jess, when it starts gittin hot."

"Maybe," Jessie said softly. "Maybe, Pap. I don't know."

††††††

Billy swore as the TV van arrived and the crew swarmed out, setting up cameras and bustling through the workers, drawing a quick crowd. "They'll want you, Billy," giggled Brenda. "You're such a quaint and colorful mountain character."

"That's why I hid," chuckled Billy. "Besides, you'd make a better story. The coal miner's daughter with a sidearm. Loretta Lynn with a silver automatic."

A terrified copperhead darted through the flames and a dozen shotguns boomed. Dan Webber screeched heartfelt curses. "You bastards!" he screamed, wincing and rubbing his bottom. "Just shoot the goddamn snakes. Somebody just ventilated my butt!"

He was almost dancing, watching the fire line. "Heads up," he yelled. "Some of 'em are trying to get through." Grimy workers scurried back to safety, and the guns thundered as copperheads tried to escape. After a few minutes the tide was stemmed, and workers crept cautiously back to the fires.

"Keep it moving," yelled Webber. "Don't let it die down." Fingers of flame shot up the mountain, following the grassy clearings. By eleven there was a hundred foot strip, a blackened ring, circling the base of Copperhead Mountain.

Webber was elated. "It's working," he yelled happily. "God damnit, Billy, it's working." He ran through the ashes, a small redheaded devil stoking the flames of hell.

††††††

Jake smashed the bottle. His eyes were glazed, his fingers numb. He lifted the rifle to continue his search. "Bastard's hid," he muttered. His eyes fell on the Nova, and he grinned. "But I know how to flush him out." He sighted, and fired. The rear window of Billy's car exploded.

"What the hell?" The trooper who had been leaning on the

fender yelled, lept for safety, and rolled as a second shot pierced the gas tank. "Somebody's up there with a rifle," he yelled. He pointed. "Up there!" A third shot blew the rear tire, and the trooper hugged the dirt. "Do something, damnit!"

The crowd scattered, running desperately for cover. Billy jumped to his feet, started to run, but Brenda stopped him. "That has to be Jake," she said, "and it's you he's after." Billy stooped and peered up through the bushes.

A trooper dived under the trees, unslinging a sniper's rifle as he rolled to his feet. Larry Blake, pale and dusty, eased up beside Billy. "Captain said to take him, whoever he is."

"It's Jake Wilde," growled Billy. "It's me he wants."

"Then stay put, damnit," said Blake. "We'll get him."

"You'll never see him," said Billy. "He'd show himself if I was out in the open."

"No way," warned Blake. He adjusted the rifle scope. "I'll stop him with this."

Two more rifle shots hit the Nova, and the gasoline ignited with a crumpling thud.

††††††

Obie spun when the rifle thundered, moving lightly across the rugged slope. He stopped short of Jake's hideout and circled to look down on him from a ledge. Jake was laughing, watching through the scope as people below scurried for safety.

"You." Obie growled, a half whisper. "It's ever bit your fault, Jake Wilde."

Jake froze when Obie spoke, and turned slowly to look. The vodka induced blur made Obie look even bigger as he loomed overhead, an angry finger pointed. Jake's jaw dropped. "Obie? You? You're the one who's been–?"

Obie was grunting, lifting the two hundred pound rock over his head. Jake screamed and ran as Obie threw the boulder, and it smashed heavily into the spot he'd left just seconds earlier.

††††††

"What's goin on up there?" yelled Blake. He crouched, staring. "Don't shoot!" Jake lept through the flames, tumbled and ran, frantically scrambled and looked back up the slope. Halfway down he dived behind a rock formation, and he screamed as his hands hit the red hot coals.

Blake ran for the mountain. "He's hurt. Help me get him down." He was twenty yards ahead of the others, climbing fast, when Jake rose from behind the rocks and fired. Blake screamed. The bullet shattered his thigh and he fell, rolling and digging for cover. He hugged the mountain, unable to retreat, and Jake's deadly fire pinned the other troopers. Billy grabbed Blake's rifle and crawled into shooting position. "He's got Blake pinned," he said. "There's not a damn thing we can do."

††††††

Obie solved their problem. From above the flames he roared in rage and sent another rock skidding down, bouncing through the fire and tumbling toward Jake's shelter. Jake yelled and ran, his pumping legs scattering the ashes.

Billy swung the rifle up to fire, but Brenda stopped his hand. "What's wrong with you?" he yelled.

"I couldn't let you kill him," she replied.

"Damn." Billy watched as the troopers moved in on Jake. "They've got him now. I'll get Blake down from there."

He ran for the mountain, crouched and weaving, toward the wounded trooper. He felt the bullet before he heard the shot. A tug at his leg sent him spinning, digging, clawing for safety in the smoking ashes. Another shot spattered and he dug faster, swearing and praying.

He heard Brenda's scream, and turned.

She was in the open, halfway to him, and Jake's grin told the story. His rifle was aimed at Brenda, and he waited.

"Don't shoot any more," Billy yelled to the troopers. "He'll kill her."

Jake hobbled closer, struggling in the deep ash for firmer footing. "Jake," pleaded Brenda, "please stop. Now, Jake. Give me the gun, and I'll take you home. Please?"

He peered at her, his lips working. Then his eyes found Billy. "No," he mumbled. "No. First I got to kill him."

"Come with me, Jake." Brenda stepped closer. "Nobody will hurt you. I promise."

"Stop!" He lifted the rifle.

Billy glimpsed Larry Blake's .38 revolver, twenty feet away, still where he'd dropped it when he was hit.

Brenda offered her hand to Jake. "Please? Jake?"

Billy tensed himself.

Jake saw. "No!" he screamed. He wheeled and aimed as Billy jumped. He missed, and cranked the lever for a second shot. Billy's scramble carried him to Blake's pistol; he grabbed it as he dove, and spun into shooting position. He stopped, looking up into the steady nozzle of Jake's rifle. It was aimed to his forehead, and Jake was grinning. Slowly, the finger closed on the trigger.

Jake was dead before he ever fired.

There was a slap of gunfire, and a small hole appeared an inch in front of Jake's ear. He toppled slowly, turning to look at Brenda as he sank to his knees.

She stood, legs spread, and slowly lowered the smoking automatic until it hung limp at her side.

Larry Blake broke the silence. "*That* is one hell of a woman," he whispered. Billy remembered, and turned to check on Blake's injury. "Just get me a stretcher," groaned the trooper. "And–Billy–go take care of her."

Billy tried to stand and his right leg collapsed. He saw the blood in his boot, cursed, and leaned on Jim's arm to walk to

Brenda. She was still standing, looking at Jake, not seeing. Billy gently took the pistol and she fell into his arms, sobbing, her shoulders heaving. He held her as he watched the ambulance attendants carry Jake's body away. "He's dead," one of them called.

"Good," grunted Billy. "Get him out of here."

Brenda watched in silence as they carried the heavy body. She twisted to look at Billy, and spoke. "I had to," she said quietly. "He was going to shoot you."

"You saved my life again," said Billy. He slipped her pistol into his pocket, and called to Jim. "Help me down off here. My leg is a little weak."

Dan was pushing the crews, shoving the flames higher, forcing the fire toward the top. Billy watched, and asked. "How's Larry Blake?"

"His thigh is pretty bad," said a trooper. "He's already on his way to Lexington." The policeman looked at Brenda. "Are *you* okay? That was a brave thing you just did."

"No. Not brave." She leaned on Billy's shoulder. "Just necessary."

The bloodstained medic appeared, looking for Billy. He cut away the boot and quickly dressed the wound. "Nothing broken," he said. "Better go to a hospital when you can."

"Tape it up good," ordered Billy. "I've still got a lot of work to do today." He stood when the medic finished, hobbled slowly on Brenda's arm, and joined Sam and Jessie.

Sam was smiling. "I told ye," he said proudly. "Brenda's jist like my Lily was. She ain't afraid of nothin." He beamed, and hugged Brenda.

"I'm still shaking all over," she said. "And I know I won't sleep for a month." She kissed Sam quickly, and sat with him on the tailgate of the truck. Jessie was staring up at the mountain.

"Fire's gittin right on up there," he observed. "If you're wonderin any, that was Obie what throwed the rock at Jake."

"I thought so," said Billy. "I had Jim warn everybody so they won't shoot him when he comes out."

"*If* he comes out, you mean," Jessie said wearily.

Billy stared at his father's face. "Daddy, do you know something you haven't told me?"

"Never mind," said Sam. "It ain't nothin, Billy. Is it, Jess?"

Jessie nodded, but kept his eyes on the mountain.

††††††

By midafternoon the fire was within three hundred yards of the crest and the mountainside was a smoking, desolate ruin. Dan pulled the crew back to the base. "It'll finish itself," he said quietly. "Nobody would want to be up there at the end." He could not face Sam or Jessie, who were glued to the mountaintop, watching for Obie.

Above the flames, the copperheads were a thick, squirming mass, disoriented and angry, and in their midst squatted Obie Cox. Sobs racked his huge body, and tears streamed freely. The snakes crawled over his feet and around his knees, tongues darting as they stood guard over their friend.

††††††

"When it starts cooling off," directed Dan Webber, "pour oil down every hole and crack you can find. Burn out the dens, and destroy the eggs."

"Eggs?" Jim grinned. "Are you serious?"

"Eggs mean babies. More copperheads. You want to get rid of them, don't you?"

Jim nodded.

"Then do what I tell you to do, Jim. If you don't, by late fall you'll have a whole fresh crop."

Jim smiled. "Dan, for an impartial, cold blooded scientist you sure are a hot headed killer. Do you want us to plow salt into the ground?"

"Not a bad idea," said Dan. "That and another fire every spring. For the next hundred years."

"You're possessed," laughed Jim. "Look, Dan, they're just copperheads. Not demons. It took a thousand years for them to get this thick, and they'll never do it again."

"You're wrong, Jim. Dead wrong. These are *not* just copperheads. Something–somebody?–has twisted nature all around, and it's all screwed up. They *are* demons, sort of. Wiggling devils. Take my word for it, Jim. Eliminate them, and their breeding grounds, and make sure this never happens again."

"You mean that, don't you?" Jim was solemn. "Is it Obie?"

"Him. Wilde. Hell, I don't know, Jim. I just know I won't rest easy until we're finished."

"Okay," grunted Jim. He stared at Dan. "We'll get started with the oil right now."

"Wait! I see something." Webber held Jim's arm. "I think it's your uncle."

††††††

Sam Cox saw the same movement, and nudged Billy's arm.

"Obie," he whispered. Jessie sighed, and reluctantly raised his eyes to watch.

Obie walked slowly out to the crest of the jutting rock, clearly visible above the flames, and lifted his arms to the sky. He stood, not moving, a dark monument above the fire.

"What's he doing?" wailed Billy. "I'll go bring him down."

He tugged on his leather gloves, tied the boot back around his ankle, and found a short axe. He moved methodically, always with one eye on Obie. On the ledge, Obie held his ground, calmly gazing upward as the flames nibbled at the base of the rock.

"Don't go," whispered Brenda. Billy stopped, perplexed, and rested both hands on her shoulders.

"I have to, Brenda. I don't know why, except that he is my brother, no matter what. In one way, it's my fault he's trapped up there." He kissed her and was gone, limping to the base for the climb. Dan intercepted him.

"You can't do it, Billy. It's impossible. The copperheads will be a foot deep, and the fire is. . ." He glanced at Billy's face. "Please," he pleaded, "nobody could live up there."

"He's still alive." Billy pointed.

"He won't be, much longer."

"All the more reason to go now," said Billy.

"He won't come with you. Don't you understand, Billy?" Webber's red face was close. "God damn it, Billy, Obie doesn't want to be saved! He won't come down! He'll stay, no matter what. If you really want to help, just shoot him! Make it quicker and less painful. That's all you can do."

Webber jerked angrily and yelled at Billy. "Damnit, he's one of them! Their leader! He thinks he's a copperhead, Billy. Maybe he is. Leave him up there. Please. Just shoot him."

"Dan," Billy said softly, "you're off your rocker. Get out of my way. That's my brother up there."

"Not anymore, Billy. Leave him. Let him die with his real brothers."

"Move over, Dan." Billy's voice was icy cold.

A shadow of a grin crossed Webber's face. "Okay. Okay, Billy. You can go. But I'm coming with you."

"Me too." Jim was at Webber's elbow, calmly tying a handkerchief over his nose.

"No," said Billy. "Your mother would–."

"I'm no baby," snapped Jim. "You need me, this time, and you'll damn well have me whether you want me or not."

Billy smiled. "All right. Let's get moving. It's getting hotter every second up there." He slapped Jim's shoulder gently.

Obie's outline, on the ledge, was blurred by rising heat waves.

Dust swirled around their feet as they climbed, working their way through glowing embers and deep layers of ash, always watching for Obie. Forty minutes later they were halfway there. Billy stopped to rest his leg and curse at the blood seeping from his boot. "Can you make it?" Jim' muffled voice came from behind the dirty mask.

"Yeah. He still up there?"

"Can't tell." Sweat poured from Webber's face, streaking the powdery soot. "If he is, he's damned hot."

††††††

Sam and Brenda huddled close to watch the three men struggle upwards, closer and closer to the fire. "What's going to happen, Sam?" she asked. "Will Obie come down?"

"Nope." Sam sighed. "Save your worryin fer them three young fools." He chewed his lip. "Obie, he ain't comin back. Not alive, he ain't."

††††††

Jessie Cox walked slowly to his truck and took his rifle from behind the seat. He opened a box of cartridges and methodically loaded the magazine. He pulled the bolt, saw the brass shell slide into the firing chamber, snapped the bolt home, and released the safety catch.

He turned lazily, shading his eyes with his hand, and propped both elbows on the hood of the truck. He leaned against the windshield pillar, focused the scope, searched the mountainside, and stopped when the crosshairs centered on Obie.

He pulled back. He lowered the rifle and looked around. All eyes were rivited to the mountaintop. He sighted again, and took a deep breath.

"Forgive me, Lord," he whispered. He squeezed the trigger. He worked the bolt and fired again, lifted his eyes, and slumped to the hood of the truck, sobbing.

††††††

The first shot caught Obie in the chest, lifting his shoulders and filling him with numb surprise. The second pierced his heart.

Webber screamed. "Look!"

Billy saw Obie stagger, then slump to his knees. He clawed toward the edge of the overlook, could not make it, shuddered and died.

"What happened?" whispered Jim.

"I think I know," Billy said wearily. "But I don't want to believe it."

††††††

Two troopers pinned Jessie's arms behind him and wrestled the rifle away. They shoved him roughly against the fender, and held him securely.

Jessie's eyes stayed on the mountain until Obie was still, then he turned to face Sam.

"I had to do it," he whispered. "He couldn't die like Uncle Obe, Pap. He couldn't."

Webber stopped Billy twenty feet short of the ledge. "He's dead," he said calmly. Blood dripped from the rock, and Obie's sightless eyes peered through the smoke.

"God." Jim's toneless whisper trembled.

On the rock, surrounding Obie, the copperheads were ready. Swaying, rearing, defiant, they faced the intruders and the flames with flickering tongues and savage tempers.

"Let's at least get his body," said Billy.

No one moved. "No. We can't." Webber's voice cracked. "It's way too late, Billy."

Flames lept at the rock, snapping and reaching, and the copperheads refused to back away. They stood guard, protecting Obie as he had protected them.

††††††

Back at the base Billy went straight to Sam. "He was dead when we got there. The fire didn't get him."

Sam stared blankly.

"We had to leave him until tomorrow," said Billy. "When it cools off we can. . .Grandpap?"

"Billy." Brenda's soft voice and her touch, gentle on his arm, turned him. "Billy, it was Jessie. He shot Obie."

"Daddy?"

"Yes. He's over there, with the police."

"What about Grandpap?"

"He's been that way since it happened." Sam muttered quietly, oblivious to all of them, his body shaking with emotion.

"Stay with him, Brenda." Billy walked to Jessie, who sat quietly with a young trooper. "Why, Daddy?"

Jessie looked up, but didn't speak.

"Why, damnit?" Billy leaned close, his voice hissing. "Why did you shoot Obie?"

"I had to save him," whispered Jessie. "You wouldn't understand, Billy."

"I sure as hell don't."

Jessie stared grimly. "I told you so. Leave me alone, Billy. Just go on and leave me be."

"Son of a goddamned bitch!" Billy slammed his fist into his hand and struggled angrily back to Brenda. "Everybody in this whole family," he fumed, "is pure damned crazy. He says he shot Obie. To save him! Hell!"

"Billy, don't jump to conclusions." Brenda held his arm tightly. "Help me with Sam, then we'll see what Jessie meant. Okay?"

"Fine. Fine and dandy." Billy slumped to the seat of a truck. "God, why did I ever come back here?"

††††††

Brenda drove Sam home and stayed with him; the doctor sedated the tired old man heavily. "It's shock," he said. "But it's mental, not physical."

"I know," she said softly. "I'll be here with him."

Billy came in at three in the morning to wolf down a sandwich, scrub his face and arms, and find new, clean boots. "How is he?" he asked.

"Sleeping, finally. He's been rambling about Obie. Sometimes it's your uncle, sometimes your brother. Billy, he keeps saying he killed both of them."

"It's a long story. I'm not sure, anymore, I've heard it all." He found a bottle of painkiller and gulped down four tablets.

"How are things going?" asked Brenda.

"The mountain is burned. We've got about fifty drunk men rolling around in the bushes, and fifty more with burns and smoke inhalation problems. It's been quiet for an hour or so, and pretty soon it'll be daylight." He hugged Brenda close. "We've got to go after Obie at dawn."

"You don't have to go," said Brenda. "Let the others do it."

"I want to. For one thing it's my job, rightfully, and I want to see the top of the mountain."

"Why?"

"Curiosity. Maybe pride. I don't know, Brenda. I want to see what's up there."

"Be careful, Billy. You're hurt, and with all the other stuff that's happened. . .I wish you'd stay here."

"No. I've come this far, and I'll see it through." He gulped down the last of his coffee. "I'll be back, soon as I can. Right now we're going after Obie."

CHAPTER 16

"YOU ALWAYS DO, JESSIE"

Fog and blowing smoke shrouded Copperhead Mountain, blanketing the peak in a gray cloud, and the littered remains of the day of fire cluttered the base.

A somber crew was ready for the final cleanup. Jim, Dan, and Billy stood quietly, peering up, planning their approach. "We may find some live copperheads," said Dan. "We'll have to go in slow, finish them off as we climb, and burn out any dens we can locate." He paused. "We've got plenty of help, Billy. You don't have to go."

"I'm coming," said Billy. "I want to bring Obie down, and I want to see for myself that this mountain is scorched to the core."

"Then let's do it." Dan waved, and the men spread into a ring and carefully advanced. The morning sun began to burn away the fog, and the smoldering peak was finally visible.

"There it is," grunted Billy. "Let's go."

A dozen well armed men approached the crest in thirty minutes. Dead copperheads were littered; the men prodded to make sure, and stepped gingerly through the bodies.

Obie was sprawled flat across the rock. His clothes were burned away, and the stench of scorched flesh hung heavy in the damp morning air. Billy was sick, retching and gagging, and he slumped weakly to the ground.

"Damn, looky here." One man was pointing with the shotgun he carried. "Old Sam has been tellin us the truth. Says 1915." Billy stood and trudged over to look at young Sam Cox's signature in the stone. Head bowed, he wondered what would become of Sam now, with the tragedy and torment weighing so heavily on his weary shoulders.

The scream wrenched him around, crouched and ready for action.

Dan Webber was dancing back from Obie's body, a wriggling copperhead clamped to his right forearm.

Billy swung, slapped the snake away, and crushed its head under the heel of his boot. His frustrations broke loose; he cursed and screamed and pounded the snake's body to a pulp, his teeth clenched in rage and his breath coming in sobbing gulps.

Jim reached him first and wrapped strong arms around his waist. "Easy," he said softly. "Calm down, Daddy. It's all over."

Billy was stiff, his hand trembling, as he pointed. "Get Obie off," he rasped. His eyes glittered. "Then bring up tires, oil, wood–any damn thing that'll burn." He kicked savagely, and the dead copperhead spun into the center of the clearing. "I want this place melted down," he whispered. "Now!"

"We'll do it," said Jim. He tugged at Billy's arm and led him away. "Just believe me, we'll get it done."

Billy broke away, cursing softly and pacing.

"Go to Brenda," Jim said quietly, "and Grandpap. They need you."

††††††

From Sam's front porch they watched the black smoke blossom from the peak of Copperhead Mountain.

"There it goes," said Billy. He was cold, and his hands trembled with fatigue and anger. "Burn it," he whispered. "Burn every damned inch of it!"

Brenda held tight to his arm.

Sam's wavery yell came from inside. "Where in the hell is everybody?"

Billy laughed with sudden relief and swung Brenda in his arms. "Grandpap's alive," he chuckled. "The world's gonna make it."

He snuggled her close as they went together to Sam.

††††††

The next day Billy waited in the courthouse hallway as Brenda met with the judge. He hugged her quickly as she came out in tears.

"They charged Jessie with murder," she gasped. "And me with voluntary manslaughter."

"Hey." He lifted her chin. "You know this is all just a formality."

She sighed. "I know. At least now we can bail Jessie out and try to figure out a defense. He admits to it but says he shot Obie to save him from a worse death. I can sort of understand that, Billy, but I don't know about a jury. "She dabbed at her eyes. "Let's go get him out, at least."

"This'll be a switch," chuckled Billy. "It used to always be the other way around."

"Then you owe him one," said Brenda. She stopped to look up at him. "You *do* believe Jessie, don't you?"

He hesitated. "Yes. Mostly."

As they walked he suddenly chuckled again.

"What's with you?" asked Brenda.

"You. You wanted a real case, and by God you've got it. It's almost funny."

"Do you hear me laughing?" she snarled.

††††††

Billy posted bail for Jessie, sent Brenda to take him home, checked on Dan Webber at the hospital, then drove back to the mountain. He parked by the burned out hulk of the Nova, and sighed as he surveyed the litter and the torn hillside. Jim, soot coated and weary, walked to join him.

"It's a mess, ain't it?"

"We can clean it up," said Jim. "What did they do to Grandpa?"

"Charged him with murder. I bailed him out, and Brenda took him home. You go rest and clean up, Jim. I'll bet your pretty wife would like to see you again."

"Where's Dan?"

"In the hospital. Don't worry about him, Becky's there, and Dan's ready to go. I just hope Becky lets him heal up some first."

"What about you? You were pretty upset yesterday."

"I'm just tired," said Billy. "Sore, exhausted, and tired of all this. Go on, Jim. I'll see you later."

After Jim was gone, Billy walked, circling the mountain, reached the back side and jumped down to the highway. He walked slowly, looking up at the darkened slopes, until a set of tire marks on the road caught his attention. The lines went off the pavement, to the right, and the brush was flattened.

"Damn," he muttered. "A wreck." He followed the trail and found Jake Wilde's pickup, its front bumper slammed into a tree. He moved closer and peered in through the closed window at the jumble of bottles and rags, the drunken clutter of odds and ends. He saw, on the dashboard, the leather journal. Billy flattened his nose against the glass for a better look.

The copperhead struck fiercely, slamming its head into the glass, chewing for Billy's head.

Billy howled, jumped back, tripped and tumbled. He crashed through the brush, hit hard on his backside, and sat gasping for breath.

"Jesus!" He wiped the cold sweat and sat for five minutes in weak relief. Then he went back to the truck, found Jake's crowbar in the back, and jerked the door open. He crushed the snake with a single blow, reached in for the notebook, and ran.

As he left, another flat head wavered from under the truck seat, and slowly emerged. The thick body uncoiled, and the copperhead dropped heavily out the door to the ground. It slithered away, and the forest was again silent.

††††††

In the safety of his truck Billy scanned the journal. The hair on his neck bristled; he shuddered as the words unfolded and Jake's efforts to control the copperheads–and to kill him–sunk in. He folded the notebook, stared back up at Copperhead Mountain for a long time, then drove to Hogtown to meet Sam and Brenda.

"Where have you been?" she asked. "You look like you saw a ghost."

"I did, sort of," he mumbled. "Or maybe a devil." He handed her the notebook. "I found Jake's truck, and this." He winced. "I had to kill another copperhead to get it. Brenda, Jake was more involved in all this than anybody would have ever believed. This book. . .it's the diary of a madman, Brenda."

She watched him closely. "Settle down, Billy. You'll get Sam all worried again."

"Don't read this unless you're ready to be scared," warned Billy. "It's. . .hell, it's impossible, but. . ."

Brenda took the journal. "It'll keep. Jessie's here. And Jim brought Karen and Dan."

Inside Billy awkwardly hugged his father. "I'm sorry about yesterday, Daddy. I didn't know what was going on, and. . . Hell, I still don't."

Jessie looked away. "Billy, I had to do it."

"He's tellin ye the truth," said Sam.

"Okay," said Billy. "I believe you both. Someday I want to hear the whole story. But it was Jake Wilde who was stirring up all the trouble, anyway." He told them about the journal, which Dan was busily reading. "He wanted to kill me over

Brenda, and he saw Obie as an enemy to the snakes. He was a simple lunatic."

"Not so damn simple," grunted Dan. He thumbed through the journal. "This explains the attacks and the strange behavior of the copperheads."

"Do you really believe he could communicate with them?" asked Billy. "That a man could talk to copperheads?"

"Ordinarily, no. *If* I hadn't seen so much with my own eyes. How would *you* explain it, Billy?"

"It weren't Jake," said Sam, sad and slow. "It were Obie."

"Obie?" Dan frowned. "How, Sam?"

"He talked to them copperheads. Set with 'em. Run with 'em." Sam's eyes were tired and bleary. "He was one of 'em, Obie was. He could go up there and not git bit, never, and they wouldn't run from him. Obie, he wasn't tryin to hurt nobody, though. He was tryin to save his snakes."

"Save them?" Billy laughed. "Grandpap, the day I came home Obe killed two copperheads."

"Did you see him do it?" asked Jessie. His eyes were weary. "He never did kill one of 'em. He always took 'em back to the mountain. Obie never wanted nobody to hurt the copperheads."

"The snakes wouldn't hurt Obie, neither," added Sam. "That's why Jessie had to shoot him. He woulda stayed up there, Obie would, and burnt to death."

"Wait a minute," said Webber. "I thought you shot Obie to keep the copperheads from getting him. Are you telling me now that they wouldn't have harmed him?"

"They wouldn't have touched him," said Jessie. "Obie was gonna burn with 'em."

Webber groaned. "Brenda, they just tore your defense all to pieces. Nobody in the world would believe what Jessie just said."

"I do," said Brenda. "That's half the battle."

††††††

After sleeping at Sam's for thirty hours, Dan Webber ate a triple breakfast, took a long shower, and drove to Brenda's office. Becky was waiting. "Have you made up your mind?" he asked.

"You just got yourself two new roommates," she giggled. "It'll sure save us both a lot of gas money."

"Great!" Dan wiggled with pleasure. "When?"

"Two weeks. I gave Brenda notice." She watched him closely. "Are you sure, Dan? Do you really want us?"

"Sure enough that I've bought a house. And a king size bed." He leaned over her chair, from behind, and cuddled her breasts.

"You better stop," warned Becky. "I might rape you."

"Right here?"

"Lock the door."

He did, and turned, grinning. "It's been a week. Brace yourself." Her throaty chuckle was his answer, and she opened her arms to welcome him.

They did not hear the door rattle, or the key in the lock.

When Brenda peeked in Becky was pinned to the wall, her legs wrapped around Dan's waist, her head thrown back, moaning and thrusting.

Brenda stepped back quickly and shoved Billy behind her as she pulled the door gently shut. "What's the matter?" he asked.

Brenda burst out laughing. "Dan and Becky," she giggled, "and they don't realize they left the shade open on the window."

She squealed and jumped as a passing car stopped with a sudden lurch, and the truck following close behind plowed into its rear bumper. Glass, chrome, and mud spewed, but neither driver noticed.

Both were staring, open-mouthed, through the office window.

††††††

††††††

Jessie and Brenda's trials were held during the October session of the Cox County District Court. Brenda's case was quickly dismissed, but Jessie was in deeper trouble.

After the testimony of six witnesses the prosecutor stood. "There are at least fifty more people who will verify the same story," he said. "I have their statements." He displayed a sheaf of papers.

Brenda answered. "We do not deny the factual evidence presented. We concede that Jessie Cox did shoot Obie Cox, in the manner described in the testimony, and we do not question any of the information presented."

The judge scowled. "Mrs. Cox, your client pleaded 'Not Guilty.' Yet you confirm the shooting. Why?"

"Because there was no murder, your honor. There was no planned, premeditated act of killing. Jessie Cox shot his son only to protect him from a worse death."

Judge Wilson peered over his glasses. "Young lady, that's absurd."

Brenda blushed. "Not so, your honor, and I will prove that Mr. Cox's actions were neither premeditated nor malicious."

"Then please do so."

Dan Webber was called to the stand and his credentials were verified. He spoke clearly, without hesitation.

"It is a known scientific fact that the copperhead snake is not aggressive, does not attack humans without provocation, and is dangerous only when disturbed." He offered printed documentation, then summarized the unusual happenings in Cox County and added his own version of the events which led to the decision to burn Copperhead Mountain. "We felt we had to totally destroy the breeding grounds, and fire was the only answer."

"Mr. Webber," asked the prosecutor, "who is the 'we' you refer to?"

"Me. Sam and Billy Cox. Jim Farley."

"I see. Is it not true, Mr. Webber, that you and this same group of men did deliberately burn the building commonly known as the Cox homeplace, and in doing so became, shall we say, slightly inebriated?"

Webber blushed. "That's true."

"Are you not, then, a close personal friend of the Cox family?"

"Yes. And I'm proud of it, too. Damned proud."

The judge hammered the room to silence. "Please refrain from profanity, Mr. Webber. Mr. Duncan, what is the point of your line of questioning?"

"That, your honor, this man's testimony is totally biased and therefore inadmissable."

"Objection!" yelled Brenda.

Judge Wilson's gavel pounded again. He called the attornies forward. "What is going on?"

"I established Mr. Webber's credentials," said Brenda. "He is an expert in his field."

"He is," agreed the prosecutor. "But he's a close friend of the defendant, and should not be allowed to testify as an expert in this case. I have no objections to calling in another herpetologist."

"Forget it," said Brenda. She shook her head wearily, and called Sam Cox to the stand. He was seated and sworn in.

"Mr. Cox," started Brenda, "I–."

"It's Sam, honey," he said. "Jist Sam."

"Okay. Sam. Did you see your son shoot Obie?"

"Nope. But I seen him jist after he done it."

"What did you think?"

"I'd have done it myself," he said quietly, "if I had me a gun and could still see good enough."

The crowd buzzed, and Brenda waited.

"Why, Sam? Tell me exactly why you feel that way."

"Jess had to shoot Obe to keep him from burnin alive.

Obie, he would have stayed up there and burnt."

"But why?" persisted Brenda. "He could have escaped at any time. Why did Obie choose to stay?"

"He was one of 'em," said Sam. "He never wanted to come down."

"Explain that."

"Obie, he was strange. He was like a brother to them copperheads, he was. He was gonna die with 'em."

The prosecutor stood, chuckling softly. "Mr. Cox, do you expect me to believe that story?"

Sam cocked his head and stared balefully at the attorney. "Ye wouldn't be a laughin, if ye'd been there, Jack. It's the truth. But. . .no, I don't reckon I do expect *you* to believe it. You ain't from these parts, and it'd be hard to tell somebody like you what it's like. But I'm talkin the truth, I swear to God."

"Anybody that's growed up here in the mountains, they'd know–better, anyhow–what I'm talkin about. Copperheads, they ain't just snakes. Not in these parts. They–they're worser, I reckon, than anything else we got around here. And Obie, he growed up hearin about the mountain and his uncle that the copperheads kilt. Somehow they was in Obie's blood."

"I believe ever damn word I've been sayin, and you ort to, too, 'cause it's the gospel truth."

Sam cut a fresh chew, and spoke again.

"Ye've all heard how Jake Wilde done what he done–devil worshippin, almost–usin the copperheads to try and kill decent people. He was crazy–drove that way by drink–but Jake *believed* he could control them vipers."

He spat. "Maybe–just maybe–Jake knowed what he was talkin about. Maybe he'd a had us all kilt if it weren't fer Obie stoppin him. They done read from Jake's book he kept. You all done heard what Jake was tryin to do."

Sam paused. "We ain't ever gonna know, fer sure, what was goin on with Jake Wilde nor Obie, but I'll tell ye one damn thing."

"If both of them men was still alive I wouldn't be sleepin none at night."

Annie Cox took the stand next, hesitant and shyly sensuous, to testify that Obie did indeed spend many days with the copperheads, that he climbed the mountain often, that he had done so for at least fifteen years. "And," she added bitterly, "he loved them snakes better'n he did his own youngens."

"Mrs. Cox," said the prosecutor, "your reputation is—well, it's said that you have had sexual relations with men other than your late husband, and—."

"Objection!" yelled Brenda. "What is—."

"Yes! Yes I did!" screamed Annie. "What would you have done if your man spent all his time lovin a damn bunch of copperheads?"

Order was restored, and after a recess Jessie took the stand. He verified that he had shot Obie, twice, the day of the fire.

"Why?" asked Brenda.

"I had to. He was gonna burn."

"Why didn't he run?"

"He couldn't." Jessie's voice cracked.

"Why not? Why couldn't he save himself?"

"He. . .Obie was. . .damnit, Obie was one of 'em!"

The gavel pounded. "We will have order," said the judge, "or we will have an empty courtroom." The buzzing stopped.

"Did you love your son?" asked Brenda.

"Yes. More than any of them. He needed me the most."

"Explain that."

"Obe, he was sort of slow," said Jessie. "The others, they was busy runnin around, doin stuff, makin it jist fine on their own. Obie, he never had nothin 'cept me and his mother, and then them copperheads. They was his life. The snakes was. He could go amongst 'em, set with 'em, and never git bit. He was tryin, right to the end, to save the copperheads. He never wanted any of 'em killed."

"It was Obie that stopped Jake Wilde and chased him off the mountain. He wasn't tryin to help us none." Jessie smiled sadly. "Nossir. Obe, he was protectin his copperheads. When I seen him, standin up on that rock, I knowed." He stopped to wipe his eyes. "I knowed he was gonna die with 'em, burn with them damn copperheads. I couldn't let him do that. Not my boy." His head dropped to his hands, and his voice was muffled. "Not the only one what needed me."

Jessie lifted his head. "So I done it. I helped Obie, one last time."

"Your honor," Brenda said softly, "the defense rests."

††††††

The jury was back in an hour, and the foreman shuffled nervously. "We know Jessie Cox did the shooting," he said wearily. "I don't reckon we'll ever understand all the rest. But whatever he has done, your honor, Jessie ain't no murderer. We find him 'Not Guilty'."

"You're free, Daddy," said Billy. "It's over. You can go."

"That right?" Jessie turned to Brenda.

"That's right, Jessie."

"I thank ye." He smiled, sadly. "Then I reckon I'll git back home. The corn's needin work." He walked slowly away, then stopped and turned. "Billy, are you gonna help me?"

Billy smiled. "I sure am, Daddy."

††††††

Jessie left the courthouse, drooped and gloomy, and drove back to the farm. He passed the house and parked the truck and walked tiredly to the family graveyard. At Obie's grave he knelt at length, then leaned back against a tree to gaze solemnly up at Copperhead Mountain. After an hour he left, moving slowly, went by to check on Annie and the children and went home to greet Georgie with an unexpected embrace.

"Jessie, what is it?" She watched carefully as his face quivered. "The trial? Billy called me and told me they let you go."

"They did," said Jessie. "They set me free, after I went and killed my own boy." He slumped to a chair.

"You had to do it," said Georgie. "It was fer his own good. I understand. Jessie, if that's what you're worryin about, I'd have done the same thing."

Jessie shook his head. "That ain't exactly what's botherin me. Georgie, I got to tell ye somethin. You got to know. Obie was yourn, too."

"What, Jessie?"

His face was bleak. "You know how Obie, he was always out roamin by hisself, walkin and wanderin, sometimes gone all night?"

"He always done that, Jessie. He wasn't good around people. He'd druther be by hisself."

"He weren't always by hisself."

"What are you talkin about, Jessie? Obie wasn't never with nobody."

"No people," grunted Jessie.

"Law, what *are* you talkin about, Jessie Cox?"

"Georgie, Obie used to stay up on the mountain. With the copperheads."

"Our Obie?"

He nodded. "Fer years. Damn near half his life. He went up there and set with them snakes, handled 'em, and walked right amongst 'em."

"He couldn't. They'd have kilt him."

Jessie sighed. "That was the problem. They never once offered to bite him."

"Why? How could he do that?"

"I don't know, Georgie. He jist done it. He scared me, goin off up there, settin on that big rock and lookin down at us. He'd set, sometimes, all day long. Jist lookin. Watchin us."

"Why?"

"I done told you I don't know. But that's how come he got so mad when they started burnin."

Georgie stared out the window at the blackened slopes. "What is it you're tryin to say to me, Jessie?"

"I didn't shoot Obie," Jessie said slowly, "to save him from the fire and the copperheads."

He stood and peered out the window, then turned, tears streaming. "I shot Obie to stop him. Because I was scared the fires *wouldn't* git him." His shoulders heaved. "I was scared he'd live, and bring them damn copperheads back down here on us again."

Georgie met his eyes. Her lips trembled, and she gulped.

"Jessie," she said softly. "You jist done what had to be done."

She sat down and went back to her sewing, nervously whipping the needle. She smiled up at him through the tears. "You always do, Jessie."

CHAPTER 17

"I HAVE SEEN TO IT"

An early spring came to Copperhead Mountain and fresh shoots poked through the blackened crust. By late May the slopes were green, lush with new grass and flowering shrubbery.

On the hillside in the valley, Billy Cox rested in the morning sun, slumped against the tractor, smoking. Across the field Jessie was still working, and the rattle of the busy diesel engine echoed.

Father and son had worked side by side throughout the busy season, readying the fields for summer crops, often laboring far into the night to complete the plowing. Now they prepared the fields for tobacco, five acres of their prime cash crop.

Billy and his father worked mostly alone, with help from Obie's oldest son and from Jim, evenings and weekends. Even Brenda had taken to the tractor, loving the smell of the fresh soil and the tanning effects of the early April sunshine.

The first calves had been delivered, and four spindly, homely young mules were Jim's pride and joy. Karen was also a willing worker in the fields, and her garden was easily the finest in Hogtown. Sam Cox celebrated his eightieth birthday by delivering a litter of seven pups, Buck's first offspring. Sam diligently worked the older mules, using them to teach Jim how to train the new ones. "Boy's a born teamster," he cackled. "He was borned fifty year too late."

The long hours and physical labor cemented a strong bond between Billy and Jessie; each developed a healthy new respect for the abilities and the staying power of the other. Income problems, for Billy, were resolved.

"We'll split it down the middle," said Jessie, referring to the farm earnings. "And I'll take care of Annie and the youngens." They compromised at thirds, with Annie to receive a full share.

Carefully, they all avoided any mention of Obie or of copperheads.

††††††

Jessie drove his tractor to a rattling stop ten yards away, and lit his pipe as he rested beside Billy.

"We're ready to start settin, Billy. Do ye remember how?"

"I'm afraid so. And I'll still hate every minute of it."

Jessie chuckled. "You always did hate this part. Too slow, I reckon, for you." He blew a contented puff of smoke. "Billy, I been meanin to tell you that I take back all I said about you last summer. About you not workin." He grinned.

"Forget it," laughed Billy. "In a way you were right. I sure never had given you any reason to think any different."

"You have now," Jessie said gruffly.

"Thanks, Daddy," smiled Billy. "I reckon you're lookin at the most contented feller you've ever seen."

"You got a good woman, Billy. That always helps."

"I know."

Jessie was staring at the mountain. "Billy?"

"Yeah?"

"Up there." Jessie pointed. "Obe. Was he dead when you got there?"

"He was. Why, Daddy?"

"I dunno." Jessie tapped his pipe on his shoe. "Here lately, since it warmed up, I been wakin up nights, worryin."

"There's no reason to. Forget it."

"I try," said Jessie. "But somethin keeps crawlin back, tormentin me."

"Well, by god, I know one thing," growled Billy. "It ain't the copperheads." He stared up at the mountain. "We scorched that place. Ever crack, ever hole. Whatever it was that Jake and Obie was into, we stopped it. For good."

"I hope so," said Jessie. He turned, and smiled. "Brenda's comin."

Billy smiled as she ran, skimming easily over the plowed ground, breasts moving in rhythm to her running, and his loins stirred.

"She's something else, Daddy," he said.

"Yep." Jessie smiled his agreement.

She arrived in a bluster of barking hounds, ragged breathing, and happy laughter. She flopped to the ground between the two men.

"No crime today?" asked Billy. "No writs or torts?"

She smiled smugly. "All caught up. I decided to come home and chaperone you two. Sam told me a woman doesn't belong out here, but I told him I'd be the judge of that."

"Truth is," said Jessie, "we're a little ahead of ourselves too. We can't start settin before Monday."

"Damn," chuckled Billy. "You mean I might get a weekend off?"

"Today too, if you want. I can finish up here before supper by myself."

"Then let's go home," grinned Billy. "We can send Sam somewhere and—."

"Whoa!" laughed Brenda. "This is a family discussion."

"Youens go on," smiled Jessie. "You got a honeymoon to finish up."

"That would take twenty more years," said Brenda. "But we'll keep trying. Come on, Billy. I get to drive!" She scrambled up on the tractor seat. "Hop on, farmer."

Billy climbed up on the fender. "Let's go. Just remember to raise the disk this time. We don't want to chop up the road. Not again."

She stuck out her tongue as the tractor sputtered to life, raised the harrows and lurched off across the field.

"Why so happy?" asked Billy.

"Secret," smiled Brenda. "Wait'll we get home."

The trip took ten minutes, with the dogs barking around the cleated tires all the way. They went straight to bed, clothes falling on the floor as they hurried, and later they laughed as the hounds brayed and scratched at the door. Billy rolled lazily and lit a cigarette and smiled as he looked at Brenda. "I've gone and married a wanton woman."

"You mean wantin?"

He chuckled. "As long as what you're wantin is what I'm givin."

"Don't you want to know my secret?"

"Yep." He lay back and blew smoke.

Brenda sat up, naked breasts thrusting. "Notice anything different?"

He inspected her closely. "Nope. Same titties." He bent to curl his tongue around a swelling nipple.

"Just wait," she wailed.

"Okay." He reached for the other breast.

"That's how it happened," giggled Brenda.

"Uh,huh," he mumbled. "How what happened?"

"That's how I got pregnant."

"Sure." He buried his face in soft warm flesh, then suddenly bolted upright. "That's how you *what*?"

"How I got pregnant." She crossed her arms under the breasts and smiled smugly. "It's true. Your second son is on the way."

"You mean you–we–us? We're going to have a baby?"

"That's what usually happens to pregnant women." She waited. "Well?"

"I. . .damn, Brenda, I. . ."

"I didn't even go to work today. I've been to see Dr. Gordon. I'm two months pregnant."

He hugged her tightly, then drew back blushing. "Was it alright for us to. . .?"

"Up until the last two months," she smiled.

"Well. . .I'll be. A baby." He grinned foolishly.

"One of those little bitty things," said Brenda. "That grows up and makes you lose sleep and spend money."

"Brenda, I'm so. . .so damned. . ."

"So damned what, Billy?"

"Happy!" he blurted. "I think I'm gonna cry."

"Then do it, so we can get back to important stuff." She smiled softly. "Are you really? Happy?"

"Lord, yes. We'll grow the finest baby! He'll be a basketball playing lawyer, as smart as you are and—."

"What else will *she* do?"

Billy grinned. "All she'd have to do, is be just like her mamma."

"I love you, Billy."

"And I love you." He rubbed her stomach. "And him."

"Her." She arched to press closer.

He stopped her with a fierce kiss. "Maybe them," he murmered.

††††††

After supper they sat on the balcony, content and subdued, looking quietly out over the hills.

"It's been good, Billy. We belong together."

"We sure do," he said softly. His voice had a slight nervous edge.

"Is something wrong? Are you worried about me being pregnant?"

"No. God no, Brenda. I was just thinking. Today Daddy said he was having nightmares, sort of, about Obie." He stared up at Copperhead Mountain. "That place still gives me shivers."

"It will always be a bad memory," said Brenda. "But, Billy, that's all it is, now. A memory."

"Yeah." He stood, stared at the dark outline of the mountain, and shrugged. "It's just. . .tonight. . .hell, I don't know, Brenda. Somehow I got this strange feeling. . ."

"Come on," she said softly. "Let's get some sleep."

He slipped his arm around her and they walked inside. As he shut the glass door he looked again, to the mountain, and could not stop the tremble which swept his body.

††††††

Dan Webber, at home in Lexington, re-read Jake Wilde's journal and became agitated. He studied the words again, wondering, struggling to understand, suddenly afraid.

He read Jake's final entry:

Tomorrow the fire comes.

With the flames of Hell they attempt to destroy our home, lay waste to the family.

I will try to stop them.

I must stop him, kill Billy Cox.

He is their leader now, the one who would burn the mountain to break my hold, kill the family to steal my powers.

Why?

Why does he fight me?

How?

How does he reach into the family, change my orders, delay the attacks I order?

He must die, this time.

Even if I am killed, I must stop Billy Cox.

My death no longer will mean the end.

The family will survive; I have seen to it.

The eggs are safe, from any man or any fire, and the new generation will carry on. I will live through them, the young, and my family will thrive.

After I have killed the evil one who would interfere. His death will open the doors.

The blackness comes.

I must now go to the mountain, to my family.

We cannot fail.

Dan reached for the phone, dialed Billy's number, then slammed the receiver down before the call was completed. He stood and paced, shaken by a growing terror, darkly afraid, shaking from a sudden chill.

Becky came in, found him, and held him close.

"It's them copperheads, ain't it?"

"How did you know?" asked Dan.

"I. . ." Becky stared, scared too, into Dan's anguished eyes. "I just knowed. And I seen that." She pointed to the journal. "Burn that thing, Dan. It's evil."

Dan smiled, a forlorn and defeated flicker. "Becky, I was studying all this, and. . .I'm not so sure Jake was just a madman."

"What do you mean, Dan?"

"I'm afraid, Becky. I'm scared as hell. What if Jake really *did* have some power over the copperheads? What if he could really tell them what to do?" His face paled. "Jake thought it was Billy who was challenging his power, but. . .Obie was the one. Becky, what if Jake was planning to do more, and what if Obie was the only one strong enough to stop him? Maybe Jessie was wrong. Backwards. Obie could have been protecting us. With Obie dead, and the copperheads still coming, the Coxes don't have any chance at all."

"Oh, Dan." Becky held him close. "You were just here all by yourself and got scared, readin all that. It's over, Dan. The copperheads are gone. The Coxes are perfectly safe." She smiled softly. "If it'll make you feel better, tomorrow let's go visit them. See for yourself."

Dan grinned and relaxed. "Becky, there must be a full moon tonight. I feel better already."

An hour later it was Becky who was still awake. She crept quietly into the den, found Jake's journal, lay it in the fireplace, and struck a match. The flames lapped at the dog-eared pages, and she waited until every scrap was burned.

"There." She stood, and shivered. "That's the end of Jake Wilde and the damned copperheads."

As she left the breeze stirred, and the charred paper fluttered across the room.

††††††

Sam Cox slept fitfully, dreaming of his younger brother and the dark mountaintop, twisting in the sheets and moaning raggedly. He woke with a jerk, wet with cold perspiration, and hobbled to the window.

Above him, a pale moon cast shadows across Copperhead Mountain, and a spring thunderstorm built in a swirl of dark clouds.

There was a low rumble of thunder, and heavy raindrops began to splatter against the windowpane. Sam sighed wearily and hobbled back to his bed.

He did not sleep again.

††††††

On Copperhead Mountain, a light rain was still falling.

It cleansed the soot from the rocks, settled the ashes, and drained gently down the slopes, nourishing the seeds for the spring blossoming.

The pattering drops washed the flat surface, exposing the scratchy writing of young Sam Cox, then covered all other traces of man's battle with the mountain. The water ran to the crevices, cleansing, refreshing the parched springs and flushing away the last debris of the two day firefight.

The trickling water was the only movement on the barren, lifeless slopes; except—at the very peak—deep under the massive rock formation, where the first of the fall eggs began to hatch. In less than an hour a dozen squirming, already lethal young copperheads were coiled together, waiting for the summer sunshine to draw them and the others up from their buried den to the familiar warm rocks of Copperhead Mountain.

The End.